HOLLOW CHEST

HOLLOW CHEST

BRITA SANDSTROM

WITH DRAWINGS BY
DADU SHIN

WALDEN POND PRESS
An Imprint of HarperCollinsPublishers

Walden Pond Press is an imprint of HarperCollins Publishers.

Hollow Chest

Text copyright © 2021 by Brita Sandstrom

Illustrations copyright © 2021 by Dadu Shin

"[i carry your heart with me(i carry it in]" Copyright 1952, © 1980, 1991 by the
Trustees for the E. E. Cummings Trust, from *Complete Poems: 1904–1962* by
E. E. Cummings, edited by George J. Firmage. All rights reserved.

Printed in the United States of America.

Library of Congress Control Number: 2020952899
ISBN 978-0-06-287074-2

Typography by David Curtis
21 22 23 24 25 PC/LSCH 10 9 8 7 6 5 4 3 2 1

First Edition

For Mom. Obviously.

i carry your heart with me(i carry it in
my heart)
—*E. E. Cummings*

In the beginning, there was Hunger, which grew teeth.
There is no other story but this.

1

THE SCREAM OF THE AIR RAID SIREN CUT OFF abruptly when Charlie opened his eyes, like a hand had come down to strangle it. The same old nightmare—sirens, dust, the hazy beams of camping torches in the dark—evaporated like smoke and left Charlie in his bed, pajamas damp with cold sweat. A stitch in his chest wouldn't let him catch his breath, as if he had been running too fast and his lungs had seized up in protest.

He saw for the briefest moment a great yellow eye looking down at him from overhead, burning and burning, before the indistinct shape sorted itself out into a streetlamp outside his window. He let out a slow, shallow breath, his side still hitching.

He felt for Biscuits blindly in the dim morning light, and she made an inconvenienced sound when his fingers sank gratefully into her warm fur.

He was safe. He was home, in bed, where he belonged, his cat tucked against his side. They were safe.

The air raid shelter was gone. The bombs were gone. The war itself was all but gone, finished, over. And yes, his big brother was still gone, but soon—so soon, one week and twelve-odd hours soon—Theo would be just like Charlie and Biscuits, at home in his own bed and safe as houses.

Somewhere outside, a dog sounded, toneless and droning, more of a wail than a howl, really. *That* was why he'd had the nightmare. Instead of a silly old dog's howl, he'd heard an air raid siren, and his sleeping mind had tried to protect him as best it could by putting him back into the depths of the Goodge Street shelter during the Blitz, sweating in the dark with too many other people and no Biscuits—

No. That time was gone. He would not think of it. He would not go back.

He stroked his cat's soft fur again and Biscuits purred groggily. *Safe as houses.*

Charlie dressed as quickly as possible, stripping off his sweat-soaked pajamas and shivering his way into a too-big shirt and an itchy wool jumper. It was a bitterly cold London morning outside, and it was only a bit better inside. Grandpa Fitz must have forgotten to get the woodstove going. And if he had forgotten, it was because he was having a bad day.

He swatted down the part of himself that wanted to sigh. Grandpa Fitz didn't ask to have bad days any more than Charlie asked to have a brother off fighting a war, any more than Charlie asked to have nightmares rather than simple, uncomplicated dreams. Some things couldn't be helped, they could only be dealt with.

But first things first. Charlie went to the wall calendar, the one that Mum had won at a raffle that displayed pictures of prizewinning vegetables. "February 1945" was spelled in fancy script over an alarmingly large squash. He picked up the pencil hanging next to it and carefully crossed off another day with a big, definitive X. Only one week's worth of boxes now stood between the Xs and the date circled in red with "Theo Comes Home!" written in Charlie's very best lettering. Taking a deep, steadying breath, Charlie rolled up his sleeves and went to show the woodstove who was in charge in this house.

The stove was unimpressed by Charlie's claim of authority, and by the time he had used up almost all their entire remaining firewood to coax it into a cheerful blaze, the sun was nudging itself over the horizon and just beginning to paint London bright as a spring day, despite the snow on the ground. It was a trick, of course. It was always colder than it looked outside these days.

"Jumping Jehoshaphat, it's cold down here," Mum said around the several hairpins held in her teeth. As she raced down the stairs, she yanked out curlers with one hand and fussed with her shirt collar with the other. "Dad, I *cannot* be late again—" She caught sight of Charlie closing up the woodstove and sighed. "Ah. One of *those* days, is it?"

Charlie nodded bleakly and rubbed at his gritty eyes.

Mum squinted at him and changed course from the teacup cupboard to Charlie, sticking the pins in her hair with mathematical precision. "Bad dreams again?"

Charlie nodded once more, not looking at her. It felt like letting her down, somehow, to still be scared of things long since over. To give her one more thing to worry about.

"Anything I can do?" she asked. A look of worry, fast as a blink, came over Mum's face, carving a line between her eyebrows that hadn't been there even a few months before, Charlie was almost sure of it.

"It's fine, Mum. It's nothing." He worked his voice into something resembling cheerful, even if it was still croaky with sleep.

"Was it about your brother?"

"It's fine."

Mum looked as if she wanted to say more—*Eleven is too young to be such an old man, Charles* was a favorite of hers—but she swallowed down the words and ran her hand over his staticky hair. Her eyes caught something behind his head and went huge.

"Is that the time?" That flash of worry again, that line between her eyebrows. "I'm going to miss that infernal bus—" Whatever else she was going to say was muffled by the toast she jammed into her mouth as she flew about looking for her coat and hat, which were hanging on the same peg by the door that they always were every day since forever.

"Have to run, love you, darling!" she called over her shoulder as she threw open the door and dashed out.

"Watch out for the ice," Charlie called after her. Visions of Mum's heels flying out from under her and sending her sprawling in the street rushed up at him, the sirens still echoing in his ears. But Mum was already around the corner and out of sight, sure-footed and unafraid.

Charlie squeezed his eyes shut until they hurt a bit, then stood up straight and walked upstairs to Grandpa Fitz's room.

Grandpa Fitz was sitting up in bed in his striped pajamas, looking at the low-lying sun through his gauzy window curtains. His left sleeve had come unpinned in the night, and he was rubbing the cuff back and forth between his fingers without looking at it.

It was like this sometimes. Grandpa Fitz would go away for a few minutes or hours or even a day, and in the place where he went, he still had his left arm and sometimes Charlie's dad was alive, or Grandma Lily, or Grandpa Fitz's first dog, Duck. It still made Charlie cry sometimes—that Grandpa Fitz was able to forget that he'd lost so very many people. And maybe Charlie was a little jealous, too. One day, maybe, Charlie would be old enough to go away like that for a little while and visit Dad, just for an hour or two. That would be nice.

If you're that old, Grandpa Fitz will be gone, too. So will Mum, so will—

Charlie slammed the door on the thought before it could finish. He would not think about it.

He rolled up Grandpa Fitz's loose sleeve and pinned it in place—when he was back to himself, Grandpa Fitz always hated having his sleeves "flop about like a sailor on leave, up to no good and dragging through the jam." Then he blew on the cup of tea he'd brought to make sure it was cool enough before holding it up to his grandfather's lips. Grandpa Fitz's whiskers glinted in the sunlight, but there was no help for that right now. Charlie did not have sufficient skill to shave Grandpa Fitz's chin for him. Theo hadn't, either, but he would always make a great production of pretending to be a barber and putting a hot towel on Grandpa Fitz's face and putting on and wiping off the thick shaving cream so they at least felt that they had done something.

He pulled Grandpa Fitz's housecoat on over his right arm and his broad shoulders, still strong as stone even if they were getting slightly stooped. Charlie got embarrassed when he had to dress Grandpa Fitz, even though Theo had never so much as batted an eyelash at helping their grandfather into his trousers and shirt if need be, but Theo was also much taller and stronger than Charlie. He could help in ways Charlie just couldn't.

But still. When Theo left to fight in the war a year and a half ago, Charlie had *promised* that he would look after the family while he was gone, that he wouldn't let Theo down, and he had kept that promise. Charlie had even convinced his mother to let him leave school for a while when Grandpa Fitz had started having so many down days so that he could look after him, at least until Theo returned.

Soon, the bright little ball of anxiety in the center of his guts whispered, *so soon*.

"I have to go to the grocer's to get things for lunch, but I'll be back in just a bit," Charlie said.

Grandpa Fitz didn't respond, but Charlie hadn't expected him to. He simply stared out the window at the dim sky as Charlie gently closed the door behind him.

He stood in the hall biting his lip for a long moment. There were things Charlie should be doing, the endless list of tasks and errands that cost just a little bit too much money, but for five minutes Charlie could ignore them. Just five minutes.

He went back into his room and got down on his hands and knees to reach under his bed, his fingers searching in the dark. Then he pulled the box out from under his bed. It was covered in a layer of dust and a generous coating of cat fur, but he could still see the outline of his fingers from the last time he'd pulled it out.

The letters inside were already starting to yellow, even though they weren't all that old. The very first one had a picture of Theo's unit in their long, dark coats and round helmets.

Dear Charlie—I'll always find you, but can you find me? (A hint: I'm the only one of these grumps smiling.)

Sure enough, all of them looked remarkably identical, but Theo was in the second-to-last row, third from the left. Charlie had circled him in pen, just to make sure Theo knew that Charlie had found him.

The letters went on:

Dear Charlie—Thanks a ton for your letters, I've been reading them to the boys who haven't been getting any from home (I knew you wouldn't mind me sharing them). Your account of the Great Christmas Story Reenactment Disaster of '43 was a big hit with the lads. In Biscuits's defense, no one can really prove there was NOT a cat present at the birth of Christ, so Father MacIntosh really shouldn't have got so worked up about it.

Dear Charlie—The army is very keen on running and jumping about, and I feel I must thank you for all those snowball fights, as they were a great preparation for basic training.

Dear Charlie—Greetings from the picturesque French countryside! At least, I imagine it is picturesque, as all we see are the insides of our tents.

Dear Charlie—Nothing much to report. Thank you for the letters. The weather is nice today, which makes for a change. Sorry to become one of those people who talk about the weather. Still, I hope the weather is nicer where you are. I hope the weather is perfect for you today. What else could I tell you, that you would want to know? Maybe it's best to stick to the weather for now. I can tell you the shapes I saw in the clouds through the window I'm stuck in front of: a cat, a crown, a sword, a wolf, a pie, a bed, another bed. Sorry, not my best.
Theo

Dear Charlie—I might not be able to write for a while, didn't want you and Mum to worry.

Dear Charlie—Happy birthday. T.

The letters had dwindled and winnowed and withered down to one postcard from Paris that had only had Theo's signature on it with no note.

And then the horrible one that Mum had wept over.

Dear Mrs. Merriweather,
It is with great regret that we must inform you that your son,
THEODORE FITZWILLIAM MERRIWEATHER, was
injured in the line of duty. He is currently receiving medical care
at L'HÔPITAL DE SAINTE MARIE. He will be granted
a MEDICAL LEAVE no later than February 10.
Yours sincerely,
Gen. C. Marshal Greene

And after that—nothing.

Why had he stopped writing? Because he was too hurt to write?

No. Charlie put the thought into a box and locked it and threw it away.

Perhaps Theo was too busy, or doing something top secret that was strictly need-to-know for the government. Or maybe the hospital he was recovering at was so far off the beaten path that mail carriers could only get there by foot. Maybe there was a whole heap of letters that he'd sent but that had gone astray, or the mail train had been hit by a bomb, or there was someone else named Charlie Merriweather in another city who kept getting his mail by mistake and was very confused by the exploits of this Theo character.

But Theo was alive. He was coming home. There was an explanation, and soon (so soon!) Theo would be able to tell him.

There were two more things at the very bottom of the box. The first was a photograph, and Charlie almost didn't look at it. But it drew him like a magnet, like it was hooked to something inside him and tugging. It was the picture of Mum and Dad on their wedding day, both of them trying so hard not to smile or move for the camera that they looked rather cross for having just gotten married. It was before Dad had a beard, and Mum's hair was much shorter and curled. Charlie's finger hovered over Dad's face, afraid to touch the photo for fear of wearing it, as he tried to match the face in the photo to his memories of him. But Dad's beard and gray-streaked hair and weathered skin in Charlie's head were at odds with the stern jaw and dark hair and grim expression in the photo. Charlie couldn't really remember Dad that well anymore, except for a few bright shards of memory that gleamed and cut like glass. But that was a secret he kept from everyone but Biscuits, to whom he would recite everything he could remember about Dad into her fur sometimes at night.

His big hands, his pipe-smoke smell, his scratchy wool jumpers, his gray-streaked brown hair.

And lastly, underneath the picture, was a bit of scratch paper with a list of things to get at the chemist's in Dad's inelegant, squarish writing. Charlie held the paper with both hands, mouthing each word silently—*tea, sugar, aspirin, iron tablets, peg hooks.*

He squeezed his eyes shut and drew in thin, shaky breaths.

"Theo will be home soon," he said out loud in a snuffly whisper. "He'll be home next week."

Out in the hall, Biscuits was awake and crying for him. Charlie wiped his face with his sleeve and opened the door.

2

BISCUITS WAS DEMANDING HER BREAKFAST, yowling in a plaintive voice and pawing at his leg with big, accusatory eyes. His cat was, in Charlie's opinion, a perfect specimen of her kind, exactly everything a cat should be: small and fine-boned with delicate triangle ears and soft, downy white fur with artfully arranged marmalade-colored patches for contrast.

"When have I ever let you starve?" Charlie demanded, bending down to rub her little ears the way she liked. But Biscuits refused to be distracted from her imminent starvation and flung herself onto the ground, languishing. Charlie dumped a small pile of kitchen scraps into her special bowl from a big container he had bought specially to keep them fresh in the icebox (and the mice out of them). But she abandoned her breakfast after just a few bites when she realized he was leaving, sneaking past his legs and out the door.

She meowed a greeting to Sean O'Leary, who was just finishing up shoveling the walk to his house. Sean and his family had lived two doors down from the Merriweathers for as long as Charlie could remember. They were in the same class at school, back when they both went to school. Like Charlie with Grandpa Fitz, Sean had been out of school for the past few months, helping take care of his younger brothers and sisters so his mum could work. He was probably Charlie's closest friend, at least since so many of the other kids had been sent away into the country to wait out the war. Mum had flatly refused to send Charlie and Theo away from home—she and one of the other mums at church had had a politely vicious row about it. "Only God is going to separate this family again," Mum had said, in a voice he had never heard her use before, or since. Mrs. Lancaster still scuttled away from her whenever they made eye contact over the church biscuits.

"Do you fancy going down to the shops after this?" said Sean, brandishing his shovel. "I've got to pick up some stuff for my mum, so I'm taking the bicycle."

Charlie raised his eyebrows, impressed. The O'Leary bicycle was in high demand. Sean was the middle of six kids, and he always seemed to be corralling a small herd of younger siblings like a long-suffering sheepdog. It always made Charlie smile to look at Sean, because he could see already exactly what Sean was going to look like as an old man: patient but almost permanently a bit exasperated.

"I can't," Charlie sighed. "I have to go to the grocer's for Mum. Grandpa Fitz isn't up to it today."

Sean nodded. Charlie didn't share with him everything about

13

Grandpa Fitz's bad days, but he had enough of a general impression to mind his business. Minding Your Business was gospel in the O'Leary house, second only to the actual Gospel. It made Sean a rather useless friend to gossip with, but more and more lately, Charlie had begun to appreciate it.

"We have to get everything ready for when Theo's home," Charlie couldn't keep himself from adding, and then regretted it. Two of Sean's brothers had gone away to fight, and neither of them would be home soon, or ever. But it had been sneaking into everything Charlie said lately, like a hiccup. *Lovely weather we're having, and Theo will be home soon. How much are cabbages today, and did you know Theo will be home soon? Our Father, who art in heaven, Theo will be home soon.*

"I'll see you at the church tonight, though?" Sean went on as if Charlie had not spoken.

"Yes," Charlie replied. Father MacIntosh had organized a group visit to a hospital tomorrow to welcome returning soldiers, and was overseeing it with the flinty focus of a seasoned general. He wanted to have a meeting tonight to make all final preparations. Absence would not be acceptable.

"Grand. I'll see you then." And, with one last heave of snow, he disappeared back inside his house. Charlie caught the sound of a baby crying before the door clicked shut.

He sighed and kicked at an ice chunk that skittered off into the street, barely avoiding braining a pigeon that was hunting for rubbish near the sidewalk. Theo would have known what to say to Sean, what quiet little gesture would convey that Charlie hasn't *meant* anything by it, he'd just been excited was all. But if Theo were here it would be a moot point anyway.

Biscuits broke his train of thought, leaping smoothly into the bicycle basket, her paws braced on the edge like a masthead. Charlie petted her gratefully and pushed the bicycle into motion, his knees stiff with cold. He went slowly and carefully, keeping one eye the path ahead and one on the ground immediately in front of him. The Blitz—German planes dropping bomb after bomb after bomb all over England near the start of the war—had blacked out and rewritten the topography of the city, making even the familiar sidewalks strange and treacherous, even several years later. Their street had escaped the bombs unscathed, but the displaced earth from a few streets over had tilted parts of the road and sidewalks like carnival mirrors, the odd edges just waiting to catch unsuspecting feet and tires.

A small pack of returned soldiers were smoking on a street corner, talking in low voices. They could only be soldiers, given their age, maybe a few years older than Theo. Even two months ago there hadn't been half as many, and the newly demobilized soldiers were rare and obvious sights on the street, either dressed still in their uniforms or in the conspicuous demob suits the government had provided to each returning serviceman: coat, trousers, shirt, and hat, all so fresh they had a self-conscious gleam to them. Would Theo already have his, or would he need to go somewhere to get it? Not that he would need it; all of Theo's clothes were exactly where he had left them in his room.

Mum had been talking less and less idly about repurposing some of Theo's things for Charlie. There were only so many clothing tickets allowed per person every year, but Charlie kept *growing*. He'd been excited as the marks for his height got higher and higher on his door frame, so excited that it had been months before he'd noticed that Mum's dresses had new darns and places where the fabric was worn thin and shiny. Charlie, in turn, kept trying to stretch his clothes to fit. Everything had to be exactly the way Theo had left it, *exactly*. If Charlie could help it, anyway, and he couldn't, always.

A precarious bit of road pulled Charlie out of his thoughts as he swung his bicycle around to avoid a gaping hole where a house and a stretch of sidewalk had been blasted away. It was only odd when he thought about it now, how one street could be as untouched as a snow globe, and the next one over flattened as if a shovel had swept it clear. He had to work now to remember what it had looked like before.

He pulled up to the grocer's and parked his bicycle next to a few others. He touched his jacket pocket again to assure himself he'd brought the ration book and the money Mum had left in a jar on the counter. He occasionally had nightmares that he had lost the little book, or accidentally used it as kindling, often accompanying dreams that he had shown up for school in his underwear and nothing else.

The shop was small and cramped inside, cans and bottles stacked high on shelves that went almost to the ceiling, a few baskets of wilting vegetables arranged a bit precariously underneath. The effect was so that it always seemed as if there had to be enough, *more* than enough, for everyone. Even as there never was.

Charlie remembered Mum's shock-slack face, the first time she had seen their rations for the week laid out on the kitchen table, how she had not been able to hide it quite fast enough before Charlie got the idea that maybe he ought to be worried. He had never really thought about food before, to wonder what would happen if there wasn't *enough*. "You can make do with anything, if anything is all you have," Grandpa Fitz had said firmly, squeezing Mum's hand tight in his own, under the table where he thought Charlie couldn't see. But Charlie had seen. And he had worried. And he had never been able to work out how to stop.

It was a thin little dark thread that was sewn up into the fabric of everything, that worry. It stitched the pieces of his life together. What would even happen if it was gone?

Now Charlie carefully picked their usual rations from off the shelves. He could pick out the correct amount of everything for two adults and one child by memory now, the weight of it in the shopping basket not even enough to tire his arm. The line moved and soon he was in front of the counter, with Mr. Short, the grocer, smiling at him expectantly.

Mr. Short *was* in fact rather short, but short like a bulldog, all compressed ham-hock muscles and determination. He had a nice, open sort of face and he was reassuring in his sameness—the same dusty apron as always, the same neat off-white shirt, the same gleam of light off his bald head.

"Hello, Charlie," he said warmly, taking the ration book Charlie offered and comparing it to his ledger. "How's your mum and old Fitz?"

Charlie pulled out the money from his jacket pocket and carefully counted it out, adding in his head. Once, the second or third time he had come on his own, there had not been enough for everything in his shopping basket, and the awful pressure of the shame had seemed to press Charlie into the floor as he tried to work out which thing to get rid of, when they needed them all. Even now he could feel the memory of it staining his neck red and splotchy. Charlie had immediately gone home and informed Mum that he was going to look for a job the next day, maybe a paper route like Sean or collecting scrap metal like Eustace. Mum had told him that for the time being, his job was to be at home to help her and Grandpa Fitz while she had to be at work.

"They're fine," Charlie replied, swallowing down the memory. And then, unable to help himself once again, he added, "Theo's home next week."

Mr. Short's whole face changed as he broke into a wide smile, deep crinkles appearing around his eyes. "Now, that *is* good news," he said, counting out change in one meaty hand. And then, almost to himself, "That is good, good news indeed." Mr. Short's crinkled-up eyes narrowed a moment later, though,

19

squinting suspiciously out the shop window.

The old woman everyone called Mad Mellie was pushing a baby's pram full of odds and ends down the street with surprising spryness. She paused outside the grocer's and began inspecting the rubbish bin.

"Oi!" Mr. Short shouted out the door. "Clear off!"

Charlie shifted his weight around, uncomfortable and embarrassed. Mad Mellie had been shuffling around the neighborhood for years, always with her pram and usually surrounded by the pigeons she fed bread crumbs. She was grumpy and dirty, but she never really bothered anyone—she hardly spoke to anyone at all besides her birds. But she *was* grumpy and dirty, and she made people uncomfortable. And that was why people yelled at her, he supposed.

Still.

"Woman's a menace," Mr. Short muttered under his breath as he finished loading up Charlie's groceries.

"Thank you, Mr. Short," Charlie said, careful to enunciate. Theo always said clarity was essential for thank-yous, and thank-yous were the cornerstone of good manners. Theo had once kicked a football straight through a glass window while playing in the street with a friend, and he had marched right up to the house in question, swept his hat off, and somehow apologized so eloquently and thoroughly that the old lady who owned the window sent him home with both the football and a slice of cake wrapped in wax paper. He'd let Charlie have a bite of it, the icing so sweet it almost stung.

"You're more than welcome, Charlie," Mr. Short said with another smile, and clapped Charlie on the shoulder. Charlie almost buckled under the weight of his hand, but he was pleased, nonetheless. For as long as Charlie could remember, every time he'd come with Mum or Grandpa Fitz, Mr. Short had smiled indulgently at him as said "Mr. Merriweather" in mock-serious tones. The first time Charlie had come into the store by himself to get the family's weekly allotment of bacon and cooking oil and milk and all the other little things that made life possible but that there were never enough of, he had been shaking so badly with nerves that his ration book fluttered in his hands like a moth. Mr. Short had looked at Charlie for a long moment and then nodded and said, "Charlie," and taken the book in calm, sure hands to fill out the logs. And he had been "Charlie" ever since.

Being treated as a grown-up by someone who mattered had made Charlie feel proud and a little embarrassed and, for just a moment, terribly, terribly lonely.

On the corner, Mad Mellie was continuing her inspection of the street's garbage, the flock of pigeons trailing after her like an ugly cape. They fluttered and squawked as he walked past to his bicycle, and Mad Mellie glared at him for disturbing them. Trying to hide behind his upturned jacket collar, he carefully settled the groceries into the basket attached to the handlebars. He avoided talking to Mad Mellie if he could help it.

"Keep your beast away from my pigeons!" Mad Mellie shouted

at him as he approached, and Charlie opened his mouth to protest that Biscuits wasn't even *doing* anything when he saw a little white-and-marmalade shadow lurking underneath Mad Mellie's favorite bench. She was stalking a pigeon with the focused intensity of a big game hunter, eyes huge, tail twitching, body slunk low to the ground.

Go home, Charlie mouthed at her, trying to shoo her away without drawing Mad Mellie's attention to her. Biscuits chirruped at him in greeting and Mellie whirled around at the sound. Before Charlie could shout that he would take Biscuits home *straight* away, he *promised*, Mellie had dived after Biscuits, brandishing an umbrella and shouting some very unflattering things about Biscuits's lineage. Biscuits streaked away in a cat-shaped blur, Mellie chasing after her down the block. Charlie pedaled as fast as he could and ducked his head down, trying very much to look like he was in no way a part of this exchange.

"*Biscuits*," he hissed as soon as he'd rounded the corner, swiveling his head back and forth looking for her little cat shape. But Biscuits had disappeared again, presumably to gloat and digest. She would show up at home for her tea when she was good and ready and not a second before. Biscuits time had very little to do with people time. "Cats view time as more of a philosophical construct," Mum had said once. "They're a bit like your grandfather that way." Grandpa Fitz had just snored louder from his chair by the fire.

Even with Biscuits off somewhere bringing more shame to

the Merriweather family name, Charlie found it difficult to stay gloomy as he rode home. The sun was bright and fat in the sky and it made him feel warmer than he probably really was, and his bicycle basket was full of soap and sugar and tea.

Seven days and Theo will be home. The thought made him pedal faster.

Charlie's good mood fizzled and died as he turned the corner to his house. A thin, reedy man in a rather upsetting hat was crouched in front of the door with an oil can, making a great production of doctoring the hinges.

"Charlie!" the man called, waving.

"Hello, Mr. Cleaver," Charlie said, getting off his bike and walking it to the house, while trying to maintain a safe distance from the man and his hat.

Charlie did not like Mr. Cleaver. It wasn't that Mr. Cleaver was unfriendly—rather, it was, among other reasons, his extreme friendliness that made Charlie keen to avoid him. When Mr. Cleaver smiled, he had what seemed to Charlie to be far too many teeth for his rather thin, small mouth. The hat was just unpleasant window dressing.

"Heard your mum talking about how this old door here has been giving you lip, and thought I'd just stop by and remind it who's in charge here." Mr. Cleaver stood, and slapped his grotesque hat on his knee for emphasis.

"Oh."

"Yes, I wasn't sure about her hours at the phone company; I know they've been letting people go all over the city, what with the boys coming back from the front. Will she be home anytime soon?" Mr. Cleaver's eyebrows bowed like a hopeful dog. "Worth sticking around for a bit?"

"*No.*"

"Ah, drat, I was afraid of that. But you know, Charlie, I wanted to say, just between us lads, that if you ever need any help around the house, don't hesitate to call! I know how difficult things have been, just the three of you, and old Fitzy feeling his age—"

"Theo will be home next week," Charlie said, parking his bike and making his way to the door, being sure to keep a safe distance between himself and Mr. Cleaver, as if he were contagious. "So we'll be fine."

"Of course, of course! And about time, too!" Mr. Cleaver looked as if he were about to slap Charlie's shoulder or ruffle his hair, and Charlie willed himself to look as prickly as possible. "Well, I'll see you all at the church meeting tonight, then, yes?"

"Yes," Charlie allowed, easing the door open and trying to slip inside.

"Lovely, well, please tell your mother I stopped—"

Charlie closed the door in his face. The hinges didn't even have the good grace to squeak in solidarity.

"Thank the sweet Almighty, I thought he'd never leave." Grandpa Fitz was in his regular clothes and fussing with the woodstove next to a pile of fresh wood. "He kept asking to come inside. Had to sing a rather inappropriate shanty about a porpoise to convince him I was dotty."

Charlie ran over to hug Grandpa Fitz, his arms barely closing around his waist. It was like hugging a tree trunk, something that had stood forever and could never fall. He pressed his face into Grandpa Fitz's soft shirt until his eyes no longer prickled.

Grandpa Fitz ruffled Charlie's hair with his one hand, and then helped him unpack the groceries.

3

CHARLIE NEVER USUALLY MINDED GOING TO church meetings, but knowing that Mr. Cleaver was lurking somewhere, waiting for his chance to talk to Mum, Charlie found that it was the worst idea he had ever heard in his entire life. He squirmed in his good shoes as Father MacIntosh stood before him and a dozen other kids from church, gazing out at the pack of them as if inspecting mustered troops.

"As you all know, tomorrow is our trip to the hospital to visit with the convalescing soldiers there. Now," he said, straightening up behind the art table in front of him as if it were a pulpit, "I know none of you would have such *poor taste*, such *little regard* for the sacrifice of both our servicemen and our caregivers that you would *run in the halls*, or *raise your voices*, or *speak out of turn*, or"—he turned his bright eyes on them like searchlights—"*loiter.*" His voice held unspeakable disgust.

Charlie was not sure what was so horrible about loitering but knew better than to ask.

The church visit to the hospital had been planned for weeks, but somehow it had still managed to sneak up on him. Stacks of newspaper were arranged on each table, and some enterprising parent had glued sheets together to make thicker paper for the cards. They were a bit bubbly and still damp in places, but satisfyingly sturdy. Pots of watercolors and even some tubes of oil paint were distributed between chairs with cups of water for rinsing and stained hand towels.

"The doctors and nurses at the hospital will be *working* while we are there, do you understand?" Father Mac continued. "You are not to distract or bother them in any way, or I will be forced to have *words* with my *supervisor.*"

"Who?" Rosie Linton asked in a loud whisper.

"He means God," Sean hissed back. Rosie paled.

"These soldiers have enough to deal with without the load of you running rampant through the wing like a pack of wild boars. Some of them may have especially grievous injuries, some of them may even seem a bit frightening. So it is important to know that if their appearance makes you feel at all uncomfortable, even for a moment, you will *not draw attention to that fact.*"

Father Mac swung around to scowl at them all accusingly, scanning them for signs of weakness.

What if Theo looks different?

Charlie slammed the door shut on the thought as soon as he had it. There were certain things he could not think about, things that stole the breath out of his lungs, that left him

27

breathing in shallows pants, unable to either concentrate or properly relax. He had to throw them out before they could take hold.

Charlie wanted to paint a garden on his card—everyone liked gardens—but of course there was no green paint, all of it long since gone to the military for camouflage coloring. So he made a blue sky in long swaths of watery paint and blew on it to dry. He added a few gray clouds—it was England, after all—and black Vs of birds.

That one wasn't very good. He picked up a fresh sheet of paper.

Well, of course Theo would look different. He might be a bit taller, he might have lost some of the softness around his cheeks. Maybe he could grow a beard now. Charlie's shoulders unknotted themselves a bit.

Father Mac was prowling around the tables, offering such helpful commentary as, "I'm not sure a painting of a graveyard sends the *precise* message of calm you intend, Eustace."

"But they're nice and quiet!" Eustace protested.

Next to him, Sean was painting his hand with a brush and pressing businesslike handprint flowers onto four sheets of paper at a time like an assembly line.

Theo would come home and Theo would be fine. This was the only truth Charlie could accept. It was the only prayer he could make, the words he superimposed over everything else Father Mac was saying. His mind covered up *missing arms* and *chemical burns* and *shrapnel* with thick strokes of carefully mixed white and brown, and painted over them with Theo's white smile with his crooked bottom teeth, his clear blue eyes, his not-quite-brown-not-quite-ginger hair, the tiny white scar on his chin where Mum said he had walked into a table and lost a baby tooth.

"That's a lovely portrait, Charlie, but remember we're making cards for people besides Theo," said Father Mac's voice behind his shoulder.

Charlie startled and knocked his elbow into a cup, upturning a stream of cloudy water that spread across the table, instantly soaking the thin paper.

Charlie could only watch as Theo's features dissolved and bled away.

At the end of the hour, everyone gathered up their cards and placed them somewhere to dry, then shuffled back out into the main hall. Charlie had lost his enthusiasm for the whole affair, and so he had taken a few gluey sheets of paper with him to finish at home. He still had half a paint set left from four Christmases ago. If nothing else, he could make a few handprint flowers like Sean, even if the stems and leaves would have to be blue.

From the next room, where everyone else was waiting for the children to finish making cards, Charlie heard Mr. Cleaver's braying laugh above the din of grown-up conversation. He scowled, the newspaper crinkling up in his fist. He was still trying to flatten it against his leg as he entered. Mum came into view, smiling politely at something Mr. Cleaver was saying. He touched her elbow to emphasize his point, and Charlie ran over to shove his painting directly in front of Mum's face.

"What lovely birds, Charles," Mum said, meeting his eyes over the card and raising one eyebrow at him. *Behave*, she mouthed silently.

"Charlie!" Mr. Cleaver said through his mustache. "How is that front door treating you? Not giving you any more guff?" He chortled around all of his teeth.

"No."

Mum nudged his shin with her shoe.

"Thank you," he added, fixing a flat smile on his face.

When Theo is here, Mr. Cleaver won't have any reason to bother Mum, Charlie thought smugly as he dragged Mum over to look at the cards where they were drying. In fact, it was entirely possible that this was the last any of them would ever see of Mr. Cleaver and his horrible mustache except for glimpses across the pews on Sunday. That happy thought propelled him all through the rest of the evening: all through Father Mac's seventh reiteration that walking quietly through hospital corridors was infinitely preferable to the fires of damnation, and all way through the cold black night and back home.

"That Mr. Cleaver is a right busybody, if you ask me," Grandpa Fitz announced as they sat down to a late dinner.

"*Dad*," Mum said, giving him a look over her water glass.

"Stuart has been very kind to us."

"Yes, a real paragon of selflessness, that one," said Grandpa Fitz, rolling his eyes.

Mum did not inform him that his face was going to stick that way, as she usually did. Instead she just looked unhappy and moved a bit of carrot around her plate.

"I was thinking we should get Theo's room ready, for when he's home," Charlie said into the silence.

Mum smiled, but it didn't look as if she really meant it. "That's a nice idea, Charlie. Maybe you could start by dusting things off in there, and then later this week we can wash all the bed linens so they're nice and fresh."

"I'm making a list of things we're going to do when he gets back, so I don't forget anything. The fish and chips place on Farthing Street for sure. The park won't be any good for picnics yet, obviously, but we can still walk by the big fountain and maybe look at the—"

"Charlie boy." Grandpa Fitz reached out his one hand to rest briefly on top of Charlie's. "It's good that you're excited for your brother coming home, but . . . I just want you to be sure you're keeping your expectations . . . realistic."

"What does that mean?"

"It means something that might happen in the real world—"

"I know what 'realistic' means. I meant what are you trying to say?"

Mum's fork scraped against her plate as Grandpa Fitz scratched

31

at his stubbly chin with a horrible, dry crackling sound that instantly made Charlie annoyed for no good reason.

"Theo's been injured—" Mum began.

"I know."

"—and he may not have . . . the easiest time," she continued gently. "At least not at first. Maybe not for a while."

"I just don't want you sewing drapes when you haven't built the house yet, Charlie," said Grandpa Fitz. "People come back from war different than they were. Sometimes there's less of them, like my old arm here. It's important to remember that—if he seems different, or if he acts a bit odd, we need to be understanding. Sometimes you can't see what's missing right away."

Charlie shoved a mouthful of potato into his mouth and forced himself to swallow it down with all things he wanted to shout at them. Weren't they at all excited for Theo to come home?

Mum's hand on his arm startled him back to the table. She smiled at him, looking rueful and fond all at once, and he wasn't really sure if it was for him or Grandpa Fitz or both. "We're all going to have to be very patient and kind with each other," she said. "For Theo's sake. It will probably take a good long while before he's feeling like himself again."

Grandpa Fitz *hmm*ed, but said nothing further.

"Come on, love." Mum pushed herself to her feet, straightening her shoulders until she looked like herself again. "Let's get these dishes cleaned, then get you to bed as well. We've all had a very long day."

＊＊＊

When Charlie finally did get into bed, he lay there in the flickering candlelight, looking about his room, unblinking. Everything had a fine, invisible coating over it, like dust—everything in his room, the whole house, the street, London. He'd stayed awake like this in the chilly dark, night after endless night, trying to memorize everything as it was so that he could tell Theo about it and how it had changed.

Here's the clock that always needed to be reset after a week because it went slow. I took it apart and put it back together, and now it only needs to be reset every two weeks, which is sort of better.

Here's the blanket Mum crocheted the first winter you were gone, and here's the hole Biscuits tore in it, and here's the darning Mum showed me how to do to sew it shut.

Here's the last school photograph I took; they told me not to smile, but I tried to anyway and my cheeks got tired so I just look cross.

Here's all the books I read so far this year; me and Sean O'Leary and Rosie Linton have been having a contest. Rosie is winning so far, but her dad has lots more books than we do, just lying around, which I think is cheating.

He rolled over onto to his side and pressed his face into his pillow.

It will probably take a good long while before he's feeling like himself again.

Charlie fell asleep listening to the sound of Mum moving around in Theo's room across the hall, a sound he'd missed for

33

so very long, and in the darkness he could pretend, just for a moment, that nothing had changed at all.

When he dreamed, he dreamed of that yellow eye burning out of the darkness and pinning him in place.

4

CHARLIE HAD PLANNED TO BEGIN GETTING THEO'S room homecoming-ready the next day, but other tasks kept jumping out of line and demanding his attention. They needed more firewood, Biscuits broke a bowl, which needed to be mended, and Charlie's best trousers ripped all down one side when they caught on a loose nailhead and had to be frantically sewn up while Grandpa Fitz chanted encouragements. By the time the trousers were decent, Charlie had to yank them on—sticking himself with a stray pin in the process—and run with Grandpa Fitz down the block to the church so they could all walk down to the hospital in a huge, shivering flock, homemade cards clutched in their numb fingers.

The pack of kids trundled down the street, winter coats and hats and scarves making their shapes indistinct and interchangeable. Father Mac led the troupe from the front and Grandpa Fitz brought up the back, keeping an eye out for any stragglers. They broke apart every now and then like a school of fish, skirting around the cratered streets and the great heaps of brick and timber and ice, and Charlie had to be careful not to step on nails or bits of glass.

There was a fresh layer of wet snow and their footsteps sloshed, leaving deep footprints behind them. A dog must have passed this way just ahead of them, and Charlie tried to match his footsteps to its paw prints as he walked. But the dog must have been enormous, as Charlie could barely match its stride, even stretching his legs as far as they would go. He was concentrating so hard that he walked right into Sean, causing a tumultuous domino effect down the line that culminated in Eustace smacking into Father MacIntosh, whose raised eyebrow sent them all scurrying back to rightness.

The hospital doors opened to envelop them in a puff of warm air that instantly made Charlie's toes start to prickle unpleasantly as the blood rushed back into them. He hopped from foot to foot as all the children presented themselves to Father Mac for final inspection, and Grandpa Fitz stood in the back.

A lady strode down the hall to stand next to Father Mac—she was what Grandpa Fitz would probably have called "strapping," quite as tall as all the men in the room and far more wide, and draped from head to foot in a soot-black nun's habit. She was more than a bit terrifying and Charlie gulped, clutching his cards a little tighter.

"This is Matron," Father Mac said, gesturing to the tall lady. "She is in *charge* and to be *minded*." They all nodded quickly, their heads bobbing like tulips in a breeze. Matron squinted down at them all. Biscuits would have been impressed by the way she changed her expression not at all while still somehow expressing that they were all being judged and found a bit lacking.

Father Mac stalked back and forth in front of his troops with rather terrifying intensity. "What are we going to be?"

"RESPECTFUL," they all said in unison.

"What are we *not* going to be?"

"NOISY, BOTHERSOME, OR UNDERFOOT."

"Where do we reconvene if we get lost?"

"THE FRONT LOBBY."

"Lift up your cards."

Eustace began to intone, "We lift them up to the Lord our God," but caught himself and shoved his handful of homemade cards up instead. Father Mac did a quick, hawk-eyed perusal to confirm that no one had shown up card-less, then turned on his heel, beckoning his troops after him as he followed Matron through the swinging double doors of the lobby.

The hospital had a very distinct smell—not a bad one exactly, but a highly unnatural one that made Charlie feel he was about to sneeze. Everything was alarmingly well-lit and very clean. Women in smart white-and-gray outfits and men in long, too-clean white jackets were walking around the pack of children as if they were rocks in a river, all with a very distinct air of knowing exactly where they were going. They had *purpose*, Charlie supposed, as a doctor nearly flattened Timothy Milligan. *Purpose coming out of their ears*, Charlie thought darkly.

Sean tugged Charlie to a halt, distracting him from his thoughts.

Matron and Father Mac had stopped in front of a wide door, both of them looking very serious and austere.

"We're here," Father Mac said in a softer but no less intense voice. "Remember this is a place of healing and calm for our servicemen. Remember the rules."

Charlie hustled through the door with everyone else. Inside was a long, narrow room lined on either side with beds and a few curtains and tables, and in every bed was a man. Most of them seemed to be terribly young, but there were a few that looked to be the same age Dad would have been.

Sean took one look at the room, handed Charlie his stack of cards, and walked out.

"Sean—" Father Mac began.

"No," Sean said simply, without turning around.

Charlie's already sour stomach seemed as if it was trying to arrange itself into new and interesting shapes.

"Carry on, Charlie," Father Mac said, his voice gruff but not unkind, and gave him a shove between his shoulder blades.

Swallowing dryly, Charlie walked up to the nearest bed and cleared his throat. "Hullo," he croaked.

The man—the soldier—didn't seem to hear him. His skin was somehow whiter than the bleach-rough sheets he was lying on, a pale blue-striped blanket tucked up neatly around his waist. He was sitting like a figurine, as if he'd been posed.

"Er, this is for you. We made them."

He held out a card—one of Sean's, which had a picture of a big tree with red leaves because there hadn't been any green paint. But the soldier didn't reach for it, so after a long moment Charlie just placed it on the bedside table next to a picture of two dubious-looking babies.

"Welcome home," he finally finished lamely, and went to the next bed, his face hot and sort of stretched-feeling, like it was about to crack open.

The next soldier had a mop of brown curls and was missing the same arm as Grandpa Fitz. Charlie almost remarked on it, but clamped his jaw shut just in time, which had the unfortunate side effect of making him appear to stare, at a loss for words, for a long moment.

"Oh, it's not so bad," the man said with a dry laugh. "Did you have something for me?"

"Oh!" Charlie's face somehow got hotter and tighter, and he presented his next card with a bit too much flourish, sending it flying.

"Now, will you look at us. A matched set!" Grandpa Fitz was suddenly there beside Charlie. He knelt down to rescue the card and placed it on the side table, sitting down at the foot of the bed. "Now, my lad, I'm going to show you my full repertoire of one-handed magic tricks, so I want you to take careful notes because I'm only doing this once, you understand?"

The one-armed soldier settled back on the pillows as Grandpa

Fitz pulled a playing card out of his breast pocket and carefully displayed both sides to him.

"You may wonder where my other arm went, naturally. The truth is that when I was learning this trick, I did it a little too well and made it"—the playing card vanished up his sleeve—"*disappear!*" The soldier threw back his head and gave a barking laugh like a seal. Charlie ducked behind a curtain tucked away in the corner and tried to catch his breath, with his eyes squeezed shut to keep anything so inappropriate as tears to come leaking out.

"Not really my scene out there, either," a voice said from behind him.

Charlie whipped around and realized he had hidden inside someone's sort-of room and began coughing up apologies like he'd swallowed seawater.

"I'm so sorry, I thought it was just a curtain, I'm so sorry, I'll leave you alone, I'm so—"

"Sorry, yes, you covered that quite thoroughly," the soldier said. "No need for it, though. Truth be told I was feeling a bit neglected back here, even though it *was* my idea to be sequestered far from the madding crowd."

"I'm—"

"If you say sorry I will be forced to point out that it's a rather odd name your parents have saddled you with, and I was raised to have better manners than that."

"—Charlie," he said, taking a breath, finally. "I'm Charlie."

The soldier smiled—he had very bright, birdlike black eyes under black-dash eyebrows that made him look just a bit surprised. It was, all in all, a very pleasant face, and Charlie liked him instantly. He shook the soldier's proffered hand.

"I'm Reginald Pemberton-Ashby, but for the love of all things holy, call me Reggie. The nurses here all call me Reginald, and I'm forever nervous that I'm about to be reprimanded for breaking a vase or some such. My nerves are thoroughly shot."

"My mum only ever calls me Charles," Charlie confided. "If anyone else does it, I get cross."

"Ah, so you understand my predicament! I don't think it's at all good for my convalescence."

"Well, I can't really help with that, either, but here." Charlie stole a pen that was tucked into the side of a chart at the foot of Reggie's bed, and after picking out the best card from his stack, carefully wrote "To Reggie, From Charlie" on the front. "Maybe that will remind them."

"I say, that is clever of you," Reggie said, smiling brilliantly. He took the card to admire it. Charlie had drawn a painstakingly detailed portrait of Biscuits next to a jug of milk—he had mixed paints until he had gotten the exact marmalade color of her spots right and placed them just as they were on Biscuits herself.

"Now *this* is a cat of substance," Reggie said, tapping Biscuits's nose. "You can *see* the plan to knock over that milk forming in her eyes."

"That's my cat, Biscuits," Charlie said, feeling terribly proud because Biscuits *had* knocked over the milk jug while having her portrait done, though thankfully there had only been the smallest bit of milk still in it and Charlie had been planning to give it to her anyway. "She's brilliant. I wanted to bring her here with me, but Father Mac said the hospital would never allow it." The priest had also added something about Biscuits being "the smallest and mightiest of all God's plagues," but Charlie didn't think such slander worth mentioning.

Reggie looked genuinely disappointed at this. "I'd *love* to have some living, breathing creature in here that doesn't try to take my blood pressure as soon as look me. You should sneak her in next time. Say she's an artist's model on assignment and can't possibly be detained from her work."

Charlie laughed, his stomach finally unknotting. His face even felt more or less the right temperature.

"May I see your other offerings?" Reggie said, gesturing to the stack of cards. "I want to admire your full catalog."

"Some of them are my friend Sean's," Charlie said, handing them over. Rocking back on his heels, he stuffed his sweaty hands in his pockets and naturally jabbed himself with yet another stray pin. He hissed and snatched his hand back out, a bright drop of blood sliding off his fingertip as he shook his hand.

"Ah, let me guess, a Sean original?" Reggie said, holding up a card that was composed of a single bright pink handprint that said just said "Hello" underneath. Reggie had a kind, easy smile and it made Charlie miss Theo so badly that he felt light-headed for a moment.

"Can I—" Charlie cleared his throat, feeling his ears get hot. "Can I ask you something? About—about the war?"

The smile slid off Reggie's face all at once. "Certainly," he said, his voice still warm and polite, even as a sort of vacant resignation settled into his eyes.

"My brother, Theo, he's coming home this week. But he . . . he stopped writing a couple of months ago. When he first left, he always wrote to me, even if it was just a postcard. But after a while, he started to write less frequently, and then he just . . . stopped." Charlie swallowed thickly, looking at the floor. "Why would he do that?"

All the warmth had left Reggie's face, and he looked somehow hollowed out, almost transparent, his skin sallow and sweaty. "Let me ask you something: What's the worst thing you've ever done?"

Charlie blanched. *That time he broke the vase Mum's grandmother had made and let Theo take the blame. That time he had yelled at Grandpa Fitz for spilling all their milk, even though he was confused and it wasn't his fault. When he couldn't find Biscuits, and the air raid sirens were wailing and wailing and they had gone into the shelter without her and he couldn't even hear himself screaming for her over the sirens.*

"You don't want to tell me, do you? Of course you don't." Reggie's voice was gentle, his pale face soft, like he was apologizing for making Charlie think of whatever the worst thing he'd ever done was. "And that's fine, because it's private, and it's hard, and hard things are difficult to speak about." He settled back on his pillows with a heavy sigh and went on, almost to himself. "But sometimes it's as if the more you don't talk about that thing, the worse it becomes, the bigger it get in your memory, and it starts to poison things."

He shuffled through the pile of cards again, pulling out at random a smeared red handprint Sean had fashioned into an unlikely heart. "You look at things you know you should love, and you feel . . . you feel . . ." His voice trailed off. He was staring at the harmless, ugly little card with something almost like horror. "I'm sorry," Reggie mumbled, his dark bird's eyes too bright, feverish. "You need to leave," he said, grabbing on to Charlie's wrist with shocking strength, the skin blooming splotchy red and white under each fingertip. "You need to leave."

"What—no—Reggie, let *go*."

Reggie looked down at his own hand where it was clutching Charlie, his eyes going wide, and snatched his hand away.

"You need to leave. *Please*, Charlie."

But Charlie was already turning, shoving his way past the curtains and out into the room. Everything was too bright all of a sudden, and loud, and wouldn't stop moving. None of it would stop. He hurried down the rows of beds, stumbling on watery legs.

Every soldier in every bed now had Theo's face, his coppery

hair, his glass-clear eyes. With each bed he passed he saw things missing: arms gone, legs gone, ears, fingers, eyes.

A memory rose gasping to the surface of his mind, a game he and Theo used to play with gingerbread men. Theo would make them run away from Charlie's greedy mouth, pleading, "Not my toes! Not my lovely knees!" in tiny, silly voices, as they tore their limbs apart. Charlie would never be able to eat another gingerbread man, he realized, with an instant and total surety.

He was going to be ill.

Charlie stumbled past Matron, her lips pursed in displeasure at his blundering, and burst out into the hall and ran all the way to the lobby, he didn't care if he was bothersome or underfoot, he couldn't *breathe*—

"It's all right, Charlie, take a breath." Sean's voice cut through the noise, and Charlie realized they were alone here in the quiet, echoing space, except for the woman behind the great front desk. "That's it, just keep breathing. Come sit down for a moment."

After a minute or an hour or however long they sat there, Charlie leaned back against the wall, too shamed to even look at Sean.

"Yeah," Sean sighed, leaning back so they were side by side. "It's like that, isn't it?"

"I'm afraid that Theo's—" Charlie squeezed his eyes shut so hard they actually hurt, but a few tears got past anyway. "I'm afraid *all the time.*"

"I don't really know which is worse," Sean said, his voice flat.

"The being afraid, or the knowing. I really don't."

They sat like that, silent and not quite touching, until the rest of the church party came back.

Grandpa Fitz didn't say a word to Charlie as they walked home, but he held Charlie's hand, very tightly, the whole way, and never once let go.

5

CHARLIE AND GRANDPA FITZ STILL HADN'T SPO-
ken by the time they were divesting themselves of coats, hats,
and gloves, putting the kettle on for tea. The room was cramped
with all the things neither of them was saying.

"Charlie . . ." Grandpa Fitz started, his voice so gentle that it
set Charlie's teeth on edge.

"I don't want to talk about it," Charlie said, his voice flat.

"It's all right if you—"

"I *don't* want to *talk* about it." Charlie set the teacups down
too hard and they rattled in their saucers like frightened animals.

That's when Mum swept into the house in a gust of snowy
air and perfume.

"Hello, boys," she called, pulling off her gloves and rolling her
head back and forth as she rubbed her neck. "I get so hunched
sitting at that desk, I'm starting to look like an old lady." She
struggled to take off her coat, and Charlie hurried over to help
her shrug her arms free. Her carefully curled and pinned hair was
wilted with snow and in the dim evening light, shadows seemed

to paint themselves under her eyes and cut deep hollows under her cheekbones. Mum's face, a face built for joy and smiles, had unfamiliar lines tugging her mouth into a frown.

And then she turned her face into the light and her face broke into a smile, and the moment was gone.

"Why do women wear these ridiculous shoes?" she asked, kicking off the shoes in question, one of which went flying and nearly brained Biscuits, who had come running in when she heard the door open. "Oh, sorry, love!" Mum swooped Biscuits up into her arms and kissed the soft fur behind her ears. "Oh, Biscuits, I must admit to coveting this lovely warm coat of yours," Mum said into Biscuits's neck.

Biscuits purred, smug and very loud, and wrapped her tail around Mum's wrist as if to hold her in place.

"How was the hospital visit?" Mum asked over her shoulder, making tea one-handed with Biscuits hoisted up in her arm.

"Fine," Charlie said, forcing his voice into a blank mask of unconcern. Grandpa Fitz gave Charlie a long look and then told the story about the card trick he had taught the one-armed soldier, carefully leaving off any mention of Charlie or Sean. Mum laughed into her tea, seeming to sense nothing amiss. Charlie kept quiet and smiled or laughed when appropriate, wishing for nothing more than to be asleep in bed so the day would just *end*.

"All right," Mum finally announced, pushing back her chair. "To bed with us. We've all got full days tomorrow." They processed up the stairs to their bedrooms, Mum carrying Biscuits on her shoulder.

Grandpa Fitz went into his room without giving Charlie any more significant glances, for which Charlie was pathetically grateful. At her door, Mum released Biscuits back to Charlie, then patted down his hair in a despairing sort of way and smiled.

"Do you want a story before bed, Charles? We haven't had one in a bit."

Charlie wiggled a toe through a hole in one of his socks. He did want a story. He wanted Mum to tuck him in and give him a mug of cocoa to sip in the warm dark until all the different kinds of sweetness lulled him to sleep so he could wake up in the fresh-fallen-snow world of the next morning, brand-new. But he couldn't, and no one else in the house needed a story to go to sleep. And besides, cocoa had been on ration for years now. It probably didn't even taste as nice as he remembered.

"No, I'm fine, Mum."

"All right, love. Good night." Mum kissed the very top of his head and slipped into her room. Charlie padded off down the hall in his stocking feet towards his room. Biscuits met him halfway and rubbed up against his shins. He bent down to scoop her up, but she darted away and pawed at the door to Theo's room.

"He's not in there," Charlie reminded her. He went to scoop her up, but she slithered away from his grip and scratched again, with an insistent *brrrrpt!* Feeling hesitant for no real reason, Charlie turned the knob and nudged the door open. Biscuits

49

squirmed through like a shot and disappeared into the darkness.

The room didn't smell right. It had that musty, un-lived-in smell of attics or garages. It was as if Theo had never lived here, never talked in his sleep here or done star jumps at six in the morning for no reason that he or Mum or Grandpa Fitz could understand. As if Charlie had never had a big brother at all.

His mind went unwillingly to Reggie, brave and funny and alone behind his drawn curtain, still shaking at things that weren't there.

He would not let that be Theo. Not ever.

Biscuits pawed at Theo's window, chittering in alarm. Charlie took a breath and crossed the room in three big steps and swept the curtain aside. He let out his breath in a rush. Across the street was a big, lanky stray dog, its head hanging low, its yellow eyes staring up at the window.

"It's just a silly old dog," he said to Biscuits, and hauled her up onto his shoulder despite her protests. "You can't fight it, it's bigger than you. And it's across the street, anyway."

He shut the door behind them a little harder than he meant to, and stood with his eyes closed in the hall for a long moment. He chewed on his lip, Biscuits's tail thrashing around against his chest.

Mum opened her door on the first knock.

"Everything all right, darling?"

"Could I have a story, Mum? I changed my mind."

Mum's smile wrapped him up warm, and she pulled back the quilt on Dad's empty side of the bed for Charlie to burrow under.

Then she settled herself next to him and wrapped an arm around his shoulders and he tucked himself into the crook of her arm, his head snug under her chin and his ear pressed to the warmth of her heartbeat. Biscuits plonked herself down with finality between their legs.

"Once there was a soldier," Mum began.

"Like Theo and Grandpa Fitz?"

"Just like them, yes, don't interrupt," she said. "A very handsome lad he was, too, and he conducted himself very nobly during the war. When peacetime came, he went home to his brothers and asked to stay with them while he recovered, and until he could find a new career. But his brothers were hard-hearted, and since he was a burden, they sent him away without a thought.

"The soldier went out in the woods and sat down beneath a great big oak tree. Now, as you can well imagine, he was feeling heartbroken and melancholy and terribly, terribly lonely. So he cut open a hand and bled three drops of red blood onto the forest floor and begged, 'Please, anyone, come and find me so I might not be alone.' But no one came, not after hours and hours, and the soldier felt even more lonesome and heartbroken than before. He was having himself a good cry, just like anyone would in his position, when a tall, thin fellow with cloven feet came up to him."

"What's 'cloven'?" Charlie asked, tipping his face up to Mum's.

"That split type of hoof that pigs and goats have, now hush. The tall, thin fellow with his funny feet came up to the man, and asked him what was wrong.

"'I'm alone and I have no skills or craft except for war,' lamented the poor soldier. 'How will I survive? How could anyone love me? What will become of me?'

"'I'll make you a deal,' said the tall, thin man, which is never something someone with good intentions says with any regularity. 'I'll give you riches so you can have whatever life you choose, if you will but agree to my terms.' Because, as you may have gathered, he was a monster, and monsters *always* want *something*."

"What were his terms?" Charlie asked, and Mum tapped him on the nose with her fingertip for silence.

"First, he had to wear a cloak made out of a bear's skin. It was thick and warm and cozy, but it smelled a little odd. Second, he had to agree to wear only the bearskin cloak and to never wash or tend to his appearance for seven years. He would always have money if he put his hand into the pocket of the bearskin cloak—"

"Bearskins have pockets?" Charlie interrupted. Biscuits chirped at him in reproach.

"It was an added feature for practicality. The soldier, it should be said, was confused by these terms, but he agreed, because he couldn't think of anything else to do, he was so distraught.

"Now, the first year wasn't so bad. He had money to pay for lodgings, and if he smelled a little off and looked a little scruffy, well, so do a lot of people. But the second year, he started to look quite rough—his beard was thick as fur and his nails got long and sharp as claws. He was quite a sight, and people were afraid of him. And even though he had money, a lot of people wouldn't let him stay in their inns or houses, and so he spent a lot of nights in people's barns and doghouses and toolsheds.

"As you can imagine, this was quite a dispiriting way to live, and the soldier was so lonely that he jumped at every chance he got to make a friend, even if it was just for a night. He shared his money with all the other poor souls who got stuck out in the barns and sheds with him, and bought them all hot meals to share. He let birds nest in his hair and beard, and rabbits and foxes and hedgehogs all burrowed into his warm bearskin cloak at night to keep warm. So for all of the bad things that happened, he was still happy because he wasn't alone anymore.

"So one day, long after the soldier had lost count of how many years he'd been wearing his bearskin cloak, he came across a man crying and wailing and really making a right spectacle of himself in the middle of the street. The soldier asked the man what was wrong, and the man went on and on about how he had no money and three daughters and how miserable life is when you're poor and have lots of mouths to feed, essentially. So the soldier fished around his pocket and brought out handful after handful of money.

"'I have lots of money that I don't really need,' said the soldier. 'You can have it if you need it.' Well, the other man was so grateful that he wept for joy and danced a jig and promised the soldier one of his daughters' hands in marriage."

"He could do that?" asked Charlie. That didn't seem a fair way to treat one's children. He was quite certain Mum would never give him away for money, even if Grandpa Fitz did sometimes joke about trading Charlie in for butter rations.

"This was the olden days, when people were still quite stupid about the whole concept of marriage and free will. So the soldier followed the man home and did his best to look friendly and marriageable, but the old man's daughters were still so put off by the bearskin cloak and the dirt and the nails that there was a lot of screaming and carrying on. The older two daughters in particular shrieked some rather unkind things about the soldier's appearance and then started crying. The youngest daughter still had some scraps of manners and simply looked very brave in the face of such poor grooming, but in a way that sort of drew attention to itself, if you understand me.

"Well, the soldier had been living rough so long that he'd sort of lost the knack for talking to people, and he was so flustered by the whole thing that he just ran away to be alone in the woods for a moment to collect himself. And then who do you suppose he should meet but the tall, thin fellow with the funny feet. It turned out that it was the very last day of his seventh year in the bearskin cloak, and he hadn't even known. Now the tall, thin fellow might have been sneaky, but he understood that rules are rules. So he had the soldier stand in the stream nearby and scrubbed him all over with soap. It took three scrubs and rinses to get all the dirt and birds' nests out. Then he cut the soldier's hair and trimmed his beard and clipped his nails and got him all kitted out in a sharp new black velvet coat and shiny boots and a crisp white shirt.

"'May I keep the bearskin cloak?' the soldier asked. You see, he'd worn it so long that he'd grown quite attached to it, and the thought of being without it made him anxious. The tall, thin fellow said it made no difference to him, and wished the soldier well in all his endeavors. So the soldier gathered up his bearskin under his arm and went back to the village where the other man and his daughters lived. Mostly because he didn't know what else to do with himself, he was so overcome by the whole thing.

"The man's two older daughters were near hysterical when they realized that the handsome chap in the velvet coat was the same man in the bearskin. *They* wanted to marry a rich, handsome man, too. But the youngest daughter was the one who the old man had promised to the soldier, so out she went to shake his hand."

"She still had to marry him?" Charlie said. "But that's not fair. She didn't even know him, and he was scary."

"I quite agree, Charles, so you'll be relieved to hear that the soldier released her from her father's promise and she went off to marry a very nice lad she'd known her whole life and was terribly smitten with. The soldier paid for their wedding and they remained the best of friends for the rest of their long lives."

"What about the older sisters?"

"Well, they were so upset that they'd missed their chance to marry a rich, handsome soldier that they flung themselves into the river, never to be seen again, and the devil was insufferably smug about getting two souls for the price of one."

"Mum! That's terrible!"

"I agree that it was a bit of an overreaction on their parts, but some families are just naturally prone to dramatics. But you'll be relieved to know that the bearskin soldier was happy and generous the rest of his days, and he gave most of his money to others to better their lives, and lived simply and was much beloved by the whole town."

"That's good," Charlie agreed. "Did he ever get to get married?"

"No, he decided that marriage wasn't for him. But he *did* find a lovely, sleek cat curled up in his bearskin cloak one night and she and all her children and grandchildren and great-grandchildren loved him and kept him company all of his days."

"I like that ending better," Charlie said into Mum's shoulder. He felt heavy all over. Like he was wearing a bearskin cloak, maybe.

"I thought you might."

It was a good story, but Charlie had been worrying a thought like a splinter since the beginning of it. "Mum . . . how could the soldier's brothers have sent him away like that?"

Mum smiled a little and brushed his hair out of his face. Those thin etched lines from before were back on her face. Abruptly, she sat up and pulled the covers back, tapping Charlie on the knee.

"You and Miss Biscuits head off to bed now, and I forbid you to dream of anything that isn't lovely, understand?"

"But, Mum—"

"*Bed*, Charles."

"Okay," Charlie said, crawling out from Mum's warm bed. "Good night, Mum."

"Good night, sweet boy. I love you. And remember: only lovely dreams tonight."

"Okay," Charlie said again, and closed the door behind him.

It was only after he had burrowed deep under his own covers with Biscuits curled up next to his pillow that he remembered he hadn't said "I love you" back.

"I love you, too," he whispered to the dark room. Only Biscuits was there to hear it, but he fancied that maybe she purred a little louder in response.

6

THE NEXT FIVE DAYS PASSED BY IN A BLUR OF frantic chores that each bled into the next as all three of them stumbled over themselves to get the house ready for Theo. Linens had to be washed and then, somehow, dried on long laundry lines that stretched across the kitchen like an inconvenient field hospital. Dishes had to be scrubbed, rugs had to be beaten so great clouds of dirt puffed out of them and promptly onto Charlie's clothes, which then also had to be washed. Floors were swept and mopped with heavy buckets that Charlie kept overfilling and spilling onto himself and Biscuits. As carefully as if they were made of glass, making note of exactly which drawer or hanger they had come from, Charlie took out all of Theo's clothes and aired them so they would be fresh, and waiting for him like open arms. And every day, Mum apologized that she couldn't help more before she left for work, fretting and wringing her hands, which only hardened Charlie's resolve to make everything *perfect*.

He did not think it would be possible for Theo's homecoming day to sneak up on him, but one morning he went to cross the day off the calendar and, with a shock like missing a stair in the dark, he saw that "Theo Comes Home!" was the next day.

The house was toasty warm and Charlie was light and bouncy as a soap bubble as he danced Biscuits around the room, fizzy with anticipation. Grandpa Fitz was already set up at the table with yesterday's newspaper, reading glasses perched delicately on his nose.

"Morning," Charlie called over his shoulder, setting Biscuits down on the tabletop so he could get the teakettle started. Grandpa Fitz waved his fingers a bit in greeting but didn't look up from his paper. Biscuits slithered over his gnarled wrist and shoved herself in front of the paper.

"Shoo, tiny hellion," Grandpa Fitz said, but he dropped the paper and scratched her under her chin. Biscuits purred loudly enough that Charlie could hear her across the kitchen by the stove. He fetched clean cups for tea off the draining board and carefully spooned a portion of yesterday's tea ration into each cup. There was something nice about being good at a job.

When he'd first started making morning tea for himself and Grandpa Fitz while Mum was at work, he had either dumped far too much into each cup so that they ran out of tea after three days, or he'd put so little in that the tea didn't taste like anything but hot water. He'd had to stand on a stool to reach the sink and have Grandpa Fitz fetch things from the cupboard. Now he knew the exact right amount of tea to use, how long to let it steep—Mum liked her tea very strong, as did Grandpa Fitz.

Charlie liked his a bit less aggressive. He took the kettle off the stovetop just as it was thinking about letting out a shriek, and poured the hot water into each cup.

He nudged Biscuits away from the cup he set down for Grandpa Fitz and she chattered at them in disapproval.

"Thank you, my lad, as always." Grandpa Fitz breathed in the steam rising off his cup and let out a loud, happy sigh. "Nothing better than a good cup of tea, is there?"

Charlie thought there were several things that were better than a good cup of tea—cakes and chocolate and films, for example—but he decided it wouldn't be polite to say so. Charlie took a gulp of tea rather than answering and scalded his tongue for his trouble.

"Have you ever heard that story about the man with the bearskin?" he asked when his tongue didn't smart quite so much. "The fairy tale? Mum told it to me the other night."

"I've heard of just about every story," said Grandpa Fitz.

"Would you wear a bearskin and never wash for seven years if it meant you'd always be rich?"

Grandpa Fitz scoffed into his teacup. "I already went for three years without washing during the first world war and I certainly didn't get rich from it."

"I *know*, but if you *could*?"

"What has rich ever done for anyone, anyway? I've had most of the good things a body can have in my life and I never needed *rich* to get them."

"Well, what if you could get something else that you really wanted? Like, like—like what if you could get your arm back?" Charlie was instantly ashamed of himself, but Grandpa Fitz just laughed.

"I never needed Old Lefty to get any of the best things, either. Why, I think it was my asymmetrical charm that first caught your grandma Lily's eye."

"But if—"

"Listen, Charlie boy, there's not a thing on God's earth that could tempt this old man into voluntarily not washing for seven weeks, let alone seven years. Why do you ask, anyway? Trying to work a way out of scrubbing behind your ears?"

"No, I was just thinking. You know. Of what would be worth wearing a bearskin for seven years for." *Like your brother coming home safe when you hadn't heard from him for months. Or your dad tucked into his side of the bed. Or your mum, lit up by sunlight, laughing and laughing in the summer heat.*

He reached out to shoo Biscuits away from his breakfast; she slithered away from his touch and poured herself into Grandpa Fitz's lap and began purring in a very loud, pointed way. Grandpa Fitz set down his tea to stroke her and Biscuits made a strange little motion with her head, as if she was butting it up against his missing left hand.

Grandpa Fitz had once told Charlie that people like him who had lost an arm or a leg or a foot could sometimes still feel it, even though it had long since disappeared. Maybe cats could, too. It warranted considering.

"I'm going out for a bit," Charlie announced into the quiet. Grandpa Fitz just made a noise into his tea. "Mum and me are making biscuits for Theo later."

"Mind the street and don't spit into the wind," Grandpa Fitz called after him, which Charlie thought was a rather odd sort of send-off, but then Grandpa Fitz was a rather odd sort of grandfather. Charlie just pulled on his Sunday jacket over his jumper and waved a mitten in reply.

Biscuits had somehow magicked herself into his bicycle basket by the time he got outside. She chattered at him for dawdling as he wheeled them out onto the street, then squinted in pleasure as the breeze ruffled her whiskers.

It did feel good to be outside. Every room in the house felt like it was the wrong size lately, as if Charlie was always taking up too much room, or not enough. His mind wandered as he pedaled down the street, dodging stray bits and pieces of glass without thinking.

The sun was out for the first time in days, and it lit up the dingy street like a fancy iced cake. Everything looked bright white, and sweet. The thought of iced cakes made Charlie's mouth water and his stomach gurgle, but sugar had been on strict ration since the war started. Mum had asked him up front if he'd rather save up their sugar rations for something special, like an iced birthday cake, or use them up on everyday treats like tea and biscuits. She had told him to take a good long time to think on it, even though he knew right away that he'd rather have simple biscuits dusted with a bit of sugar every Sunday than a fancy cake he'd only get to taste maybe once or twice a year.

"I think that's both very practical and very wise, Charles," Mum had said. "There's something to be said for delaying your pleasure of something, but I think we've had more than our fair share of that already. There's also something to be said for having something nice up front, too." And she had kissed the top of his head and they'd spent the afternoon making the biscuit dough and rolling it out flat on the countertop and cutting it into neat circles. It had rained all day and he got to pop one of the biscuits hot and sweet into his mouth right out of the oven. It had been a good day.

All he needed from the grocer's was an orange, and even though fresh fruits were rationed along with everything else, Charlie didn't feel the same heavy pressure that came with buying a regular week's worth of groceries. Orange drop biscuits didn't need any sugar. They used honey instead, from good sturdy English bees, and the juice and rind of the orange. They didn't taste quite the same, and they were soft and melty instead of crispy and crumbly. But they weren't bad. And after five years, he had gotten used to them. He had gotten used to a lot of things. You could get used to anything, really, if you found a way not to think about it too much.

He put the orange on the counter, and Mr. Short went through the now-familiar ritual of checking the ration book. The grocer was making idle talk, but Charlie couldn't bring himself to do more than nod and smile in return. He felt strange, for some reason. He was excited to make the biscuits. He didn't know why he felt almost angry looking at the small orange rolling slightly on the counter. Outside, Biscuits pawed at the glass, her mouth opening wide in a silent meow of reproach.

"Now, now, Miss Biscuits, we're almost done," Mr. Short said, waving at her.

Charlie realized, now that he thought about it, that in his mind the idea of sugar and the idea of his brother had gotten all tangled together, that some part of him had assumed that when one came back, so would the other. But Theo would be home tomorrow, and sugar was still gold-dust precious. That was all right, though, he thought, tucking the orange under his arm and heading back out to his bicycle, waving to Mr. Short through the glass. There were other kinds of sweetness in the world.

He tapped the wicker basket between his handlebars, and Biscuits leaped up into it with an impatient chirp. He felt a bit ridiculous, cycling back from the grocer's with a single orange rolling around in his basket. But it left enough room for Biscuits to ride as well, one of her back feet braced precariously against the fruit.

Charlie was stretching his arms in a wide arc when an enormous black rat scuttled across the street just as Charlie rounded the corner, something that looked terribly like a piece of bird wing clutched in its sharp teeth, and Charlie swerved to avoid it. Biscuits screamed bloody red death at him or the rat or both, and it was all Charlie could do to keep from flattening poor old Mad Mellie where she was examining something in the street.

He wrenched the bicycle to the side to avoid the old woman and crashed right into her pram, knocking it over and sending the odds and ends she had collected flying in all directions.

"I'm sorry! Are you all right? I'm so sorry!"

"You keep your beast away from my pigeons," Mad Mellie snapped, quite calmly, from where she was, nary an inch from the middle of the street. Charlie looked down to find his basket empty save the orange, and Biscuits slinking towards the flock of blue-and-gray birds. He could tell that her intentions were not noble.

"Biscuits!" he shouted, dropping his bike to chase after her. "You leave those pigeons alone! They're not for eating!" Biscuits flicked an ear backwards towards his voice, but otherwise ignored him. Charlie had to run to grab her by the scruff of her neck right before she pounced at a particularly fat and vacant-looking pigeon. Biscuits hissed at him in betrayal and twisted out of his grip, streaking away from him to sulk by his overturned bicycle.

"Think on your sins," Mellie said to Biscuits as she passed by on her way to her bench. Biscuits scornfully ignored her. Mellie held up her find from the street so Charlie could see. "A *shilling*," she said proudly, twisting it so it glinted in the light. "Tonight you feast, my lovelies." Charlie thought the last bit was probably intended for her pigeons.

Pocketing the coin, Mellie began the business of gathering up the contents of her upended pram. Charlie hurried over to help her, but she slapped his hand away when he went to reach for a chipped blue vase. "No, no, no, you'll just put them back all out of order. You tend to my birds while I set this mess to rights." And she fished a small bag of very stale bread crumbs out of the depths of her jumpers and shoved it into Charlie's limp hands. "Go!"

Charlie jumped, his hands snapping closed around the bread crumbs. The pigeons instantly swarmed him. The fluttering of their countless wings against his ankles made him feel equal parts squirmy and happy. They were sort of funny, once you got past the hungry look in their beady eyes.

Charlie, keeping a careful eye on Biscuits and the twitching tip of her tail, dropped a few bread crumbs on the ground and immediately caused a kind of pigeon riot, coos and feathers flying violently. Charlie yelped and clutched the bag to his chest, which didn't help.

"If you're going to feed them, you have to feed them *all*, or the little ones will starve," Mellie said without looking up from her hunt in the bushes for something that had flown there during the collision. Charlie quickly threw another handful of bread crumbs to the other side of the pigeon swarm. Feathers, gray and black and green and lavender, roiled like a tiny, chirping sea.

He looked up to ask Mellie if he was doing it right and saw her lifting the chipped vase up to the light. He realized that it wasn't plain and gray like he'd thought, but a very dark blue, covered in a layer of dust. With the sunlight pouring through it, it shone a lovely inky blue, the color thrown onto Mellie's face and making her, just for a moment, lovely, and faintly magical. Then she brought it back down again and the vase was just a dirty, dusty vase with a chip in it, and Mellie was just strange, unkempt Mad Mellie in her three mismatched jumpers and men's boots. He thought, suddenly, of the soldier from Mum's story, forced to wear a bearskin for seven years because nobody wanted to take care of him. She carefully placed the vase in her pram and hobbled over to the edge of the sidewalk to gather up some jam jars than had rolled near a drain. She was singing under her breath in a surprisingly strong, clear alto.

Charlie sprinkled some more bread on the ground, this time leaving a larger pile for the big bully pigeons to fight over, and quickly tossing more for the straggler pigeons while the bullies were distracted. A particularly slow pigeon with a wing that stuck out at a slightly odd, wrong angle still missed the crumbs and Charlie had to repeat the process, practically dumping some bread on the vacant-eyed pigeon's head to make sure it got its share. It cooed obliviously, then gulped down bread, happy as a clam. The clumsy pigeon had rather lovely feathers, once you actually looked at it, Charlie realized. Its green neck shimmered in the light.

"I think . . . I *think* I like your pigeons, Mellie," said Charlie. Almost as soon as the words were out of his mouth, the pigeon suddenly launched itself into the air and tried to land on Charlie's head. Perhaps he might have spoken too soon. Charlie batted it back towards the ground before it could relieve itself on his coat, but it was already swooping unevenly towards the ground again.

"Pudge can't fly anymore," said Mellie, tossing a pair of rusted gardening shears in the far back of the pram. "But Bertie looks out for him." Charlie was about to ask who Bertie was when a gray-lavender pigeon dive-bombed him like the Red Baron and snatched a chunk of bread crumb out of his hand. The fighter plane pigeon landed dramatically next to the glazed-over-looking pigeon, and delicately shoved the piece of bread at Pudge's beak. The other pigeon happily pecked the bread and ate it up, leaving a bit of it for its benefactor.

"They're friends?" Charlie asked, tossing some crumbs to the other side of the bench so the flock would leave Bertie and Pudge alone while they ate.

"Mmm," Mellie agreed. "Pudge is special, and Bertie's smart. A good combination, that. Makes all sorts of things possible."

"How's Pudge special?" Pudge was nice enough, Charlie thought, but "special" was perhaps stretching it a bit.

"Pudge," said Mellie proudly, straightening up, "is a veteran."

"Come again?"

"Pudge was a carrier pigeon in the war. He brought key intelligence back from the front. They stuck him and all the other pigeons in little boxes on a plane and dropped them over the French border. Most of them died or were eaten, but Pudge came back with a secret message from French Resistance fighters, even though a Nazi hawk mangled his wing. He made it all the way home. All the way back to England, can you imagine? He never lost the message."

"How did he know where to go?" Charlie asked, staring, incredulous, as Pudge attempted to eat a small rock.

"All homing pigeons are geniuses at exactly one thing: finding their way home. It has something to with magnets or ice caps or something. Drop them anywhere in the world and they still know where their roost is."

How could they do that? Charlie wondered. What did it feel like? Was it like a bright trail of light only they could see? A machine hum they followed to its source, a vibration in their tiny bones? Or was it more like an invisible thread, tugging them through the air towards home? He imagined a bright, golden string stretching from the house all the way across the ocean to Theo, and Theo following it like a mountaineer.

"How do you know all this?" Mad Mellie did not seem the sort, in Charlie's admittedly inexpert opinion, to be privy to communication tactics from the Allied forces.

"My boy, David, trained him. He trained them all. He was so proud of Pudge that he wanted to give him a well-deserved retirement."

"I didn't know you had a son," said Charlie, and he was surprised to find that he was quite angry with David, wherever he was, for letting his mother live as she was.

"He died right after," she said flatly. "The Blitz. You know how it was then. Lots of people gone, all at once. Lots of people's sons."

Charlie did not know what to say to this. What was there to say? He looked at Mellie with her three sweaters and her pram full of junk, and he thought that she was terribly brave to keep trying to find lovely things, *worthy* things, where everybody else just saw trash, and pests. Things that only glowed if you made the effort to hold them up to the light. He felt infinitely worse for knocking over the pram, but he still stood by his decision to crash into it and not her.

"I'm sorry about your son, Mellie," said Charlie, and he was. *My dad died in the Blitz, too*, he almost said. Millie didn't look at him, but she nodded as if she had heard him, although she didn't pause in her collection.

"Still, at least death was instant for him. The wolves didn't get him, did they? His heart was safe, at the end."

"Wolves?" Charlie said. He'd heard Grandpa Fitz and his old soldier friends talking at one of the church meetings about how sometimes the stray dogs and rats and foxes around the battlegrounds had grown to frightening size feasting on all the dead bodies that didn't get buried fast enough. But he'd never heard them mention wolves. And besides, he wasn't supposed to cavesdrop on Grandpa and his friends anyway—he'd overheard them back when he was smaller and used to hide under the refreshments table with Biscuits. And he had tried very hard to forget that particular story. It was too horrible.

Now, Mellie was squinting at him as if he'd just spoken in

tongues. "What was that?"

"You said something about wolves."

"No, I didn't." Mellie began gathering blankets and pigeons into her pram.

"You did, you said you were glad—"

But Mellie just glared daggers at him from under her shapeless wooly hat and scuttled down the street like an offended crab.

Just because Charlie felt bad that people called her Mad Mellie didn't mean it wasn't somewhat warranted, he thought. He grabbed Biscuits and deposited her in her basket before she could get any more ideas about Pudge, and turned his bicycle towards home.

"Have a nice day, Mellie," he said over his shoulder as he started to pedal off.

"Guard your heart, boy," Mellie called after him. "And lock that cat in an attic somewhere!"

Charlie ignored her, but the whole way back, he imagined he was following the tug of an invisible silken thread, thin as a spider's web, pulling him home.

Grandpa Fitz was worn out from all the extra chores, though he blamed it on not sleeping well the night before and went to bed early, as soon as dinner was over. Charlie and Mum listened to his shuffling footsteps in his room overhead until they eventually stopped, and the house filled with warm, close quiet of being the only ones awake. When Mum took out the ingredients for orange drops biscuits, it felt somehow like the two of them were sharing a secret.

Mum was in charge of the dry ingredients, which she assembled in front of her in neat little regiments according to their corresponding measurement for how much was needed. Charlie was in charge of the orange, cradle to grave, and he ran the cheese grater along its sides until his arm ached and there was a fat pile of orange rind shavings in the bowl. Then he sliced open the pale, naked orange (he was very careful with the big kitchen knife) and squeezed each half until the juice slid down his hand and into a little glass bowl, where he carefully picked out the pips so he could pour the juice into the big mixing bowl with the butter, egg, zest, and salt that Mum had assembled.

Mum hefted up a heaping bowl of flour to put into the sifter to carefully sprinkle the flour into the dough in a light, steady dusting so it wouldn't form clumps and bubbles—and the bottom of the sifter simply fell out into the bowl in a puff of flour and faint *pwuh!* sound, like someone getting the air knocked out of them.

"Oh my." Mum stood staring uncomprehendingly at the remaining piece of sifter in her hand. Charlie laughed, and swatted at the little cloud of flour on his shirt, which simply smeared, and reached for the next ingredient so Mum could deal with the errant flour.

He opened the jar of honey Mum had bought specially from one of the neighbors whose sister lived in the country and kept bees. It was a surprisingly dark amber color, almost brown, but it caught the firelight and seemed to glow a churning, molten gold. Charlie remembered, out of nowhere, that when he was very little he used to believe with perfect certainty that Mum's dangly amber earrings were made from frozen honey, and he was forever afraid that they would melt when Mum stood in the sun.

Charlie turned to tell Mum, only to find she was facing the wall, her hand pressed tight against her mouth, her eyes closed.

He opened his mouth, his hand reaching out, to say—something, anything. *Mum, it's okay, it's only biscuits, they'll be fine, it doesn't matter, Theo won't mind, I don't mind, it's all right, everything will be all right.* But he found he couldn't. It was as if in that moment he had become too tired to even hold his hand up, as if he hadn't slept for days, he didn't *want* to, he was so *tired*. He just wanted someone else to be in charge, someone else to take care of things.

And then, sweeter and more precious than sugar: *Theo.* Theo would be home tomorrow, and Theo would fix it. For the first time, the realization didn't bring excitement but *relief.* Relief as acute and straightforward as standing still and guzzling cold water after running very fast for a very long time on a very hot day. *Theo will be home tomorrow.* The cool, crisp clarity of it unfroze him, shook off the exhaustion that had settled into his limbs as suddenly as it had come.

Charlie gently took the broken sifter out of her loose fingers and set it aside and began to stir in the mound of flour, the wooden spoon knocking softly against the side of the bowl. In a minute, the flour was mixed in the rest of the batter. In two, the crumbs and pockets of floury air were smooth, the dough thick and sticky with honey, studded through with shavings of orange peel like speckles on an egg.

"There, Mum, see?" Charlie said, touching her elbow with one hand, careful not to get flour on her sleeve. "It's perfect. Everything's fine."

Mum let out a shaky breath, but when she turned to him, her eyes were dry and her smile was just as it always was, the same little crinkles at the corners of her eyes.

"So it is, darling. Let's put them on the tray, shall we?" And they let a spoonful's worth of dough drop off the tip of the spoon onto the baking tray until it was full, and then Mum slid it into the oven, whispering, "In you go, boys" and winking at Charlie.

Charlie started to wash the bowl, even though he did not want to, because he knew Mum liked doing the washing-up even less than he did. But Mum came up behind him and slipped an arm around his shoulders and left a lingering kiss on the top of his head, and whispered, "I'll take care of that, Charles. You go to bed. You've done more than enough for one day."

7

THE TRAIN STATION WAS HOT, DESPITE THE WINTER, so crowded was it with people, all of them packed in along the edges of the platform, all of them holding one great breath. There was a string of bunting hanging above the platforms, limp as a dead thing. Hand-drawn Union Jacks were stuck to every surface like limpets. A picture of King George that someone had painted for the occasion had gotten stuck somehow up in the rafters, and he almost appeared to be waving down at the gathered crowd, which was heartening in an odd sort of way. Charlie noticed all of this as he tried to calm the vibration in his center. Still, his leg would not stop bouncing.

A girl a ways off from Charlie hefted up a sign that had "Welcome Home!" painted on it in big red letters so the soldiers could see it from the train. Charlie could have made a sign, but really the biscuits he and Mum had made were much better. Theo would see that when they got home. He would see how much they had missed him, and how many rations they had saved, and he would know that Charlie had taken care of Mum and Grandpa

Fitz for him. He would know that Charlie hadn't let him down.

Charlie tasted blood, and looked down at the thumbnail he hadn't known he was gnawing at. He stuffed his hand in his pocket. He tasted blood again. He put his hand back in his pocket again. Beside him, Mum, too, was fiddling, with her necklace, twisting it back and forth between her fingers, her eyes watching the hands of the clock sweep slowly from twelve to one. Grandpa Fitz alone seemed relaxed, his cap tilted down over his eyes so he could drowse up against the station wall if the mood took him. Charlie had wanted to smuggle Biscuits into the station in a picnic basket—she would have known how to unknot the hard, tight ball of ice that was lodged like a fist in the bones of his chest—but Mum had said in no uncertain terms that cats and train tracks were not meant to become acquainted.

Charlie tasted blood again. Grandpa Fitz's big hand came down to rest on his shoulder, and Charlie let his thumb fall away from his teeth, flushing.

"Now, you remember what I said, Charlie boy," Grandpa Fitz said, tucking his cap under his good arm. Charlie nodded, and clenched his fist tight in his jacket pocket, worrying the ragged edge of the nail. *People come back different than they were.* He felt the tackiness of blood under the nail and wished again for Biscuits. And then, as if summoned by the thought, a shape that was definitely an animal appeared just at the edge of Charlie's vision.

As he twisted to see it, a hum of whispered chatter spread through the whole station in a ripple and for a moment Charlie thought they were all as surprised as he was to see a stray animal, whatever it was, on the platform. Then he felt it: the unmistakable vibration rising up through the soles of his feet. The very first promise of a train coming down the track.

Charlie was distracted from the noise by the creature, slinking into view again, a shadow, low to the ground. He could see now it was a dog of some kind, very big and very dark, and it was snaking between people's legs without any kind of lead. It was there and gone and there again, and Charlie's gaze followed it in and out of view. The sight of the loose dog so near the tracks, which were beginning to tremble in time with a steam engine's wail, made his heart stutter with worry. Soft, living creatures shouldn't be that close to churning steel.

The buzzing noise of the engine and the crowd built and built and built into a continuous drone. Charlie slid out of Grandpa Fitz's grip and started towards the dark shape.

"Charlie—"

He could see the shape of the train now, the flat round face of the engine. He was close enough to see the dog's tail swish between a set of knees. He started forward, but the train wailed again and the dog darted away. What if it was someone's pet that had gotten off its lead? It could be lost here forever in this crowd.

The train had slowed and was overflowing with soldiers— they were half out of the car windows, pressed flat up against the doors, their pale faces crowded like apple blossoms on a branch. Charlie thought he heard Grandpa Fitz call for him again, but if he looked up, he would lose sight of the dog, and the train wasn't all the way stopped, even though soldiers were already squirming off the train, running to people waiting on the platform.

The train made a full stop and the doors opened with an audible *whoosh*. Charlie could see the dark fur of the dog's back, it was so *big*.

Men poured onto the platform, everyone bumping into each other, all rank and file abandoned and forgotten.

Charlie made a grab for the scruff of its neck, but it ducked around someone's cane, and Charlie bumped into the soldier the cane was attached to.

"*Watch it*," the soldier said in a snarl, his body trying to bow in around his stiff, bandaged leg.

"I'm so sorry," Charlie said, looking up past the nondescript wool uniform at the man's haggard, whiskered face. "I was just— Theo! Theo, it's you!"

And so it was. Charlie's brother's hair was cut short, and he was thinner, and he looked somehow pale and sunburnt at the same time. But it was so obviously his brother that Charlie couldn't believe that he hadn't seen him the moment he stepped off the train, like a beacon.

Charlie forgot about the dog, forgot about Mr. Cleaver, forgot about the lines on Mum's face and the blank absence in Grandpa Fitz's eyes and launched himself at his big brother, his arms wrapping themselves tight around Theo's ribs. Charlie's heart was louder in his ears than the train, drowning out Theo's own heartbeat, even with Charlie's ear pressed up against his chest.

Theo is home, his heart proclaimed with every thump, *Theo is home, Theo is home.*

"I knew you'd be back, I knew you'd always find—"

"Charlie." Theo pried at Charlie's grip, his hands strong as iron as they yanked him off. "Charlie, get off." He shook himself free of Charlie's embrace, sending Charlie spinning into Grandpa Fitz, who had finally caught up to them.

Theo shouldered his bag and limped away towards where Mum and the rest of the crowd were waiting with their banners and signs. His left leg dragged behind him a bit as he walked, stiff and unbending. *THUMP*-drag. *THUMP*-drag. *THUMP*-drag. Theo didn't look back at them as he went.

"What have we got to remember, Charlie?" Grandpa Fitz said, his hand on Charlie's shoulder anchoring them both to the earth, even as the ground seemed to go all topsy-turvy under Charlie's feet.

"Sometimes you can't see what's missing right away," Charlie intoned. But it didn't matter, Charlie said to himself, the thought tight and fierce in this throat.

Even if there was something missing, Charlie would find it.

∗∗∗

In addition to the biscuits, Mum had prepared a special welcome-home feast with carefully saved-up rations.

Theo, however, bolted from the table to retch into the sink after just a few bites of potato.

"Of course, it's too rich for you after the nonsense they've had you eating," Mum said, brushing his hair off his forehead with a damp cloth as he clutched the counter. "I'm sorry, my love, I didn't think."

Theo shrugged her off, but his cheeks were burning crimson under his clammy skin, and he wouldn't look at any of them afterwards. Charlie had eaten his portion of potato when Mum said it was all right, but it didn't taste as good, and his chewing was too noisy in the embarrassed silence.

Charlie was brimming with things he wanted to say to Theo but couldn't. He kept stuffing food in his mouth to keep from speaking in front of Mum and Grandpa Fitz. They were just for Theo's ears. He couldn't let Mum know that he knew she was worried and exhausted all the time. That he knew why Mr. Cleaver kept sniffing around like a stray dog. That he knew Grandpa Fitz was only going to get worse, not better.

He hadn't thought to imagine this part, the part where he couldn't talk to Theo yet, *really* talk, get to work fixing everything.

"Do you remember that time I threw potatoes at you, Theo?" was all he could think to say, and then words were spewing out of Charlie's mouth like he was ill with them. "But I missed and hit

Grandpa Fitz right in the eye? And it was like he had an eye patch made of mashed spuds?" Charlie had half a mind to try it again now, just to make Theo laugh, but Mum fixed him with a hawk look across the table and shook her head once, eyebrow raised.

"I remember," Theo said, moving his carrots about with his fork without actually eating them. "It seems like such a waste now." He stabbed a carrot so hard the tines of his fork screeched against the plate like blackboard chalk. "Almost as bad as throwing it all up."

"Oh, love," Mum said, and reached out to touch his hand. He let her leave it there for a moment before drawing his hand away and hiding it under the table. The four of them sat in the silence that followed for a long minute, then there was a soft tread near Charlie's feet and he looked down to find Biscuits staring up at him, her eyes enormous in the dim light.

Biscuits was right. Sometimes the only thing for it was a cat.

Charlie scooped her up, pushed himself away from the table and up onto his feet, and walked over to carefully deposit Biscuits in Theo's lap. Theo looked at her uncomprehendingly. But Biscuits was used to working around the inadequacies of humans and shoved her head against his limp hand over and over until he lifted it and began to pet her as if trying to remind him how. His hands, always so steady and so sure, seemed enormous and clumsy as they patted at her. He was still looking at her as if he had no idea what she was or how she had gotten there.

Grandpa Fitz picked his fork back up and began to eat in a particularly deliberate way, his face smooth and impassive. After a moment, Charlie and Mum followed suit. Biscuits's loud, performative purrs were enough to drown out the scraping of their fork and knives. When the rest of their plates were empty, Theo set Biscuits down on the ground, a little too hard, where she proceeded to situate herself with great precision in front of the fire and began to clean her face.

"I think I might just go to bed," Theo said, pushing away from the table. Charlie and Mum both rose with him.

"We put clean sheets and blankets on this morning, so it'll be nice and fresh for you," Mum reassured him.

"And I put some comics on your nightstand," Charlie added. "Only the fun detective ones, not the boring stuff Sean O'Leary likes. D'you want to read one together before bed?"

"Maybe tomorrow, Charlie. I'm too tired."

Grandpa Fitz reached out his one hand and gently tugged Charlie back into his seat. At Mum's worried look, Charlie tried to school his crestfallen face into a smile.

"Sure! Tomorrow! After your party, I mean."

Theo looked at him searchingly for a moment, then back to Mum.

"The welcome-home party, darling. At the church, remember?" She took his limp hand in hers. "Everyone is just so happy you're home, love. They want to see you, that's all. You won't have to do anything."

"Fine," said Theo, but he was already heading to the stairway. He had to step onto each stair with his good leg, then his cane, and then sort of swing his bad leg up after him like a lump of wood. Charlie didn't want to think about what it would be like to get back down them again. He sat on his hands to keep himself from running over to help. Theo was embarrassed, he could tell, even though Charlie wanted to go to him and shake him and tell him it wasn't embarrassing, not at all, that it wasn't his *fault*.

When Theo's bedroom door finally clicked shut overhead, Mum sighed, her shoulders caving in like a loose sail. Charlie's stomach churned as if he was about to be sick, too. He was embarrassed, or ashamed, or something like it that chafed and burned under his skin.

He was embarrassed for Theo, and ashamed of himself for *being* embarrassed.

But he was embarrassed *for* Theo, not *of* Theo. Theo had to know that, he *had* to. And if he didn't, Charlie would prove it to him, whatever it took.

"Remember what we said, love?" Mum asked, squeezing Charlie's hand. "We're all going to have to be very patient and very kind with each other."

Charlie nodded hard. "Patient and kind," he agreed. Grandpa Fitz smiled, a little sadly, not saying anything.

Patient and kind. He carried it with him all the way up the stairs, pausing for a long moment in front of Theo's door. Not to knock, just to listen to the sound of Theo moving behind it, of so many nights of wishing made real. He and Biscuits crawled into bed, still savoring the noises of a house with four people in it again.

Go ahead and try, his mind whispered to whatever nightmare thought it could haunt him now that Theo was home.

In the night, Theo cried out from his room, but when Charlie and Mum ran into the hall, bleary with sleep, Grandpa Fitz was already there, still dressed. "Just a nightmare," he murmured, and waved them back to their rooms.

Back in bed and clutching Biscuits like a teddy bear, Charlie begged the nightmares to come back to him, that he hadn't meant to pass them on to someone else.

8

CHARLIE HAD NO INTENTION OF DWELLING ON the night before, not on Theo's first day home. He had far too many plans.

"Come on," he shouted, and yanked Theo through the kitchen— Theo's new cane accidentally knocking them both on the shins. Theo already looked more like himself out of his uniform. Charlie even imagined his hair had grown a little overnight. The cane would take some getting used to for Charlie, but Theo was still adjusting to it, too, his grip on it always shifting and uncomfortable. They would both get comfortable with it eventually, Charlie was sure. "We're going to the park."

Theo winced. "Charlie, I don't really want to bother with all that right now."

"Come *on*, it'll be brilliant, you'll see. We'll stop by the fish and chips stand on the way, and we can see the fountain with the lion head and—"

Theo sighed, and yanked Charlie against his side in a one-armed hug.

"You're so much taller," Theo said. Charlie straightened up proudly. He'd grown six inches, at least, since Theo had left. "You used to fit right here," Theo went on, looking at the crook of his arm as if he'd misplaced it and couldn't understand where it could have gone.

To distract him, Charlie tugged him towards the door, shoving hat and gloves and coat at him and then leading him out into the light. The sun had taken note of the occasion and shone cheerfully over smatterings of fat, fluffy clouds.

"My God," Theo murmured, his mouth hanging open slightly as he looked around him. "I'd forgotten." Charlie looked around the street he'd pulled them down because it was the shortest way to the fish and chips stand. The rubble of what used to be three houses, all pressed right up to each other, had been mostly cleared out. A chimney and a chunk of wall with a window that was miraculously intact, the glass not even cracked, were all that remained. Charlie found it hopeful or very sad, depending on his mood. "The Gillies used to live right there. I don't even remember, did they . . . ?"

"No! No, they're fine! They made it to a shelter. They moved in with Mrs. Gillie's sister and her family, in Kent or somewhere. They're fine."

"In my mind it all still looks like it did when I was a kid," Theo said, shaking his head. "When I would think about home, I would think about it like it was before, not like . . . this."

Charlie, not liking this grim line of thought, grabbed Theo's hand again and tugged him quickly past the ruins.

"Slow down, Charlie, I can't keep up," Theo said after a block or so.

Charlie fell back, embarrassed. He had been planning on challenging Theo to their customary race to the top of the small hill before the park, but he realized, watching Theo wince and pant, that that had been stupid.

"Theo . . . ," he said, ducking his head. "Can I ask . . . what happened to your leg?"

Theo stopped halfway up the hill, his breath jagged and loud. "A grenade went off near me," he said after a moment. "It hit a barrel that was nearby, and when the barrel exploded, little bits of it went flying everywhere. Shrapnel, they call it. All these bits of metal were sticking out of my leg, but they couldn't take them out right away because I would have bled to death. And when they finally did take them out, a bit of it was stuck in the bone too deep to remove, so"—he gestured at his stiff leg—"here I am."

"They just left it in there?" Charlie asked, horrified. *"Why?"*

"I don't know, Charlie. The doctors just said they'd done all they could without taking the whole bloody thing off."

Charlie fiddled with his scarf. He had planned to take Theo to their favorite bookshop after the park. He'd been saving up his pocket money so they could each buy something. But as he watched Theo, grim-faced and pale, labor up the hill he had always taken at a sprinting run, it didn't seem like a clever idea at all, bringing Theo out here. It seemed silly.

This whole plan had been silly.

"Mum said you have a job?" Charlie said after a long minute. His face felt hot and clammy despite the cold.

"A mate from another unit got me a job at a factory, the one that makes parts for cars, over by Dale Street. It's a long bus ride, but the pay's not bad."

"Rosie Linton's sister works there," Charlie said. "Or she did; they let a whole mess of people go last month. She was really upset."

Theo nodded. "The women took over when all the men were gone because of the war, but now that we're back, they're giving the jobs back to the men."

"But that's not fair," Charlie said, stopping. Was Mum's job at the telephone company going to let her go, too? What would they do for money?

"Maybe not, but it's the way it is." Theo carefully avoided an icy patch of sidewalk, so intent he did not even look up to notice Charlie worrying his lip between his teeth. If Mum lost her job, Theo could still take care of them. They'd be okay. He exhaled.

Not that that helped Rosie's sister, he thought.

"It's good, though," Charlie said, mostly to himself. "Because I know Mum is worried, about—about money stuff. She pretends she isn't, but she is. And I want to help, I *want* to get a job, but someone needs to be around when Grandpa Fitz gets bad. I *would* get a job if I could, Theo." It was suddenly, desperately important that Theo understood that.

"Oh, Charlie," Theo said, and tugged Charlie back into

another one-armed hug. Charlie wished, with a stab of longing so sharp it took his breath away, that he was small again, as small as when Theo went away and Charlie fit perfectly into his arms. "You did the best you could." Theo let him hold on for a while longer until Charlie was certain he was not going to cry, then huffed, "I need to sit down for bit. How much longer do we have to stay out here?"

"We can go home now, if you want," Charlie said, smiling so Theo did not hear the catch in his voice.

"In a minute," Theo said, sitting down hard on a bench. "Still figuring out how to use this bloody thing." He gestured with the cane. Then he leaned his head back and closed his eyes, letting the sun fall on him. Charlie took the opportunity to take in his brother's face, the face he'd been imagining for so long.

Theo looked different. His cheeks were thin, with deep hollows under each cheekbone. The new-penny color of his hair seemed to have dulled to a nondescript brown. His freckles were as stark against his pale skin as spilled ink. Charlie could not stop staring at him, drinking in each change and cataloging it, comparing it to the picture of Theo in his mind.

"Why did you stop writing letters?" he blurted out.

Theo's face remained blank, unreadable. Finally, he opened his eyes and said, "There was just . . . nothing to say. People keep expecting me to say something, but I never know what it is. It's like I'm missing all my lines from a play. None of this seems *real*," he said, gesturing around him. "I don't *recognize* anything.

Yesterday I saw Mum from across the room and I thought, *Who is that?* I recognized her, but it was like they'd cast someone else in her role."

Charlie had absolutely no idea what to say. He thought of Grandpa Fitz, sometimes calling around the house for Grandma Lily, as if she were still alive. He thought of the bearskin soldier, washing off seven years' worth of dirt and worry in the river.

Right now, Theo didn't remember who he was, not really. He'd been a soldier so long that he didn't remember right away how to be anything else, like a big brother. But that was all right, because Charlie would remind him. He would bring Theo back to himself.

"Come on," Charlie said, taking Theo's hand again. "Let's go home."

9

CHARLIE GRABBED THEO'S HAND AND LED THE way in through the doors at church. His cheeks hurt from grinning, but he couldn't make himself stop, especially when the two of them, followed by Mum and Grandpa Fitz, walked through the high archway and into the gathering room.

Everyone had come, just like Charlie knew they would.

It began as a sort of ripple through the gathered neighbors, then Mrs. O'Leary burst into tears and ran over to cup Theo's face in her hands. She reached out to squeeze Mum's shoulder, and she kept trying over and over to say something. But instead, she made a small, strangled sort of noise and ran from the room, her hands pressed over her mouth.

Sean, smiling tightly at Charlie, went after her. Theo's hand in Charlie's felt very hot and clammy. The congregation dissolved into a rush of smiling people all trying to clap Theo on the shoulder or hug him or shake his hand. Charlie was smiling, too, even though Theo was squeezing so tight his fingers ached.

Father Mac cleared his throat in the way only Father Mac

could, the sound sending an instant hush over the room as if they were all readying for prayer.

"Thank you, everyone," he began. "We are here today to celebrate our neighbor Theo Merriweather's safe return from the war to us, to his family, and to his community. In a time when so very many young men are returning to stays in hospitals if they're injured, or to soldiers' homes if they have no families to care for them, or even not returning at all, we—" Father Mac cleared his throat again. Charlie was alarmed to see his eyes were bright with unshed tears. After a long pause, he continued, his voice steady and clear. "We are so very thankful that Theo is home where he belongs, amongst those that love him. Let us pray."

Everyone bowed their heads and closed their eyes as Father Mac started droning a prayer, but Charlie peeked up at Theo standing next to him. Theo was staring ahead, his expression flat and closed off. His hand in Charlie's had gone slack. Not soon enough, the prayer was over.

"Beth, this must be your eldest!"

Charlie stiffened. He had forgotten to warn Theo about Mr. Cleaver. But maybe that was best. This way Theo could see exactly what he and Mum had been dealing with all the time he'd been away.

Mr. Cleaver grabbed Theo's shoulder and shook it vigorously. "Stuart Cleaver, great friend of your mum's here, great friend! We do so admire our Beth, don't we, Charlie!"

Charlie, having learned from Biscuits, did not dignify this with a response.

"Oh, erm, nice to meet you," Theo said. Charlie was afraid the assault would alarm Theo, and was relieved that it hadn't. In fact, Theo looked more annoyed than anything else. Charlie almost smiled.

"You too, old boy, you too," Mr. Cleaver said, beaming around his mustache, and he launched into a long description of how smashing Mum was, except it sounded as if he was describing some strange, poor woman Charlie had never met. "Such a delightful soul, so full of guff and bluster! We are so terribly lucky that Bethy is here with us—the church, I mean, the community. Terribly lucky."

No one but Grandpa Fitz called Mum "Bethy." Ever.

Mum looked pale and miserable under her smile. Blood rushed in Charlie's ears.

He tugged on Theo's hand. Theo looked down at him, eyebrow questioning. Charlie jerked his head at Mr. Cleaver, scowling. Theo rolled his eyes and went back to nodding vaguely at Mr. Cleaver.

There were other people here, people Theo actually knew and liked, and Mr. Cleaver and his ridiculous mustache were sucking up all of his time and attention away from everyone who could help Theo remember who he really was, now that he was home. What Theo needed was to be reminded how much he belonged here, among people who knew him. Not humoring Mr. Cleaver, drawing into himself more and more with every word.

This wasn't how any of this was supposed to go.

Grandpa Fitz finally extricated Theo by grabbing Mr. Cleaver about the shoulders and steering him away, launching into a long and detailed story about the door hinges. Charlie kept waiting for Theo to say—*something*, but every time there was a moment for him to speak another person came up to say how happy they were that he was home and wasn't everything exactly as it should be now? Theo would only nod and smile and look at them as if he couldn't understand why they were speaking to him. It was like was watching a party for a ghost.

Less than an hour later, Theo said abruptly, "I'd like to go home now."

At that, everyone there made pleasant goodbyes and shuffled back into their coats, Mum looking fretful and apologetic. Outside, the noise and light of the party spilled out into the street for one exaggerated moment, suspending the four of them and everything around them in amber—the velvety gleam of Mum's lipstick, the silver glint of Grandpa Fitz's eyebrows, a new scar hidden in Theo's hair that Charlie hadn't noticed before—before the door swung shut and brought down murky darkness like a curtain.

Dinner was quiet, too.

Charlie kept waiting for Theo to bring up all the people he'd seen at church, all the old ladies who had fussed over him and tried to inundate him with church gossip, or even Mr. Cleaver and how horrible he was, but Theo only gave short, murmuring responses to everything, and once again went to bed early. Though they could all hear him walking in endless thumping circles around his room upstairs.

Later, when Grandpa Fitz had dozed off by the fire and all the dishes were washed and put away, Mum pulled Charlie to sit next to her on the stairs.

"I know it's hard, love," she said, taking his hand and folding it between hers. "There's no instructions for this part."

"I *want* to be happy," Charlie said to the floor. "I *want* to feel like everything is perfect now that Theo's back. I just . . ." He scrubbed at his face with the cuff of his sleeve.

"Sometimes, Charles," Mum said, her voice quiet as she twisted her wedding ring back and forth on her finger, "you have to pretend to feel something until you actually do. You have to trick yourself into believing it, into feeling it."

"That sounds horrible." Charlie sniffed. Mum laughed and pressed the heels of her hands against her eyes for long moment. Finally, she looked back at him.

"Nothing's more horrible than giving up, darling. Or not much, anyway." She sank down so she was even with Charlie, taking his sticky hands in hers. "We're not in charge of the weather, Charles. Or traffic, or accidents, or other people. The only thing we're in charge of is what we do in this exact moment. We can't change what we did in the past, and we don't know what we'll do in the future. Ourselves, right now. That's all we've got."

"Ourselves, right now," Charlie repeated.

"You and me," Mum said, pressing her forehead against Charlie's, "we're going to be just fine." He had been so excited for Theo to be home, had wished for it for so long, that he had never thought to cherish being the center of Mum's attention, had never thought to wonder how it would feel when it changed. He missed it. He was ashamed that he missed it, but he did. When it had just been him and Mum against the world.

They sprang up in alarm when the *THUMP-drag* of Theo's cane announced his descent down the stairs.

"Darling, is everything all right?" Mum asked, turning, a furrow of worry blooming between her eyebrows.

"Fine," Theo said, distracted, and Charlie had to jump out of his way as he continued to descend to where they were sitting with no signs of stopping. "I just wanted to check the doors and windows. I couldn't remember if we'd locked them."

"We did, dear," Mum reassured him, but Theo yanked on the doorknob anyway. He went to the kitchen windows next, rattling them in their frames. Theo nodded to himself, then pulled on the front door again.

"Theodore," Mum started, but Theo didn't even pause, moving to each window in turn again. By the fire, Grandpa Fitz had woken up and was watching Theo's progress with an unreadable expression.

"Don't worry, Bethy, Theo and I will keep each other company for a while. You go on to sleep. You've got work tomorrow, and it's been a long day."

Mum's lips were pressed so hard together they looked white, and Charlie grabbed Mum's hand as they both went upstairs. As they got to the top, Charlie could hear Grandpa Fitz murmuring quietly downstairs, interspersed with the occasional terse mutter from Theo.

"Do you—do you need a story, Mum?" Charlie asked at his door. "I could tell you one, if you need. I could think of one."

Mum's eyes shone like glass in the dim hallway light, and she pressed her fingers to her mouth, just once.

"Oh, Charles," she whispered, then came over to kiss the top of his head. "I'm all right, my sweet boy. You go to sleep. Dream only of lovely things."

After Charlie had crawled into his cold bed, he waited in the dark, trying to think of a story he could tell Mum, in case she needed one tomorrow. But the only ones that would come to him were all about monsters waiting in the dark.

10

CHARLIE WAS UP EARLY THE NEXT DAY BECAUSE it was Theo's first day of his new job at the factory, and Charlie was determined that it would go perfectly. And Charlie had a plan.

The idea had come to him in the night, while he had been lying awake, braced for air raid sirens even as he knew they would never come. Theo just needed exactly what Charlie needed: for things to be normal again. Everything so far had been about celebrating that Theo was home, but what they all *really* needed was for it to be as if Theo had never left. So Charlie was going to treat this day if it were just like any other, and treat his brother as if he hadn't been gone so long that Charlie had grown six inches, as if Theo didn't have an injury, or a frown that never left his face. Confidence bubbled up in Charlie as he got dressed, made his bed, and threw open the curtains to find whatever sunlight was to be had. He could fix this.

Before the war, Theo and Charlie had both been in charge of feeding Biscuits. So that's where Charlie was going to start. Simple.

It shouldn't have surprised him that Theo was already up, but it still did. Before the war, Theo had always slept in as late as possible, and he was impossible to wake without an alarm or Charlie vigorously jumping on his bed. But here he was, sitting at the kitchen table and watching the closed front door with a nameless expression. He wondered if he had ever even gone upstairs last night.

"G'morning, Theo," Charlie said around a yawn, the words stretching between his jaws like taffy. "Did you sleep at all?"

"A little," Theo said, but his shoulders were tight, and Charlie wondered if he was lying.

"You'll probably be so tired after your first day of work that you'll fall asleep straight away tonight."

"Yes, maybe."

"I was thinking," Charlie said, fiddling with the hem of his jumper. "D'you think you'd want to take over Biscuits's supper? Like before? She eats scraps now, not tinned food, but she likes it, and Grandpa Fitz says she's probably supplementing her diet with mice, which is disgusting, but she seems happy."

Before the war, there had been loads of tinned cat food in all different flavors, but once the rationing started, the government had deemed it "nonessential," which was both stupid and incorrect. Mum had even helped him write a letter to the local MP explaining that Biscuits was a necessity to their family, and should be fed as such. He had never received a reply. "I won't be forgetting that come the next elections,"

Mum had said darkly.

"Sure," Theo said after a beat. He looked a bit surprised, but not upset. That same confidence bubbled back up inside Charlie, and he had to turn around to hide the grin splitting his face. As if to underscore the point, Grandpa Fitz trundled down the stairs with a great deal more noise than was strictly necessary.

"Great. So, the way that you do it is—"

"I know how to put food in a bowl, Charlie," Theo snapped, and Charlie bit his lip. He stole a glance at his brother's face out of the corner of his eye. Theo looked more like Mum than Charlie did, with wide, expressive features made for laughing. A frown looked unnatural on him; it was an expression that belonged to someone else.

"Oh, I made you up a lunch." Charlie pointed to the bag on the counter. "Last night. For your first day. It's just there." He swallowed hard, and resisted the urge to pick at a loose thread on his sleeve.

Theo's bright blue eyes flashed to Charlie's, then his whole face spasmed into a smile.

"Thanks, Charlie. Thanks for looking out for me."

"Merriweathers look out for each other," Charlie said, his cheeks and neck going hot.

"Yes, we do," Theo said. His stiff shoulders relaxed a bit, and his coppery hair gleamed in the morning light.

***

That night Charlie woke to the sound of air raid sirens in his head again. He was out of bed and in the hall, searching desperately for Biscuits in the dark, when the sirens turned into Theo's voice, screaming over and over and over again.

Mum was already in the hall, her face a pale oval in the dark, with purple smudges under each eye.

"Go back to sleep, Charles, I'll take care of it."

"It's fine," Charlie said quickly, "I don't mind. I can help."

"Go back to your room, Charles, I mean it." But Mum was already going into Theo's room, so she wasn't there to see Charlie waiting in the hall next to the door.

The sounds of Theo's dream kept hitting Charlie like a fist, over and over. He could hear a lot of thrashing around and something falling to the ground and breaking, followed by a loud, heavy *thump*.

Then silence.

The silence went on, stretching out in front of Charlie like a viscous thing, like honey or syrup. He was caught in it, couldn't shove his way through it, it stuck his feet tight to the floor. And then he heard something that sounded almost like Mum's voice, but hoarse and muffled and wrong-sounding somehow, and the silence broke and he was crashing into the room, the door banging into the wall behind him as he threw it open.

"Stop!" Charlie screamed, his voice high and tiny in his ears.

"Theo, stop it, wake up!"

But Theo's eyes didn't seem to see him, didn't seem to see either of them, not really. He kept flinching away from blows that weren't coming. His hands were closed around Mum's arm, his thick fingers digging into her pale skin. Charlie shouted wordlessly, pulling on Theo's arm with his whole weight and pummeling his fists against Theo's back when that didn't work.

"Mum!" Charlie's voice ripped its way out of his throat. Her face was getting red, almost purple, as she bit her lip so hard Charlie saw blood, her fingers scrabbling at Theo's, trying to pry them loose. He was going to break her arm if he didn't stop. She was trying to say something, but no words were coming out.

And then an arm was dragging Charlie away and hauling on Theo's arm. Grandpa Fitz kicked at the back of Theo's knees so he lost his balance.

"Help me hold him, Bethy." Grandpa Fitz's voice was calm and even. Mum, breathing hard, eyes streaming, grabbed Theo's other arm and together they held Theo against the wall until his body suddenly went limp.

"There now," Grandpa Fitz sighed, easing Theo down to his knees. "You're all right, lad. You're all right. You're home."

Theo's thrashing stilled until he was slumped in their arms. And then he was weeping, tears and snot streaking down his face while ugly, gulping noises came out of his mouth.

"I'm sorry—Mum, I'm so sorry, I didn't—"

"I know you didn't, shh, love, I know—"

Charlie closed the door on the sound of them. No one seemed to even see him go, all of them so wrapped up in the monstrous thing that Theo carried around with him. He heard Theo crying, loudly and then very quietly, through the wall for another hour.

11

CHARLIE PAUSED IN THE HOSPITAL LOBBY. HOW had it only been a few days ago that he had sat next to Sean on that bench over there, so scared that something bad had happened to Theo?

But something bad *had* happened to Theo, hadn't it? Something he wouldn't talk about, wouldn't explain.

But maybe there was someone who could.

Behind the big desk in the lobby was a lady, looking at him suspiciously over the tops of her glasses. But she seemed to forget about him completely when a woman in a fancy hat covered in fake flowers and, horrifyingly, a small stuffed bird came in with a cloud of perfume and demanded in a cut-glass accent to speak to a "real doctor" about her bunions and not the "backcountry charlatan" she had been subjected to last time. The lady with the glasses straightened her shoulders like she was about to start a fist fight, and Charlie took the opportunity to slip through the second set of doors and down the corridor.

He hadn't really been paying much attention to the path they'd taken last time to the ward that housed the soldiers; he had just followed everyone else in line. But he found he recognized a wall with a huge blackboard covered all over in names and numbers, and remembered they had turned left just past it. And then there was the room, the same soldiers lying in the same beds. Keeping his head ducked down to avoid any curious gazes, his neck hot and blotchy, he made his way as quietly as possible down to the drawn curtain and cleared his throat.

"Pardon me? Reggie?"

The curtain was yanked back, and Reggie was staring at him owlishly, clearly unable to place him. Then the penny dropped, and his look of confusion spread into that bright smile Charlie recalled.

"What an unexpected pleasure. It's Charlie, yes?" He seemed genuinely happy to see him, even after how horrible Charlie had been to upset him and run away.

"Hello," Charlie said, bright red and frozen with sudden shyness. "I'm sorry for bothering you."

"Nonsense, you're easily the most interesting thing I've seen all day. Sit, sit," he said, gesturing to the foot of the bed.

So Charlie did, and he was indescribably pleased to discover that his card with Biscuits painted on it was displayed on the little side table, next to a little cup with a single yellow carnation in it.

"What brings you by?" Reggie asked.

"I was wondering—" Charlie started, stumbling over the

words. It seemed so silly now to have bothered Reggie, now that he was actually here. "I was wondering if maybe I could ask you something. About my brother, Theo. I know you don't know my brother, but he's a soldier, too. He was, I mean. He's home now. But he's . . ."

"Different," Reggie said, his voice gentle.

"Yes." Charlie's voice sounded like it belonged to someone very, very small.

"It's all right, you know. To be sad about that."

Charlie did not reply. He wasn't sure it was all right. He didn't *feel* all right about it. He felt sticky with shame.

"Bad things happened to your brother, Charlie. I don't know him, you're right, but I know that. He can't talk about them right now. He might never be able to talk about them. And I know you probably feel rather helpless, don't you?"

Charlie nodded, miserable. Reggie patted his shoulder, his dark eyes kind.

"I know you love your brother, anyone can see that. He sees it, too. But you probably . . . oh, how to explain it?" Reggie rubbed at his eyebrow, frowning. "I suspect that when he looks at you, he doesn't just see his little brother. He sees everything that changed whilst he was gone. You're different, too, I'm sure, than you were when he left. Your mum is older, the shops on your street have moved around. Everything is the same, but everything is *different*. And that just makes *him* feel even more different. He doesn't know where he fits in it all anymore."

"But he's home," Charlie said. "He fits with us, right where he always did."

"I suspect you are all discovering that that isn't completely true," said Reggie. "But that doesn't mean it always will be. Give each other some time. I imagine it took time to learn how to live without him. It will take time to learn to live with him again, too. Lucky for Theo, he's got a good brother to look out for him. To look out for his heart."

Here, Reggie seemed to lose his train of thought, his eyes going unfocused, looking at something quite far away past Charlie's head.

"Yes," he murmured, almost imperceptibly. "Maybe. If they didn't eat it."

Charlie froze, certain he'd misheard. "Eat . . . what?"

"What?" Reggie flinched, as if Charlie had moved to strike him.

"You said 'if they didn't eat it.' Eat what?"

Reggie smiled again, but there was an edge of wrongness to it, like he was working very hard to remember the mechanics behind it.

"You'll have to forgive me, Charlie. It's this time of day. I'm usually under— That is, I'm usually asleep by now. I sleep quite a lot these days. It's making me a bit foggy."

"I'm sorry," Charlie said, pushing himself up. "I'll let you sleep. Thank you, for talking to me."

Reggie's smile gained a bit of its old warmth, but there was

109

something like panic building behind his eyes. Charlie ducked past the curtain as Reggie pulled the blanket over his head, and as Charlie left, he remembered how he had felt when his football had hit his great-grandmother's vase: that he had just broken something fragile and precious that couldn't be replaced.

12

CHARLIE WAS STILL BLEARY FROM SLEEP AND THE same weary, ink-dark dreams by the time he got Grandpa Fitz awake and downstairs. They were both of them blurry around the edges, Charlie with sleep and his grandfather with confused reverie. Theo was still upstairs, no doubt catching up on whatever scraps of sleep he could steal in between his bouts of restlessness.

Biscuits chirped to get his attention. She was pacing in front of Grandpa Fitz, the way she did when she noticed him doing such improper things as not petting her when she demanded. Grandpa Fitz was drooling just a bit, as he sometimes did when he was having one of his bad days or was simply very tired. Charlie reached out with a napkin to clean it off his chin, but Grandpa Fitz's hand shot out and trapped Charlie's wrist in a vise grip halfway across the table.

"Hollow Chest, that's what we called it."

Charlie tried to pull his hand away. "Huh?"

Grandpa Fitz made a grumpy noise and let go of Charlie and

dragged the back of his hand across his mouth to dry it. "I said that Hollow Chest is what we called it, back in my day."

"Called . . . you called what?"

"What's wrong with your brother. Hollow Chest."

"What's that?" As soon as he asked, Charlie was suddenly quite certain that he did not want to know what Hollow Chest was.

"It didn't happen to me. Do you know why? My secret?"

Grandpa Fitz slapped at his chest. His fingers poked at his shirtfront until he fished out a thin gold locket that Charlie had never seen before. He held it out to Charlie.

"Well, open it, boy. Of the two of us, you're the only one with two hands and nothing but time."

Charlie took hold of the locket, nearly dragging Grandpa Fitz across the table when he forgot for a moment that it was still attached to Grandpa Fitz's neck. Inside was an old, yellowed photograph of a plain young woman, who looked like she had very little patience for getting her picture taken. She looked a bit like Mum, although Mum was prettier.

"My Lily. She was a nurse at the hospital where they dumped the bits of me they'd scraped off the field. That first night, when they took my arm . . . I could *feel* it, like hooks sinking into the meat of me. They kept saying that I had to hold on, that I couldn't give up yet, but all I thought was, what's the point when my arm's gone? What's the point when I'll never ride a horse or swing a cricket bat again? What's the point when I'm just going to die of infection in three days anyway?

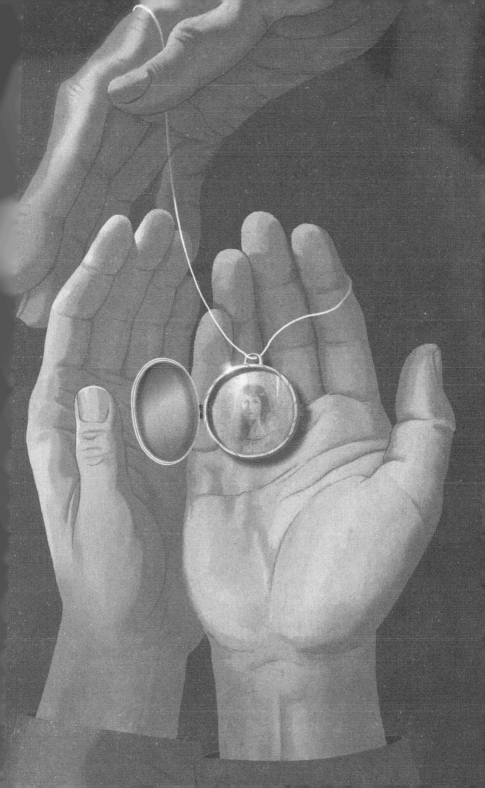

"And in walks Miss Lily, spitting sparks she was so cross with someone or other, and told me that if she caught me feeling sorry for myself, she would upend a mop bucket over my head. Tiny little thing she was, you might remember, barely as tall as an umbrella stand. Maybe another lad wouldn't've thought she was much to look at, but *I* wanted to look at her. I thought she was *exactly* enough to look at. My own dear Lily, she kept the dark at bay.

"I'd handed my heart over to her for safekeeping before I even knew which way was up. She never let it go after that; there wasn't anything in the world what could've torn it out of her grasp, not even me. Oh, Lily."

Charlie felt very strange, listening to this. It occurred to him that Grandpa Fitz had lived a whole life that Charlie had never known about, and probably would never know about, and so had Grandma Lily, and so had Mum and Dad. And so had everyone, really, everyone in the flat on the one side of their house and the cobbler on the other, everyone on their street, everyone in London. So many stories that he would never know, that maybe *no one* would ever know, except the people who had lived them.

It made him feel sad and sort of wondrous at the same time. But mostly sad. He had never met Grandma Lily. Grandpa Fitz didn't always remember that.

The old man had gone quiet, staring at the locket he now held gently in his one leathery hand. He was awake-dreaming—that's what Mum called it when he went off in one of his memory trances, and this seemed like a nice one, so Charlie didn't wake him. He just cleared up the remains of the meal, leaving a cup of tea for when Grandpa Fitz came back from his memories. He always did, eventually.

And sure enough, as sudden as waking from a dream, Grandpa Fitz started and blinked, looking around as if surprised to find himself sitting at the table. He shook his head briefly to clear it, a gesture so familiar it squeezed at Charlie's heart with unexpected tightness.

"What were we talking about, lad?"

"Um, Hollow Chest?" Charlie said.

Grandpa Fitz looked up and squinted at Charlie across the table. "About . . . what?"

"Hollow Chest," Charlie said quietly, glancing over his shoulder at the stairs. "You were saying that's what's wrong with Theo?"

"I don't know what 'Hollow Chest' is. . . ." He looked at Charlie askance. "What I do know is that what's ailing your brother isn't something you nor I can fix for him. It's not a broken bone that you can set right."

"But just now—just now you said that Theo had 'Hollow Chest,' and that you didn't because of Grandma Lily—"

"Oh, Charlie boy, you know I talk nonsense some days." Grandpa Fitz straightened and ran his hand through his short gray hair. "I wish there was a simple explanation for what's going on inside Theo as much you do. But it's a swirling mess in there that we can't get at. All we can do is be here for him until we can't."

Charlie's neck went cold. "What do you mean, 'until we can't'?"

"All I mean is that we all have to realize our limitations. We can only try to meet him where he is."

"Meet who where he is?" Theo asked. He was on the stairs, dressed in his new work clothes, his hair combed and gleaming like a new penny.

"You, at that fish and chips stand near your work," Grandpa Fitz said without missing a beat. "For lunch."

"I won't have time, Charlie," Theo said with a sigh, pulling on his coat. "It's too far to bloody walk with my leg, in case you hadn't noticed."

"Mind how you talk to your brother," Grandpa Fitz said, straightening his shoulders so he seemed to take up the whole room. Theo ducked his head and became very interested in the buttons on his coat. The silence stretched out between them all.

"Do you want me to make you a lunch, Theo?" Charlie called just as he was walking out the door.

"No, I'll buy something on the way," Theo said over his shoulder.

"Okay, bye!" But the door closed on his voice.

Biscuits was mewling next to her food dish, demanding breakfast and attention.

"There's nothing for you until I make lunch, I'm sorry," he crooned, stroking her soft ears and under her chin. Biscuits nipped painlessly at his shin, unconvinced, then got up to stretch her paws as high up the wall towards the icebox and the container of her food as she could.

"There's nothing up there, Biscuits, I swear to you."

Biscuits made a sound like a baby crying, a sound Charlie hadn't heard before, and he scooped her up into his arms, feeling her all over for cuts or scrapes. But she squirmed loose and landed on the floor with a *thunk*, then scrambled over to paw at her empty food dish. She made the baby cry again, and flung herself belly-up on the floorboards.

"What is it? Are you hurt? Did you step on something? Did you fall?"

She flipped back onto her feet and screamed at the icebox again.

"There's nothing in there, Biscuits, look," and he took out the jar and opened it to show her—a single portion's worth of scraps at the very bottom of her ceramic food jar.

But that had been last night's dinner for her. He'd been careful, he'd *checked*. The only reason it would still be there was if she hadn't eaten last night. If no one had fed her—

Theo. He'd promised, he'd said that he would feed her. A spike of pain shot through Charlie, an echo of what Biscuits must be feeling, a hand that had grabbed his stomach and twisted into a fist. He turned on his heel, frustration churning in his guts so hot it burned like acid.

"Theo!" Charlie opened the door and chased after him, his toes going cold and then numb as his stocking feet were instantly sodden with slush. The buildings loomed up on either side of the street, like they were leaning in to get a better view. "Theo, did you feed Biscuits dinner last night?"

"Charlie, I can't be late for work, shove off."

"No!" Charlie grabbed Theo's arm and spun him around.

"Don't bloody sneak up on me like that," Theo said, his voice a snarl that might as well have dripped gore for how deeply it cut. How could Theo have forgotten about Biscuits? He knew that she had been there with Charlie when Mum started going away to work at the phone company, when Grandpa Fitz started going away to the fog of memories in his brain, and, finally, when Theo went away to war. How could he know that and treat her like she didn't matter?

"She can't tell anyone when she's hungry, it's our job to take care of her—"

"You haven't got a job, Charlie."

"You said—" Charlie's breath was coming in a thin, trembling gasp, his throat burning, his eyes burning, too. He *would not* cry. "You told me that it was my job to take care of everyone, and I did, I was good at it. Now you're back, and you can't even—"

Theo started stalking away. And before he could even think about what he was doing, Charlie had scooped up a wet handful of slushy snow and lobbed it at the back of Theo's head.

Charlie was braced for Theo to scream and curse and shove Charlie into the snowbank, to shove slush down the back of his shirt, like he might have done before the war. He was not prepared for Theo to crumple with a choked-off wail. He was not prepared for him to clap his hands over his ears, to curl into himself like a piece of paper in a fire. His good knee buckled, but his bad knee couldn't; it stayed locked and slid out from under him. Theo tilted horribly, and tried to catch himself with his cane, but it slid on the ice and out of his hand. Theo fell like a tree, his legs smacking hard into the sidewalk while his elbow caught in the snowbank.

He pressed his face into the ground and began rocking.

"No," Theo moaned, his fingers digging hard into his own shoulders. "No no no no no nonononononono."

"Shh, Theo," Charlie said, his eyes flicking up and down the street. Neighbors were starting to peek out of windows. A couple on the other side of the street hurried past, the man wrapping his arm around the woman as if afraid Theo was going to launch himself across the street at them. An animal somewhere had started a low, eerie howl, as if in reply to Theo. Charlie wanted to shout at them that it was *his* fault, not Theo's, to just mind their own business, but Theo just started rocking faster.

"Theo, it's okay, just come inside, I didn't mean it, I'm sorry, Theo—"

A strong, wiry hand grabbed hold of Charlie's shoulder and yanked him backwards. "Theodore," Grandpa Fitz said in a firm voice. "Theodore, can you hear me? I'm right here with you, Theodore. You're home. You're safe."

Grandpa Fitz crouched down next to Theo, not quite touching him, his voice low and soothing, like it had been the time the Mortons' pony had gotten spooked and bolted into the street, getting her reins hopelessly tangled in the fence.

"You're home," he kept repeating. "You're safe. Is it all right if I take your hand?"

Theo made a strange groaning sound, but seemed to nod his head, his eyes still squeezed shut. Grandpa Fitz took careful hold of Theo's fingers, gently prying them loose from his shirt. The old man swayed a bit without his arm to balance him; looking up, he jerked his head towards Charlie, who rushed over to steady him from his other side.

"Charlie and I are going to help you up now, and we'll go inside and get a nice cup of tea. Does that sound all right, Theodore?"

Theo nodded mutely. Grandpa Fitz kept a tight grip on Theo's hand as Theo slowly uncurled and laboriously got to his feet. He hobbled like an old man back down the walk and inside, Charlie and Grandpa Fitz balancing him on either side.

As Charlie turned to close the door, he caught sight of the dog that had been howling. It was a couple of streets away, silhouetted against the graying snow. Somehow, even from so far away, Charlie could still see every one of its teeth.

Grandpa Fitz half carried Theo up the stairs and into bed, and called in to Theo's work to tell the overseer he was ill. Charlie fed Biscuits, and made pot after pot of tea. When he couldn't stand the heavy, stifling quiet that had fallen over the house a moment longer, he hopped on his bicycle and rode to the shops. He would buy biscuits, the real kind, made by someone else with too much sugar and milk, he didn't care if it took all of his pocket money. He would get something special for Theo, and Theo would know that Charlie was sorry, that he hadn't meant it, that he would never do it again.

The only shop where he could get the special kind he liked was quite far away, and he had to make a large sort of square around the worst of the bomb-damaged neighborhoods, skirting around the cratered streets and the great heaps of brick and timber and ice. It looked like giant children had been playing with blocks and dirt, gotten frustrated halfway through the game, and begun throwing things. Whole swaths of streets had simply been upended, and had to be avoided or else his bicycle would either run into a ditch or wind up with glass and nails stuck in the tires.

So he had to go out of his way, past the hospital again.

And if he hadn't, he might not have seen the wolf.

A man—a soldier, surely, his trouser legs hanging loose and empty just below the knees—was being pushed along the sidewalk by a woman, who was talking in a nonstop stream of cheerful babble. She either didn't notice he wasn't talking back, or was choosing not to notice. She did not seem to notice the monster slinking along behind her, either.

It was as if the last two weeks finally slipped into focus in his memory, and he knew that he had seen it before, so *many* times. The dog at the train station, twining between the soldiers. Outside his house, an hour ago, watching his brother cry. That great yellow eye, burning and burning. None of those half-glimpsed shadows could have prepared him to see it with his waking eyes, with the protective layers of sleep and distractedness stripped away.

Hysterical laughter bubbled up in his throat. Not only was he a monster who hurt his injured brother, but he was also apparently having nightmares during the day. The wolf—that, Charlie decided, was what it had to be—was all wrong, too big and too skinny, almost as tall at the shoulder as the man in the wheelchair, its hips and ribs sticking out at jagged angles to its body. It looked almost as if it had been broken and reassembled by someone more concerned with speed than precision. It was barely a wolf. How could he ever have mistaken it for a dog? How could he have ever seen it and not known it for a monster?

It kept pace with the woman pushing the wheelchair, its feet leaving deep paw prints in the snow. And even though Charlie could not accept that what he was seeing was real, he could not deny that whatever it was, was getting much too close to the woman and the soldier. And before he could stop himself, he was crying out.

"Hey!" Charlie shouted, his fingers so tight around his handlebars that he could feel his pulse in his fingertips. "Behind you! Look!"

The woman paused, glanced over her shoulder in alarm, then shot Charlie a dirty look.

There was nothing there.

Charlie gawped like a fish. It had *been* there, he had *seen* it—but now, there was nothing. It didn't matter that it had been more real than ever this time; the monster had, once again, winked out of existence as neatly as a bad dream.

"You're a nasty little boy, did you know that?" the woman was yelling at him. "You ought be ashamed of yourself, trying to make fun of a war hero."

"I wasn't—"

"I would be ashamed to call you mine," she continued, and Charlie was alarmed to see thick, glassy tears welling up in her eyes. The man in the wheelchair said nothing. He did not seem to be fully awake, even though his eyes were open and he was sitting upright. It was as though something essential were simply absent. "What if this was your father? Who raised you to be so cruel?"

Charlie wanted to tell her that his brother *was* a war hero, that he would never be cruel to a soldier. But that wasn't exactly true, was it? Wasn't his brother the war hero curled up in bed because Charlie had thrown something at him and made him think he was back in a trench? Hadn't Charlie done that?

"But there's—it was there!" He looked around frantically to the people around on the street, who all avoided his eyes and scurried around him. A flash of grinning fang and dark fur sliced through the corner of his eye, and he whipped around back to the woman and the soldier, pointing. But there was nothing.

There was nothing.

The woman shoved at her eyes with the back of her hand and sniffed loudly, then quickly pushed the soldier in the wheelchair away down the sidewalk.

"Don't mind that horrid boy, darling," she said to the man, smoothing his hair with one gloved hand. She didn't glance behind her again.

A man in a smart suit and a felt hat bumped into Charlie, making him startle so badly he almost tipped over his bicycle. Then there was an odd snuffling noise, like a wolfish snicker, right next to Charlie's ear. He whipped around in a panic, but it was gone.

The man glared down at Charlie before joining the flow of people on the sidewalk, none of whom, clearly, had seen any wolf.

I'm going completely mad, Charlie realized. *Seeing things that aren't there, that's what mad people do.* He was breathing too fast and too shallow; black spots seemed to be flashing across his eyes. He couldn't be mad, he wouldn't allow it. Who would help Mum? Who would look after Grandpa Fitz? Who would help Theo remember who he was and make their family whole?

Charlie dug his hands into his hair, looking around helplessly for—what? For a wolf that was well and truly there, to prove to himself he hadn't gone mad? He caught his reflection in the wide hospital window, a small figure in a too-tight jacket.

And, just behind him, a hulking furred shape.

The wolf smiled, wet and white.

Cold washed over every inch of him. He could *smell* it, a heady, acrid smell that almost made him light-headed.

Another soldier was sitting on the steps of the hospital a few yards away from him, smoking a cigarette. He caught Charlie's gaze and shook his head once, the movement small but very deliberate. He looked at Charlie with dull, hollow eyes, and held a finger to his lips.

Hush, his eyes seemed to whisper. *Don't let it know you see it.*

Charlie dragged his eyes over to the wolf and then back to the soldier. *You can see it, too?*

The man nodded slowly, then took a long drag on his cigarette.

Charlie dropped his hands to his sides. He forced his shoulders to relax, and the scant inch of skin at back of his neck felt so exposed that he had to bite down on his cheek, hard, to keep from cowering into a ball. Keeping his eyes locked on the soldier, Charlie reached blindly for his bicycle. He had to look down for a moment to get on, and when he looked up again the soldier just flicked his cigarette away, got onto his feet, and walked away in the opposite direction.

Charlie rode home so fast, the streets seemed to blur. And as he pedaled, the strangest thing began to happen: with each block, the wolf seemed to vanish from his memory. He remembered that he *thought* he had seen a wolf. He remembered the woman crying, and that there had been nothing behind her. But why would he have seen something that wasn't there? And he *remembered*, he remembered the certainty that he had seen *something*. But there could not possibly have been a wolf, and he didn't remember *seeing* the wolf, only that he had believed that it was there.

The other soldier, the one with the cigarette, he could have just been telling Charlie to hush, that he was upsetting people, that he was causing a scene, that he needed to leave.

By the time he got home, he was shaking with cold, and he could not decide if it was comforting or terrifying that he couldn't remember anything about the wolf—not its shape, its size, its color, what it had done. He remembered being terrified of it, but not why.

Charlie dumped two meals' worth of scraps into Biscuits's bowl and waited by the fire for Mum to get home. He sat so close to the flames he almost set his jumper alight, and still he never seemed to get warm. His eyes burned. The dust of hopes and memories that had covered everything had turned to ash. They had been ash all along, really, Charlie just hadn't been able to see.

He saw now.

He was seeing far too much.

It wasn't until much later that he realized he had never gotten the biscuits.

13

THE NEXT DAY, CHARLIE COULDN'T SEEM TO shake himself loose from the treacly haze of dread. It was as if he was trapped in that moment between sleeping and waking when he couldn't yet remember what was real and what was a dream. Had he gone past the hospital and seen a wolf? Or had he gone past the hospital and had a momentary hallucination and accidentally played a joke that was taken badly?

He had gone past the hospital and there had been—

But maybe there had been nothing. Just sad people outside a hospital. He was tired, he wasn't sleeping well, he had fought with his brother, he had gotten confused; that dark thread of worry, again, of fear, was just getting tangled into a new shape—

But there *had* been a wolf.

There had been. Hadn't there? What could he possibly have confused for that?

He could not talk to Theo about the wolf. He would not upset Reggie again. He refused to tell Mum about the shame of the snowball. He might have asked Grandpa Fitz, but Charlie found he could not bear the thought of his grandpa responding with blank incomprehension, or worse, patient indulgence. So, after Theo had left for work without incident, and after Biscuits had been fed, the soft, wet *plap* of scraps against the bowl as loud as breaking glass in the silent kitchen, Charlie poured two portions of tea into a thermos, squeezed into two jumpers, put on a hat and mittens, and went out into the morning to try and find some answers.

Leaving his bicycle leaning against the side of the porch, he walked down the street, careful to avoid the deeper piles of slush and the slick patches of ice. The icing-sugar snow of a few days earlier had been dirtied and melted into a grimy, wet wool blanket that clung to everything with a gritty, oily sheen. Charlie felt grubbier just walking about in it. There were so many things—buildings, streets, people—that should have been in their proper place and simply *weren't*. They weren't anywhere. They were just gone, scraped out, a missing tooth he couldn't seem to help worrying.

He was almost to the corner when he heard an urgent yowl and looked back to find Biscuits standing at the edge of a slush puddle like a marooned sailor. Charlie sighed. Bringing Biscuits into a flock of pigeons didn't seem wise, but she had that look that meant she would just magic herself outside again if he put her back inside the house.

"I don't think Mellie will be thrilled to see you," he warned her. Tucking the thermos under his arm, Charlie rescued her from the snow and carried her to safety. She insisted on being escorted the rest of the way to Mellie's bench, where he set her down on the cobblestones.

"*Behave*," he said, pointing at her with the thermos. "These are *friend* pigeons, not eating pigeons."

As if to test her sincerity, a pigeon—Pudge, Charlie could tell, from his dragging wing—waddled in front of Biscuits and cooed. Biscuits turned her back on both Charlie and the pigeon and stared with great intensity at a light post.

"Tell your beast that if she gets any bright ideas I'll dunk her in holy water, see if she dissolves."

For someone so distinctive, Mellie was surprisingly good at sneaking up on people. Biscuits flicked an ear backwards but otherwise ignored them both.

"G'morning, Mellie," Charlie said around a yawn that he covered with a lobster-claw mitten. He proffered the thermos to her. "I brought tea."

Mellie squinted at him from under the edge of her droopy hat. "You'll be wanting something, I suppose."

Charlie's face got hot despite the cold, but he kept his head up. "Yes, but that's not why I brought tea."

"Why did you bring it, then?"

"Because it's cold out, and it's breakfast."

Mellie stuck out her chin and squinted at him again, a lot longer this time. Then she snatched the thermos out of his hand and led him over to the ground in front of her bench, where she spread out a musty-smelling blanket for them to sit on.

Charlie took the thermos back and poured some tea (overly strong, maybe, now that he smelled it) into the lid that doubled as a cup.

"Cup or thermos?" he asked, holding them out.

"Cup, I'm not a *barbarian*," said Mellie, holding the lid in one gnarled hand, with her littlest finger sticking out.

Charlie didn't mind being a barbarian, so he slurped some hot tea out of the thermos. Steam drifted in lazy curls around their faces as they sipped, the street still waking up around them. The pigeons were puffed up against the cold and huddled together in feathery clumps. Biscuits continued her observance of the light post, disdain dripping from each whisker.

"So," Mellie said at last, setting down her cup (Charlie refilled it for her with what was left in the thermos), "what did you need from a mad old woman, boy?"

Charlie glanced around for anyone nearby, and then again for any eyes that were gleaming in places they shouldn't have been. He licked his lips. He should have brought more tea.

"I don't really know. I just—I don't really have anyone else to talk to. About my brother. I used to talk to Sean—you know Sean O'Leary, he's got freckles and he's always wearing that funny hat? But Sean's brothers died in the war and now he won't talk to me about Theo, or anything about the war, really. He just pretends like he hasn't heard me. And I've been seeing all sorts of strange things . . . I feel a bit like I'm going mad—"

"And you reckoned you'd go straight to the expert, eh?"

"No, that's not— Well, I don't know. Sort of. I guess . . . You see things differently to other people. And lately it feels like I am, too."

"What have you been seeing, Charlie Merriweather?" Mellie grabbed his arm in one bony hand, her eyes gleaming almost like a cat's.

"Nothing," he said, trying to jerk his arm out of her grip, but her fingers were tight as iron around the creaking bones of his arm. "Nothing, that's not what I meant." But when she refused to let go, he admitted, "I'm just imagining things, that's all, I haven't been sleeping well—"

"What have you been seeing?" Her voice came out in a hiss, and she yanked him close enough that he could see each of her bared gray teeth.

"I thought I saw a wolf," he said. "It's probably just some dog that lives in the neighborhood, I've been seeing it at night, hearing it howl. . . . But every time I see it, I keep thinking it's something else. And in bed at night, I keep thinking I hear the air raid sirens, but of course I don't and . . . I just feel like I'm losing track of what's real."

Mellie dropped his arm as if he'd burned her. "You get away," she said, scrambling to yank her tatty blanket off him and scuttle across the bench to her pram. "You forget them, do you hear me? You forget them and you forget me. They've gotten a whiff of you now and they won't stop, not till they've eaten it, and they won't get mine, too. They *won't.* They tried before, and I won't let them get close again, not ever."

"Mellie!" Charlie said in a yelp, and made a grab for her sleeve.

"Get away!"

The pigeons startled up like a dust cloud, wings flapping at his hands and face so hard he had to curl up with his hands over his head until they swooped away, quick as a school of fish.

That's why they call her Mad Mellie, he reassured himself. *She sees things that aren't real. This is what I get for trying to talk to her.* Charlie sat up on the blanket; the gray buildings loomed up on either side of him, as if the whole street was about to collapse in on itself. *But she isn't mad, is she?* He had seen that for himself.

He scooped Biscuits up and stuck his face in her soft fur, breathing in her familiar animal smell until he was brave enough to set her down and stand up. Mellie was gathering up her things in a frenzy, tossing blankets in her pram in preparation of fleeing.

"Mellie," he said, stepping forward to touch her elbow, very gently, with one hand. "Mellie, please."

Her whole body seemed to collapse in on itself, her already hunched shoulders sagging towards her ribs.

"I suppose there's no point now, is there? In trying to protect you from them. They've got your scent now."

"Who does?"

"The *wolves*, boy. The war wolves. They've been eating hearts longer than you or I've been alive. They're *professionals*, connoisseurs."

132

"The war . . . wolves?"

Mellie nodded, her eyes terrified and enormous. "*Enormous* wolves, wolves the size of bears—horses, even. The others said they couldn't see them, but I knew they could. They just didn't *want* to see them, so they told themselves the wolves were something else—hunger, thirst, hallucinations. But they're *real* and I saw them. And when I didn't see them, I heard them, snuffling around, chewing things up and spitting them out. But I was vigilant."

At that, Mellie poked Charlie hard in the chest, right where his heart was *thump thud*-ing against the cobblestones of his ribs, like soldiers' boots stamping in parade formation. *Thump-THUD. Thump-THUD.* "*Constant vigilance* is the only way to keep your heart safe, you remember that, boy."

"What do you mean, keep my heart safe? What do they want with my heart?"

"The less you know about them, the better," Mellie said.

"*Hollow Chest,*" Charlie whispered. Grandpa's words, the empty sound in Theo's chest when Charlie met him at the train station . . . "That's what it is, isn't it? It's when they take your heart. They did it to Theo, I know it. That's why he hasn't been the same—that's why he won't get better. He can't get better, can he? Not if his heart was taken—"

"Not *taken*, boy. *Eaten.* Consumed. Where else would they put it? Have you ever seen a wolf with pockets? Of course not. Only prey animals have pockets; predators have teeth and gullets."

"How do you know? You don't *know* that it's—that it's gone entirely—"

"It is gone. Complete and entire. When you eat an apple, do you just take a bite and leave the rest on the tree? No. There's no cure, there's no coming back. All you can do now is guard your heart and let him go."

"I can't do that. He promised that—that he'd—"

"Promises don't survive a wolf's teeth any more than hearts do. Let him go."

"But you don't *know* it's Hollow Chest," he insisted. "It could be anything, he's just tired, he's not himself. He was hurt by the—by the shrapnel, he has these *nightmares*, it would be too much for anyone. It could be any of those things." Charlie was babbling, the words tripping over themselves in his mouth; his hands were shaking where he kept shoving them into his hair and yanking them back out. His scalp was starting to ache.

"If it was any of those things, you wouldn't be here asking," Mellie replied, unmoved. "You wouldn't be seeing them."

"But it doesn't make sense—" He broke off again, pacing back and forth in front of Mellie's bench, sending pigeons scattering. He couldn't see straight. He couldn't *think*. "What does it mean, though, a missing heart?" he asked, spinning back to Mellie. "You'd be *dead* without a heart, you couldn't live without it."

"That's the *point*, lad, keep up," Mellie snapped. "That's not living, is it? Spend so much time without your heart, you become cut off from everyone. Being so alone, it's not—" Mellie broke off, and rubbed her gnarled, knobby hands over her face, smearing around some dirt across one cheek. But when she looked up, her eyes were as clear and as focused as he had ever seen them, gleaming like cut glass in the light. "Charlie," she said, taking his hand in hers, "let him go. It's the only way you can still save yourself. Let him go."

Charlie wrenched his hand out of her grasp, so hard he went reeling back out into the street.

"You don't know anything!" he shouted. "You're just a mad old woman making up stories." Charlie yanked Biscuits up off the ground and ran back towards home, tears blurring in his eyes.

Mellie didn't say anything. She didn't chase after him. It was as if she'd been expecting him to leave her.

Charlie kept his eyes locked on the street ahead of him all the way home. He did not see any dogs, any wolves. He did not see anything except the same cobblestones and bricks he saw every day. He did not see anything except the same city that had always been there.

But then again, whole chunks of that city were gone, whole chunks of families, of people's bodies, of *hearts*—

No. Don't think about it.

When he got home, he did not watch his brother out of the corner of his eye. He did not wonder if Theo's chest was hollowed out, the heart digesting in a monster's belly. He did not put his hand to his own chest and feel the thumping muscle there and wonder if it felt the way it should, or if he would feel the same thing if he touched Theo's chest.

When he lay awake in the darkness of his room, it was not because he was afraid to turn on a light and let anything lurking in the darkness know he was there. When he got up around midnight, it was only to get a glass of water, not to check the street for too-bright eyes and the clicking of claws on cement.

Voices downstairs stopped Charlie on the landing, and he ducked down just out of the edge of the light cast by the dying fire. The shadows and the stairs hid him from view.

"He's my son, Dad. I'm not sending him away when he needs me the most."

"Bethy, listen to me. He is not safe. We love Theo. We know it and he knows it. But what if I hadn't been there last night?"

"But you *were* there—"

"But I won't always be, Bethy. Those dreams are going to outlive me, love. I'm an old man, and getting older by the day. Even if I'm around, I may not be in a fit state to help for too much longer. You have to consider all your options, Bethy."

Charlie could not remember a time without Grandpa Fitz. He could not imagine a world that didn't shift to fit his shape. Charlie squeezed the webbing of flesh between his thumb and forefinger until it stung and he could breathe right again.

Mum made a strange sound somewhere between a sigh and a quiet sob. Then she gave a choked-off huff of laughter. "I suppose I could always take Stuart Cleaver up on his offer."

"That's not what I meant."

"But it's the truth. I thought we could get by until Theo came home, but if he loses his job, or if he needs to go away to . . ." Her voice trailed off.

"Listen to me, love. What if it's Charlie who wakes him up next time?"

"I'm not discussing this any more tonight."

"Bethy, *please*—"

There was a scraping sound as Mum pushed her chair back from the table, and he could hear her pacing circling closer to the stairs. Charlie crab-crawled as fast as he dared back into the hall and then sneaked back into his room. He heard the doors to their rooms click shut, first Mum's, then Grandpa Fitz's.

His head knocked against his door with a soft *thump*.

Hollow Chest, he thought, pressing his hand against his own chest where his heart beat a steady thud against his palm. *War wolves*.

If Theo had it, Hollow Chest, if a war wolf had eaten his heart, he would never get better. How could he? Hearts couldn't grow back. Could they? No, no more than Grandpa Fitz's arm could grow back. If something was gone, the only way to fix it was to get it back—

But how could he?

He thought of what he'd seen outside the hospital, and at that moment, it was as if the memory finally slipped into focus. He remembered the wolf. The great hulking shape of it, and how it had smelled strongly, not of dog or of anything he could put his finger on, really, but something distinct. There was no mistaking that smell for something else. Charlie had an odd feeling that he would remember that smell until the day he died. And he remembered the sound of its snickering laugh, and the eyes of the soldier as he held his finger to his lips.

Don't let it know you see it.

But maybe that was exactly what he needed to do. Mellie said the wolves—that's what she had called them, war wolves—had his scent now, that they could find him anywhere. But maybe he could find them, too. He could see them now, and he knew with sudden certainty that he would never forget them again, or mistake them for something else. He knew that trick now.

The stray dog, always howling. The soldier in the hospital, Reggie, his black eyes going wide with terror. The bearskin soldier, weeping in the woods and spilling blood from his hand so someone would come find him. An idea began to form in Charlie's mind. It wasn't a *plan* by any stretch of the imagination. More of an experiment. Just a test, to see if it would work.

He didn't get back into bed. Instead, he pulled on his warmest clothes and two pairs of socks and sat down to wait. He waited a long time.

But finally, maybe an hour later, maybe more, the entire house had gone quiet. His stocking feet were silent on the floorboards as he made his way down the hall.

Light was seeping from the space under Theo's door as he

crept past. Charlie paused for a moment, but kept walking.

Boots, hat, mittens, Sunday jacket all went on over his clothes. He was just easing open the door when a sound from behind him made him spin around, frozen.

Biscuits shook herself loose from the shadows and made another soft mew.

"You shouldn't come," Charlie whispered, the dark room heavy with silence all around him. "It might not be safe."

Biscuits mewed again, louder this time, the threat plain in her voice.

"Fine, fine, shh." He held the door open for her and she dashed between his ankles and out the door. He closed the door as soft as he could behind them and together they went out into the cold night and all its hungry shadows.

14

CHARLIE WASN'T SURE HOW THIS WAS SUPPOSED to be done, but he started walking in the direction of the hospital, where he'd first seen the wolf. His path took him down a long, thin alley that smelled of smoke and something less nice. It was very dark—neither streetlamp nor moonlight could peek over the high walls that loomed up on either side of him.

When he finally emerged from the tunnel-like alley, he was in a small clearing between several buildings, with more alleys leading away in all directions like spokes on a wheel. He turned around in a slow circle three times, looking for a hint about where to go next until he made himself dizzy and had to sit down on the cold ground for a moment.

Biscuits chittered a reproach at him and then butted her head up against his chin. He clutched her warm little cat body close to him, shivering in the night air.

"It'll be okay," he said into her coat. He hoped he wasn't telling a lie.

When the alleys stopped spinning around him, he stood up

on shaky legs. Maybe no one else could see the wolves, but the wolves could see him. And if they could see him, then they could hear him, too.

"War wolves?" His voice was thin and small and he coughed until he felt a bit braver. "War wolves! I know you're there." He did not, in fact, know they were there, but pretending to know what he was doing seemed like the best way to muscle past his own fear. Mum had said that sometimes you needed to pretend to feel something until you could feel it for real. Charlie could pretend to be brave. "I need to talk to you."

Nothing happened. Charlie's breath puffed out in the air and Biscuits paced fidgeting circles around him. Charlie had anticipated this. In Mum's stories, one could never just *summon* the person or thing they really needed to talk to. You always had to give something to get something, which seemed fair enough.

Mum had pinned a tiny scrap of white fabric to the inside collars of his jacket that had his name and address written on it, in case he or the jacket ever got lost. Carefully, his fingers clumsy with cold, he unpinned the little note and let it fall to the ground, where a breeze swiftly bore it away.

He pulled off one mitten with his teeth. Biscuits squeaked in alarm.

"Trust me," he said, then stuck the very tip of the safety pin into the very tip of his pointer finger. His finger was too numb for it to really hurt, so he watched the dark bead of blood well up with exaggerated slowness on the pad of his finger. Then he pressed the pearl of blood into the snow.

"I need to talk to you," he repeated in a whisper.

"Now, what on earth would a nice boy like you want with the war wolves?"

Charlie spun around so fast his coat flew out around him. Standing behind him, head cocked curiously, was an old, rickety wolf.

He had only seen the wolf outside the hospital for a minute, but he was certain that this was a different wolf, its scraggly fur and rangy legs distinct even in the dark. Its eyes, which were even with Charlie's, were clouded and milky, and it made Charlie extremely uncomfortable to look at them. And there was that smell again, so distinct, somewhere between leather and rotting leaves. A musky animal smell, but with something bitter and metallic underneath.

"I can see you," Charlie breathed, almost to himself. "I'm really seeing you."

"You're to be commended," the wolf said, its black lip curling in a rictus smile. "It takes a specific kind of stubbornness to decide to see my kind. Most of you humans refuse to remember the sight of us, even as we are right in front of you." His voice sounded almost velvety, completely at odds with the rest of him. It was a gentleman's voice.

Charlie thought about that first glimpse of the wolf, how trying to remember it had been like trying to hold Biscuits when she didn't wish to be held, how the memory had tried to wriggle out of his grasp. Sweat bloomed across his neck and chest and upper lip, despite the cold.

"My name's Charlie." He could not think of anything to say, now that a war wolf was actually here, and he decided to stick with facts he knew to be true. "Who are you?"

"I know who you are, Charlie Merriweather." Charlie found that this also made him extremely uncomfortable. "You aren't the first Merriweather whose heart my kind have tasted."

"No one's tasted my heart," Charlie said, sounding a lot braver than he felt. But this, at least, he knew was the truth. His heart was making itself known loudly and very quickly in Charlie's chest. Charlie suspected his heart knew a predator was nearby and would have fled like a rabbit if it weren't confined to his rib cage.

"No?" The wolf took a step closer to Charlie and sniffed the air. Charlie looked at his ghostly eyes and wondered if the war wolf was blind. "Hmm. Perhaps not eaten. But I can sense a few tooth marks on your heart. Don't worry, they'll scar up nicely, just like your grandfather's. A heart that's healed is tougher meat—an awful lot of work to soften up. You should thank whoever nibbled on you."

"No one's been *nibbling* on my heart," Charlie protested. He became suddenly aware of a quiet sound, a bit like someone tearing a piece of metal very slowly. "Who are you?" he asked again, still trying to find the source of the noise.

"My name is Dishonor," said the war wolf, leaning down on his front paws in a creaky bow. "A pleasure to make your

acquaintance." His muzzle was completely gray, and when he licked his lips, Charlie could see that most of his teeth were missing. He had only one great fang left, crooked and a little misshapen. He stared at Charlie with his rheumy eyes and Charlie was not quite as certain as he had been that Dishonor was blind.

"And you're a—a war wolf?" Charlie looked down at his feet and found the source of the ripping-metal noise. Biscuits was planted between his ankles and she was very, very angry.

Dishonor nodded his enormous head. He was drooling slightly, like Grandpa Fitz sometimes did. Charlie did not think it would be wise to mention it.

"But . . ." Charlie trailed off, uncertain. "But the war is nearly over. We've won. Why are you still here?"

"War wolves go where the war is," said Dishonor. "The soldiers, the ones who get cracked open, oyster-like, they keep the war inside now. Like pearls. All of them broke off little pieces of the war to keep with them. Some people stole bigger chunks than others. Greediness should be repaid in kind."

Charlie resisted the urge to chew his thumbnail bloody. He wanted very much to run, as far and as fast as he possibly could. But the war wolf was still speaking.

"I know you must look at me now and think, *Who could fear this old beast?* But I assure you that I once was the mightiest of all my pack. I ate for centuries, whole decades of nothing but noble hearts laid out for me like a feast."

"You look . . ." Charlie tried to think of a polite way to say it. ". . . old."

Dishonor sighed, and sank down to his haunches, his knees creaking loudly in the open air. "War just isn't what it used to be. Now, the *Templars*," he wheezed, "*they* knew how to die. There was never a heart tasted better than a shamed knight. Nobody can get that kind of flavor anymore. It's gone out of vogue, I suppose. Ah, well." He sighed again, blowing out his lips, white whiskers shivering.

Charlie *hmm*ed in agreement, having very little idea of what Dishonor had just said.

"Anyway," the wolf said, shaking out his ruff so that a cloud of dust flew off him. "It is the fate of the forgotten that they are never able to forget. The old days, and all that. You had a request, I believe."

"Yes," said Charlie, although having seen a war wolf in person now, he was a little less sure of his conviction that they were the sort of creatures he wanted to see ever again in his whole life. Dishonor just stared at him, quite patient. His tail had begun to wag slightly. It did not make him look anything like a dog. In fact, the doglike gesture in such an undoglike countenance made Charlie wish that there were war shepherds, or even war terriers, instead of the beast laid out before him, bony and heavy-pawed.

"I . . . I wanted to talk to you. About my brother. His name is Theo Merriweather and, well, I think you ate his heart. Well, not *you*, but, you know. War wolves did. I want to know if there is a way to fix him. Please," he added, Magic Words and all.

"Eaten is eaten, Charlie Merriweather," said Dishonor, not unkindly. "You seem like a bright young man. I'm sure you can appreciate that."

"But I was thinking maybe I could . . . you know . . . buy it back? Bargain for it?" Monsters in the stories Mum told loved a good bargain, almost as much as they loved contests. Charlie couldn't think of a contest he was likely to win with a war wolf— maybe a contest of Smallness or Thumbs-Having. Neither did he think he had much with which to bargain. But monsters in stories always wanted *something*, and Charlie had always been good at finding things.

"I'm afraid it's almost certainly digested by now." But Dishonor's tail had begun to wag just a little faster than before. He seemed like a wolf who was trying very, very hard not to look hungry. Which, of course, only made him look hungrier.

"But what if I could give them something they really, really wanted? What about then?"

"Now, what," said Dishonor, his tail going still and his milky eyes going very bright, "do you possibly have to offer a war wolf?"

Charlie's mouth had gone dry. He tried to swallow down all the paper lining his throat, but found he couldn't. At his feet, Biscuits dug her claws into his ankle, like she was trying to get his attention. Or distract him.

Charlie coughed, soft enough to clear his throat, then hard enough to spit out the words he was afraid to say. "Anything you want. Anything I can give you."

Dishonor's tail was wagging again.

"Interesting," said the war wolf.

"Please," said Charlie.

Dishonor rose up on his creaky haunches, then stood up to his full, great height. His maybe-blind eyes looked right into Charlie's as he padded closer, sniffing loudly. Coming closer—far too close, Charlie thought, much, much closer than a war wolf should ever be—he sniffed until his pointed nose bumped into Charlie's chest. Charlie could feel it all the way through his jacket and jumper, a sharp lump of ice sucking up all the warmth in his body with each deep breath. Safe in his chest, Charlie's heart fluttered—*thump-THUD, thump-THUD*—like it was trying to shy away from Dishonor's nose. *Thump-THUD, thump-THUD.*

"A brave heart," Dishonor said quietly, "and strong." His mouth spread open in a wolfish grin, and the teeth he still had left were terribly, terribly sharp, each one stuck in his gums at odd angles, like knives dropped blades-up into a snowbank. "A prize indeed. A proper meal. How long since I had a valiant heart to feed upon? How long since my brothers and sisters shouldered me aside to feed on scraps?" Drool was dripping from Dishonor's jaws in thick ropes, melting the snow into hissing vapor where it fell. "Why shouldn't I?" he murmured. "Why shouldn't I have it?"

A sound like several glasses breaking at once cut through the air, and Dishonor flung himself back from Charlie, bits of spittle flying through the air, burning Charlie's skin wherever it landed. Dishonor howled pitifully, pawing at his nose, which was dripping blood from several long, thin scratches.

Standing between Charlie and Dishonor was Biscuits, puffed up as big as she could possibly go, ears flat against her little skull, screaming her battle cry and what he was certain were extremely rude words in Cat. Normally when Biscuits puffed herself up like this Charlie thought she looked silly. Charlie did not think that now.

Dishonor growled, raising his ragged hackles like he was going to answer her challenge. Then he abruptly sat down on his haunches and sighed heavily.

"Your small companion makes a fair point," said Dishonor, licking his bleeding nose with a long, gray-pink tongue.

"Did you take my brother's heart?"

"We don't take. We accept."

"What do you mean?" said Charlie sharply.

"We aren't thieves, we don't steal. An eaten heart is a heart freely given."

"You're lying." Charlie had thought he was going a bit mad for days now, but clear, crisp certainty crystalized inside him, unbreakable: Theo would never have given up his heart to one of these things, not for anything, not ever.

"I don't have to do anything so gauche as lie, Charlie Merriweather. You'll realize that. Soon enough."

But Charlie found that he was tired of this game. "Can you fix him?"

"I cannot, no."

"Do you know who can?"

Dishonor pawed at his nose and shook his head. Biscuits leaped away from the spray of blood and spit, landing on Charlie's feet with a thump. "I do not know if one of the consumed *can* be 'fixed,' much less if they *may* be. But I am not the one to ask."

"Who should I ask, then?" Charlie very much wanted to scoop up Biscuits and bury his face in her fur, and he shoved cold hands in his pockets to keep them from grabbing on to her like a life preserver.

"I am the least of the war wolves now, and for matters of diplomacy you must speak to the greatest. And there are so very many of us to keep track of here. We require supervision, else we'd cull entire flocks. The leaders of my brothers and sisters hold council in the War Room. To speak to them, you must go there."

"Where's that?"

"Oh, it changes. Slipperier than an oil slick to pin down, and I don't merit an invitation to those meetings anymore."

"Then how am I supposed to find it?" asked Charlie indignantly.

"Our leaders' emissaries might be able to point you down the path, but *I* certainly don't know. And unless I'm getting a taste of heart out of it, I can't see why I should be inclined to look into the matter for you. That is, unless . . . ?"

He made a vague gesture with his bloody nose, and Charlie

clapped a hand over his heart, a bit as if he was about to salute the Union Jack.

"No, then," the wolf said, resigned. "I thought not. Pity. Your heart smells . . . *wonderful*." Dishonor closed his eyes and breathed deeply. Biscuits yowled a reminder at him. Dishonor flinched, and clambered up to his feet. "Well, I think that concludes our business, Charlie Merriweather. Give my regards to my siblings when you see them. *If* you see them," he added, smiling smugly.

"Thank you for your help," Charlie bit out, his jaw trying to clamp shut over the words.

"It was my pleasure." Dishonor gave a little wolf bow, then padded off down the alley, blending into the darkness, so Charlie could not say for certain when, exactly, he disappeared.

15

CHARLIE WAS NOT SURE WHEN HE WOKE UP THE next morning whether or not he wanted it to be a dream. On the one hand, if he *hadn't* dreamed up Dishonor and the war wolves, then he was no closer to fixing whatever it was that was broken in Theo. On the other, if he *had* dreamed it, then he didn't have to worry about either him or his heart ever having to see a war wolf again, and he could go back to sleep.

But he knew, deep in the gurgly part of his stomach, that it hadn't been a dream. He knew it in the way his heart lurched at the remembered sound of Dishonor's voice. He knew it in the way Biscuits sat hunched up over his feet, eyes roaming the room and tail lashing restlessly. But mostly, he knew it in the way he could feel the scars and tooth marks on his heart. He hadn't known they were there before (When had he gotten them? What wolf had gnawed on him when he hadn't known to look, what to see?), but now he found he couldn't help but feel them. They seemed to ache and catch, scraping up against his ribs and lungs a little bit, like how Mum's nails sometimes caught her nylons and made little snags in them.

But Mum knew how to stop the snags from tearing with clear nail varnish. Charlie wished he knew how to stop the scars on his heart from hurting everything else.

He shook his head to clear it; he had bigger things to worry about now. "How are we going to find the war wolves?" he whispered to Biscuits. His cat didn't answer, which he took to mean that she didn't know, either.

Grandpa Fitz was already up by the time Charlie sneaked downstairs, Biscuits a heavy warm lump in his arms. It was going to be a bad day, Charlie could tell. Grandpa Fitz's left sleeve was undone and hung loose and empty down his side. Charlie set Biscuits on the table—she cried and tried to climb back up his chest immediately—and rolled and pinned it up the way Grandpa Fitz liked it, then wiped up a bit of drool from his whiskers with the hem of his shirt. Biscuits butted her head against Grandpa Fitz's shoulder and mewled for attention while Charlie got breakfast ready.

When he came back with steaming cups of tea and a small bowl of gruel, the cat had her paws braced on the old man's chest and was grooming his beard with grim determination. Grandpa Fitz blinked at her and made a strange motion with his left shoulder. Charlie knew he was trying to pet her with his missing hand, and his scarred heart twisted in his chest. As gently as he could, he picked up Grandpa Fitz's hand and placed it on Biscuits's back. It sat there, limp and heavy, for a long moment before it began to stroke up and down her soft coat. Biscuits mewled and rubbed her head up against Grandpa Fitz's chin.

"Would you like some breakfast, Grandpa?" Charlie asked, sitting down next to him at the table.

Grandpa Fitz's eyes took a moment to focus on Charlie's face, then his blue eyes cleared and he smiled.

"Charlie boy. Yes. Yes, that'd be nice."

Theo thumped down the stairs as Charlie was helping Grandpa Fitz get his last spoonful of gruel up to his mouth. Charlie found, suddenly, that he could not bear to see his brother, to look in his eyes and see what had been taken from him, to know the gaping emptiness where everything Charlie loved best about him was supposed to be. He listened to Theo's footsteps get closer and then farther away, until they were just an echoey shuffle in the front entryway. Apparently he didn't need breakfast. Or company. Charlie leaned his head down, his eyes stinging. His mind was like an animal trying to escape a locked room, running circles and bumping up against what Dishonor had said to him last night.

Theo, his head thrown back, laughing in the sunlight. Theo, weeping in the dark of his bedroom. Theo, hoisting Charlie high on his shoulders, so high that he could touch the ceiling. Theo, his heart stolen from his chest.

He listened as the front door opened, and then shut.

***

"It's gruel," Charlie said, apologetic.

"Hmm." Mellie squinted at the mug he'd handed her in a rather dubious, Biscuits-ish manner. She scooped up a spoonful and sniffed it, then shrugged and tucked in. Charlie sipped tea from his thermos and tossed bread crumbs for the pigeons.

"Where's your hell beast?" she asked, setting aside the empty mug.

"She's looking after my grandpa."

Mellie nodded and resettled herself on her nest of blankets, then draped an extra one over Charlie's legs. He looked at her in surprise, but she was ignoring him again. Yes, she was definitely very Biscuits-ish this morning. They sat in companionable silence for a while, flicking bread to the birds.

"You're heavier this morning than you were yesterday," Mellie said at last. "You've got an anchor round your neck."

"I think I might've done something stupid," said Charlie. "Or I'm *going* to do something stupid."

Mellie didn't reply, just waited. Charlie picked at a hole in the blanket. If he had a needle and thread he could darn it for her. Mum had shown him how.

"I talked to a war wolf last night."

Mellie's knuckles went white around the bag of bread crumbs, but otherwise she didn't react.

"It said if I could find where the leaders of the war wolves

155

meet—the War Room, he called it—he said if I could find it, then maybe I could get them to fix Theo."

"It's a special kind of fool who hammers nails into his shoes and then complains that his feet hurt," Mellie said. She turned on him, her eyes bright and furious. "It's an even bigger fool who serves up his heart on a platter to a beast who likes the taste of heart meat."

Charlie squeezed his eyes shut and wished for Biscuits so hard it hurt.

"But done is done and the past won't unbreak itself, will it? What are you going to do, you brave simpleton?"

Charlie stopped picking at the hole. "Find them, I suppose."

"And how do you intend to do that?"

"I don't know," he said, wretched. His tea had gone cold and he wanted his cat.

"Well, I may be able to help with that."

Charlie jerked his head up to stare at her. "How?"

"After the nonsense you were talking yesterday, I had my suspicions about how your night would go. And I realized that you were always going to do this, fool that you are, whether I helped you or not. So I might as well help. It won't save you, and it won't make it hurt any less in the end, but . . . well, everything hurts in the end. That's living for you." Mellie paused for a moment, then shook herself out of her reverie. "Anyway, I've sent Bertie out on reconnaissance. When he gets back we might have some answers."

Charlie knew, in theory, that it was ridiculous to feel a surge of hope at the fact that a pigeon was out on an information-gathering mission for him. But he felt, all the same, just a tiny bit lighter.

16

TAP-TAP-TAP.

Charlie's eyes opened to the dark of his room. There was a heavy, warm weight on his chest and sharp points digging little pinpricks into his skin. Something soft flicked against his ear. Biscuits.

Tap-tap-tap.

Biscuits slunk, so slowly, closer to the window. Something was out there. Testing the glass.

Tap-tap-tap.

Charlie couldn't breathe. Biscuits's small bulk seemed to weigh a hundred kilos on his chest. He could turn to see what was on the other side of the window. That's all it would take. Just tilt his head a little bit to the left and then he would know. But the knowing, he was absolutely sure, would be worse.

Tap-tap-tap.

Biscuits's weight coiled tighter, her little claws digging deeper into his chest, and then—

Tap-tap-SMACK.

Biscuits thudded hard against the window, almost flying out when the latch gave way against her intent little body. Charlie bolted upright, grabbing on to Biscuits half by her body and half by her tail, which only made her wail louder. Scratches bloomed up and down his arms as he hauled her back onto the bed.

A pigeon flapped in off the window ledge and onto Charlie's bed. It was sleek and almost purple in the dim light. Its black eyes caught the gleam of the streetlight, staring back at Charlie like beady little mirrors. The pigeon made a soft, authoritative chirp.

Charlie did not reply.

The pigeon chirped again, this time with a distinctly put-upon tone, and pecked at Charlie's knee. Biscuits, now recovered from her ordeal, gave a yowl of fury and lunged, but Charlie managed to deflect her with a well-aimed pillow. She thunked onto the ground somewhere to the right, screeching in indignation.

"B-Bertie?"

The pigeon cooed and twitched a wing in what Charlie could sort of believe was a tiny pigeon salute.

"Bertie, I don't know what Mellie's told you, but—*Biscuits, no!*—but this reconnaissance had better be worth it."

Bertie pecked at Charlie's knee again and hopped back onto the window ledge. He gave another chirp and then promptly dive-bombed back outside. Charlie scrambled to the window, shoving his head out into the cold night air. A distant coo had him squinting down towards the sidewalk under the streetlamp across the street. Scrunching up his eyes, he could just make out two tiny, smudgy shapes outlined against the watery light.

Apparently Charlie and Biscuits were being summoned. Pigeon reconnaissance must have gone well.

It was a questionable idea, following strange pigeons about in the middle of the night, on the assurance of a woman called Mad Mellie, to look for monsters that spoke politely and ate only hearts. Charlie knew this. But there was a dusty little cinder of hope, deep in his insides, that had begun glowing just a tiny bit brighter with Bertie's appearance. It had been so long since it had flared to life that Charlie had all but forgot about it. And while the rational part of his brain suspected that this was a fool's errand that could only end in disappointment or disaster, the rest of him was so hungry for some scrap of hope that things might get *better* that he decided he didn't care.

Biscuits seemed to sense his resolve and growled from the floor, disapproval setting her fur on end like a bottle brush.

"Well, *I* don't have any other ideas. We're following the pigeons unless you have another suggestion."

Charlie pulled his Sunday jacket on over his pajamas in the dark, tiptoeing down the hall on silent stocking feet, dodging past the creaking floorboard by Grandpa Fitz's room and the light coming from under Mum's door even though he was sure she'd fallen asleep hours ago.

He was almost to the stairs when a sound came from Theo's

room. It wasn't a scary, nightmare sort of sound; it wasn't an awake sound, either. Just a kind of mumble. Theo's door didn't even squeak when Charlie nudged it open, like the whole house was holding its breath around him.

Theo was curled up on his side, his good knee pressed against his chest, as if he were cradling a wound there. He looked a lot smaller than a person as tall as Theo had any right to be. The covers—sheets, blankets, the quilt Mum had made three years ago—were balled up on the floor.

Theo made the sleep-mumble sound again, then shivered all up and down his body. Charlie reached for the bedclothes, but jumped, his throat tight and burning, when Theo made the noise again and rolled over suddenly in his sleep.

He was afraid of Theo. Shame bubbled up inside him, thick and soupy. It was an ugly thing, to look at yourself and see something so poisonous lurking within you. Like looking in the mirror one morning and seeing another face staring back.

He knew what sorts of things Theo had been through. He'd seen the newsreels, heard the things grown-ups whispered about when they thought he couldn't hear. None of this was Theo's fault.

But it didn't change the fear.

When Theo twisted once more, restlessly, and turned his face towards the sound of Charlie breathing, Charlie turned and ran.

He shoved on his boots at the door, biting down a yelp as he discovered a bit of half-melted snow in one of the toes. He eased the door open, but despite Mr. Cleaver and his stupid oil can, the door still gave a bit of groan as it opened. He froze, but no other sounds came, no rush of feet or voices. This was the second night in a row he had sneaked out of the house. *It shouldn't be this easy*, he thought, feeling suddenly wretched.

He made himself hold still to close the door, pressing until the latch just barely caught. Then he spun around, searching in the dark for the two little shapes. Bertie cooed again and Charlie followed the noise like the sonar on a submarine.

The bird was standing at attention, goose-stepping in little circles in the dim circle of light from the streetlamp. Next to him, Pudge was settled in a round, feathery lump, apparently haven fallen asleep waiting for them. Charlie grabbed Biscuits more out of instinct than anything else as she torpedoed towards Pudge. He shoved her up onto his shoulder, where she dug her claws in a bit harder than he thought was strictly necessary.

"So . . . ," he started. "Where to, um, gents?"

He didn't want to be outside in the cold in the middle of the night. He wanted to go home and go back to bed and pretend there were no such things as war wolves or veteran pigeons or Hollow Chest. But Biscuits settled and wrapped herself, scarf-like, around his neck, her body was rigid and warm, and the warmth seemed to seep into his skin until he could see Bertie and Pudge a little clearer against the cobblestones.

Bertie jumped into motion and flapped very dramatically before gliding a few yards down the street. Pudge fluttered his wings enthusiastically, but only managed to do a rather pathetic-looking series of looping hops. Biscuits made a derogatory sort of growl.

"How on earth did you even *get* here?" Bending down, careful not to jostle Biscuits, Charlie scooped up Pudge, cradling him gingerly in both hands. The plump pigeon weighed almost nothing. It wasn't wise, he thought, to put one's fate into the care of something so very breakable.

"Well, I guess we might as well go, if we're going, right?"

Bertie, apparently satisfied, once again launched himself into the air and took off down the street. Two tiny hearts beat machine-gun fast against Charlie's skin as he ran, matching his steps to their determined rhythm.

Bertie swooped and dived, taking corners so closely Charlie was certain his feathers would be knocked clean off. They veered off the main streets and into a narrow, looming series of alleyways. The walk wasn't tended back here, and his feet kept slipping in his heavy boots—twice he slid and lost his footing, landing heavily on his knees, which sparked bright with pain. He kept his hands raised high above him to keep Pudge safe. Biscuits, instead of leaping to safety, just dug her claws in tighter to his skin. Perhaps she would become permanently attached, and he would forever after have to request tailors to accommodate for the cat who lived on him. Could that keep you out of the army? Was there a medical term for it? Cat-Shoulder?

Charlie nearly stepped on Bertie, who was sitting in the middle of the alley, fluffed up against the cold. Biscuits launched herself, none too gently, off his shoulders, landing next to Bertie. The pigeon hooted, his beady eyes glinting a warning. Biscuits ignored him and began washing her face.

"Why're we stopped? Where are we?"

Pudge flapped and squirmed in Charlie's hands. Charlie let go and the bird plopped onto the ground, narrowly avoiding Bertie, who scuttled out of the way. Pudge waddled over to an overflowing rubbish bin, picking through the bits that had fallen to the ground.

"Pudge, get away from that!"

He'd found a dirty bandage crusted with old blood, and Charlie kicked it away from the pigeon, who cooed and chased after it.

Charlie turned his attention to a door that opened up into the alley, which stood slightly ajar. A strange smell was coming from inside—a nose-searing antiseptic smell, and, under that, something sickly sweet and unpleasant. He found that he very much did not want to go in there, that he would rather do almost anything than discover the source of the smell.

But while Charlie considered the numerous and varied things he would rather do than look anywhere near the inside of the building ever in his life, Pudge had nudged it open wider and waddled inside, his head bobbing back and forth, oblivious and *so* stupid.

"Pudge!" Charlie hissed, shoving Biscuits and Bertie away from the crack in the door with one foot. "Pudge, get back here!"

But Pudge did not come back, and Bertie flew over his head and Biscuits sneaked over his foot and Charlie had to follow or get left behind, alone, in an alley, where there was a rubbish bin full of dirty bandages.

Just inside, in a sort of mudroom, a tarnished brass plaque mounted on the wall underneath a picture of King George read:

Mary, Queen of Peace Convalescent Hospital

Charlie almost laughed in desperate relief. All of this, secret pigeon meetings in the dark, just to come back to the hospital he'd visited a few days ago. Bertie must have taken them around the back way.

Charlie cracked open the inner door. Ladies in their neat white-and-gray uniforms and funny little hats marched past, most of them either talking very intently to each other or looking at little clipboards, quite serious. There was something reassuring about them, all the same and all so busy with their neat hair and fresh red-lipsticked mouths, even in the middle of the night. They looked, Charlie thought, like they knew what they were doing. Which put them one up on him at the moment.

What was he supposed to do? What *could* he do? Ask a nurse if she could point him towards the Hollow Chest ward? Was that why Bertie had brought them here? And even if it was, what was he supposed to say? Skinny nine-year-olds in their pajamas and winter boots didn't seem to command the most respect, even if they *were* wearing their Sunday jackets and had very good reasons for being there.

"Are you trying to find someone, love?"

Charlie yelped, his stomach somewhere in the vicinity of his wet boots. The nurse looking down at him was older than Theo, but not so old as she had looked at first, with her fancy hair and lipstick. He wasn't sure if she *actually* looked a bit like Grandma Lily, or if it was just the nurse's cap and the general air of having somewhere to be.

"Yes," Charlie said, stepping fully into the hallway. "But I . . . I don't know where to look."

"What's your name, then?"

"Um. Charlie. Charlie . . ." He knew spies always used false names on their missions, and while Charlie didn't really think he was *spying* exactly, he was definitely in *snooping* territory. Best not to risk it. It only took him a moment to remember the name of the soldier he'd met, which wasn't enough time to decide whether it was a good idea before he said, ". . . Pemberton-Ashby."

"Well, Charlie, I'm Aggie. You stick with me and you'll be fine, yeah?"

"Aggie?"

"It's short for Agatha, which is a rubbish name to foist off on a girl, but what can you do? Mend and make do, right?" Aggie took off the down the hall, the heels on her shoes making her sound like a very small, efficient horse, clip-clopping down the white hallway. "Well, come on, then."

Charlie jumped again and hurried after her. There wasn't a cat or a pigeon to be found anywhere. He felt, suddenly, very much on his own.

17

"WHO ARE WE LOOKING FOR, THEN?"

"My brother." Charlie felt immediately terrible for lying about being related to Reggie; it felt very disloyal to Theo. "He's . . . he's sick. I wanted to see him."

"Of course you do, you're a good lad, even if your fashion sense is a bit avant-garde."

Charlie smiled like he did with the old ladies at church. As long as the birds had brought him here, he might as well try to see what they had found.

"All right, Charlie Pemberton-Ashby, let's see where we're storing your brother." Aggie had click-clacked her way up to a massive blackboard, covered from floor to ceiling with little boxes done up in white paint. Some boxes looked freshly washed and black as soot, but most of them were so smudged and smeared that the scribbles inside them looked a bit like the cave paintings Charlie had seen in history class.

"Pacely, Paget, Peckford, Pemberton. Pemberton-Ashby, Reginald."

"That's him."

"Ah! The dashing lieutenant! You should have said. He's *well* memorable. You know, you're the first family that's come to visit him, which is a shame, chatterbox that he is. Never shuts his yap about his poets and philosophers, does he?"

Charlie opened his mouth to reply, but promptly choked on whatever lie he had been about to say when he spied a set of cat-sized paw prints stamped down the corridor and under a curtain towards where he could smell something vaguely resembling soup, and tea. At some point in just the last few minutes Biscuits's feet had become acquainted with some *very* white chalk.

He looked up to find Aggie had already begun striding off. He got a move on, keeping a nervous eye out for a set of chalky cat feet and making sure to stay close to the nurse.

Aggie ushered him into the long, clean, white room Charlie had visited before. It smelled a bit like soap, with something sharp and a bit headachy underneath. The lights were mostly out for the night, but he followed her to a wedge of yellow glow coming from a small desk lamp set up by a metal hospital bed in the far corner. Reggie's curtain was pulled back to reveal where he was sitting up in bed, his dense black hair neatly combed except for where it was sticking up in the back. His black-dash eyebrows were furrowed and he was frowning in concentration at a fat book propped open on his lap.

"I've brought someone to see you, Lieutenant." Aggie waited

for Charlie to announce himself, nudging him with a pointy elbow when he did not.

Reggie looked up with a pleasant smile that burst into a wide, surprised grin. "Charlie! What a delightful surprise!"

"Young Charlie here said it was imperative that he visit his brother, so I thought we could bend the visiting hour rules a bit, just this once," Aggie explained with a wink.

Charlie wanted to die just a bit. He was bothering a stranger now on his mad quest, not just Mellie and her pigeon familiars. Reggie was a real person with real hurts and real reasons for being in Mary, Queen of Peace Convalescent Hospital. Charlie was about to run for the door when Reggie set down his book to beckon him over. He looked so genuinely pleased to see him that it somehow made Charlie feel both better and infinitely worse.

"Well, it's simply lovely to see you again. I admit, I was afraid I might have scared you off after last time. But a bit late for a visit, though, isn't it?"

"I guess so," Charlie said to the floor.

"Well, good of you to come, all the same. Ward sister, would you be so kind as to give my young brother and me a moment?"

Aggie smiled and went off somewhere else to do something that was probably very important, but not before shoving Charlie towards the bed.

There was a long minute of silence during which the man looked at Charlie and Charlie looked at the floor and no one said anything at all. It was very unpleasant.

"You know I'm not your brother, right?" Charlie finally said. He knew that sometimes soldiers got confused, like Grandpa Fitz did, although Mum said that was mostly because Grandpa Fitz was old and not because he had been a soldier.

Reggie settled himself back on his pillows and looked Charlie up and down. One of his thick eyebrows was set at a jaunty angle. "I am aware of that, yes."

"Oh. Good."

"Would you care to tell me *why* the very nice Nurse Aggie seems to be under the impression that I am your brother?"

"Um. It's a bit . . . complicated."

"Well, lucky for you I am more than just a bit clever."

"Right, well . . . My brother, my *real* brother, the one I told you about? Theo. I know you said to be ready, that he might be . . . different." Charlie felt too hot; his jumper was too scratchy against his skin. His dry fingertips kept catching against the wool. "Everyone told me that. And I *was*, I was ready. But it's more than that. It's not just that he's different, he's . . . there's something wrong." He looked up, meeting Reggie's eyes. "He's *missing* something, do you understand?"

"Missing something," Reggie repeated, his voice quiet and strange. Charlie watched Reggie's hand creep across his chest to rest against the dip of the ribs where his heart was.

"My grandfather called it Hollow Chest," Charlie continued.

"Hollow Chest," Reggie said, his voice rolling each syllable around like a pebble. "Yes. Yes, that sounds right."

"Then you know about . . ." Charlie's tongue was thick and dry as clay in his mouth, a swollen, lifeless thing, the wrong shape for its task. He couldn't think of a way to be clever, he was too tired and desperate, and so he decided to take a chance. He lowered his voice to a whisper and said, "You know about the war wolves?"

Reggie flinched as if Charlie had hit him, curling around the hand braced against his chest as if cradling a wound from further harm.

"I've been seeing them," Charlie went on. "I talked to one, and—"

Reggie jerked and looked up. Charlie could not begin to read his expression. He had gone very pale, his skin almost the same color as the bedsheets. He smiled, but it wasn't a happy sort of smile. It looked like he was in pain. He began to rub at his arm.

"Well, I can't say as I was expecting that. Do you know what I've got, Charlie? Why I'm in here?"

Charlie shook his head. He knew that sometimes things went wrong with people that you couldn't see on the outside, but the man looked quite healthy, for all that he was wan and beginning to break out in a sweat.

"Battle fatigue, they call it. It means my body's fine, but my head's a mess. They don't know what to do with people like me, so they keep us here and have fine people like the esteemed Nurse Aggie look after us."

"What do you mean, your head's a mess?"

"I forget where I am, sometimes. I'll wake up, think I'm still out in a foxhole somewhere. Some days I stay in bed all day and some days I stay *under* my bed all day, although less of that of late. I get mixed up about what's real and made up sometimes, what actually happened and what didn't." At that, his eyes went a bit unfocused, and his fingertips ghosted over that spot on his ribs again. "But I know the wolves were real. I'd heard someone else talking about them, but didn't start seeing them myself until just before I came home. Even then, I didn't think they were really there, until the night . . ."

Reggie trailed off, staring very intently at nothing Charlie could see. Charlie swallowed. He didn't have to wait long for Reggie to continue. "We'd just finished a push into German territory. We'd lost a lot of men, I was lucky to be alive. That's what everyone told me, anyway. I didn't feel lucky. It felt like I was being punished, staying alive when everyone else . . . They came in the night, that first day after the offensive started. There were two of them. One of them held me down—the weight of it on my chest, I thought it would crush me. The *sound* it made, when they took it . . . The medic couldn't find anything wrong with me the next day. But . . . I knew it was gone."

"Your . . . your heart?"

Reggie nodded grimly. He jerked his head to a stethoscope that was hanging from a corner of the metal bed frame.

Uncertain, Charlie picked it up.

"Listen," Reggie said, tapping at his chest with one hand.

Charlie gulped down a thick knot that had tied itself up in his throat, and fit the stethoscope to his ears. He had vague memories of when Mum had been certain he had pneumonia, but the doctor had listened to his chest and assured her it was only a bad cold. Flicking his eyes around to make sure Aggie wasn't on her way back, he pressed the flat part of the stethoscope to Reggie's chest the way that doctor had.

Nothing.

"You see? They ate it whole."

"Don't the doctors notice?"

"They hear what they expect to hear, just like all of us. I'm breathing, I'm speaking, I'm eating, so I must be alive, so I must have a heartbeat, so they believe that they hear one. It's an impressive exercise in hope, really." He was quiet for a moment. "Or self-delusion, I suppose."

"Do you know—" Charlie had to untangle the knot in his throat again. "Dishonor, the wolf I met, it said that if I could find where the war wolves meet here in London, that I could talk to them, maybe get my brother's heart back."

At this, Reggie coughed, but said nothing. When he didn't speak, Charlie asked, "Do you know how to find them?"

"You don't have to find them. They're always there. They've

always *been* there. Most people just don't know how to see them."

Charlie felt cold and hot at the same time, imagining Dishonor lurking in the shadow of every memory. That dog, the one outside his window, the one he saw again at the train station, slithering between all those soldiers and their fresh, battered hearts . . .

Charlie's own heart sank, heavy as a stone.

"But the rats came first," Reggie said finally. "If I was trying to find the wolves again—which I wouldn't, because I may be addled but I'm not *mad*—I would try to find the rats first."

"Rats?" Charlie was not particularly afraid of rats, but neither did he have a particular fondness for them. He had learned in history class that they had helped spread the Black Death, and ever since, they had possessed a certain sinister air for him.

Reggie nodded. "They came first, I remember. I could see their eyes in the shadows. Their feet made these little pattering noises on the ground beneath our cots, in the shadows of the foxholes we dug. They were there after the wolves, too. I could feel their tails sliding over me, looking for leftovers. . . ."

Charlie shuddered, but made himself form the words. "When they . . . when they took your heart . . ." He found did not know how to end the question, or else he just couldn't bear to.

"It wasn't . . . it wasn't what you might think." Reggie seemed almost outside himself, as if he were listening to someone very far away. "I was thinking about my father, actually, my mother and sisters, when the wolves appeared, I thought that I might . . . I thought . . ." Reggie's voice trailed off, his eyes unfocused.

"Your family?" Charlie prompted him, as gently as he dared.

Reggie started, looking surprised to find Charlie still there. "It's good. Good they haven't seen me like this."

"They haven't come to see you?" Charlie asked. "Ever?"

Reggie became terribly interested in smoothing the dust jacket of his book. "They don't, er, know I'm here, exactly."

"What do you mean, not exactly?"

"I didn't . . . tell them. When I came home."

Charlie felt panicked by this, though he couldn't say exactly why. "Do they know you're alive?"

"Yes! Yes. I'm almost—yes, of course they know. Or, they know I'm not dead. I suspect they believe I'm still in France."

"Why would you ever do that? How could you not tell them you'd come back?" Charlie immediately felt ashamed, prying into someone's private life like he had any business to, but he also remembered those horrible days when Theo's letters had stopped. How after that every letter from anyone else in the post could have been the one that told him and Mum and Grandpa Fitz that Theodore Merriweather was never coming home.

"They wouldn't want me. Not like this. I'd be, I'd be . . . an embarrassment to them, a burden. They're better off this way, and so am I."

Mellie's voice echoed in Charlie's ears. *That's not living, is it? Spend so much time without your heart, you become cut off from everyone. Being so alone.*

"I don't think it's true, that they're better off. If you really were my brother, I would want you to come home. I wouldn't mind if you went under the bed sometimes." But another voice, different to Mellie's and infinitely nastier, whispered that Charlie seemed to mind the things Theo had been doing, an awful lot.

That's different, he thought, pushing the voice aside, but a squirmy little seed of uncertainty was starting to spread roots in his stomach.

Reggie was rubbing at the skin of his arm again, so hard Charlie was certain he would have bruises. "I can't stop you from doing this," he said at last. "And I can't tell you what to do. But, Charlie, I want you to listen to me. The wolves are dangerous. I know you know that, but please *remember* it. I can't imagine anyone—*recovering* . . ." Reggie trailed off again, the same as he had when he'd mentioned his family, but he wasn't silent for long. "I don't know, maybe it's possible. But whatever this . . . Dishonor told you, the wolves won't play fair. They don't have to. You must think very carefully about *why* they would let you try to get your brother's heart back. They want something from you, as much as you want something from them, or they wouldn't bother. Be *careful*, Charlie—"

"How are we doing in here, lads?"

They jumped as Aggie strode back into the room, her heels clicking against the floor. She took in the sight of them, both pale and bit shaky.

"Oh, fine, fine," Charlie said reflexively, even as he knew she wouldn't believe it.

Aggie's warm, firm hand was on his back. "I think we should let your brother get some rest now, Charlie."

"Do you know what the oldest medicine in the entire world is?" Aggie asked. She kept her warm hand on the middle of Charlie's back, pushing him around various corners and down various halls until they arrived at a long, narrow room filled with long, narrow benches around long, narrow tables covered in clumps of white-and-gray-and-lipsticked nurses chattering away or hunched over bowls of soup or asleep on their folded arms.

"No?"

"A hot cup of tea, and that's the truth. They teach us that in school. Ask anyone if you don't believe me." Aggie steered him towards an unoccupied bit of bench. "You wait right there and I'll prove it."

Charlie's feet could only just reach the ground when he sat on the bench, and it made him feel even smaller than he already did. He wanted to fold up his arms and go to sleep, wake up to discover he was still in his own bed and had never had this unbelievably stupid idea. Maybe if he slept long enough, he would wake up to find out the whole war had been a terrible dream, that Theo had never left, they were all still whole.

Aggie plunked a chipped white mug down in front of him, sloshing a bit of tea onto the tablecloth. The mug was so big Charlie could barely fit both hands around it as he dragged it to his lips. Hot steam curled up against his face in an almost

Biscuits-ish sort of way, which made him feel a bit warmer.

"Were you a nurse during the war, too?" Charlie asked after he'd slurped down a fortifying amount of his tea. He wasn't sure how old Aggie was, if she was old enough to have been a nurse long. Mum didn't wear makeup except for special occasions, and Aggie's made her look like a poster of a lady, not quite real.

"Oh, yeah. I worked on a hospital train before I was a ward sister here. A year I was on that bloody thing, right out of training."

"Hospital train?"

"It's a train that the army turned into a sort of moving hospital to get soldiers from the field hospital to the big hospitals. Let me tell you, the only thing worse than a soldier whinging about how he's been shot is a soldier whinging about how he's got *motion sickness*. Get their feet off the ground and they all turn into little old ladies."

"Was it scary?"

Aggie waved one hand, as if shooing the suggestion away. "No, I was so busy I didn't have time to be scared of anything. There's no cure for scary like a job that needs doing, I'll tell you that for free."

Charlie took another sip of tea. "Have you ever heard of Hollow Chest?"

"Hollow what?" Aggie cocked her head at him, a bit like one of Mellie's pigeons.

"Hollow Chest. My granddad was talking about it. He said he knew some people who got it during the Great War."

"What, like asthma?"

"I don't think that was it."

"Well, it's not anything I ever heard of during training, but these military types should come with a translator with all the gibberish they talk. Do you know what the Australian soldiers call a rifle?" Charlie shook his head. "A *bang stick*." Aggie rolled her eyes so hard Charlie was a bit worried she might strain them. "Not the most creative lads God ever saw fit to give life, the Aussies. Now, let's have a chat about why you're in a hospital in your jim-jams and snow boots in the dead of night, hmm?"

Charlie tried to inhale a mouthful of tea. "Uhm."

"Yes?"

"I was just . . . I'm trying to help my brother."

"Your brother's fine, love. Or he will be fine, at any rate. He's alive and he's recovering. He's got the very best looking after him, and he's got a pretty all right brother keeping an eye on him, if you ask me."

Charlie didn't feel like a pretty all right brother just now. "But . . . he hasn't been the same since he got back."

"And he might not ever be the same, Charlie, but that's growing up. Are you the same as you were this time last year?"

"I dunno," Charlie said into his tea.

"I very much doubt you are. I know I'm not the same as I was when I first stepped onto that train. My pop used to tell me all the time that he and my mum had to take time every year to get to know the person they'd married, because every year we change a bit. The trick to marriage, he told me, was if you could both learn to love the new person, not just the person you remember."

"But I'm not married to my brother."

"I am well aware of that, thank you. What I mean is that just because someone changes doesn't mean something is wrong. It means you love them for who they are, not who you want them to be. And I always listen to my pop because he's very clever— almost as clever as me." Aggie winked at him, nudging an elbow into his ribs again. Then she looked up and the grin promptly fell off her face.

"Oh, bother, Matron's coming."

The intimidating lady from his first visit, the one who Father Mac had said was *in charge*, came striding into the room, her black clothes flapping with the force of her walk, this time with a strange, ornate hat adorning her head. She looked a bit like an industrious cannonball, flying through the room with great purpose.

But it wasn't her stride Charlie was looking at. Nor, apparently, was Aggie. They were both looking at her hat. Or what appeared to be a hat.

"Oh no," they whispered in perfect unison.

Pudge sat atop Matron's head like a smaller Matron, plump and majestic. Matron did not seem to be aware of this fact. Pudge, in turn, did not seem to be aware that Biscuits was creeping along behind Matron, her eyes bright with bad intentions.

Charlie made a frantic shooing gesture under the table at his cat, but she either couldn't see or didn't care, so focused was she on the hunt. A strange thing was happening to the other people in the room. They were all going silent and very pale, making little grabbing motions with their hands that they kept choking off as Matron turned the glaring beacon of her bright, dark eyes on them. Charlie slid down low in his seat.

"What on earth has gotten into you lot?" she asked in a clipped, booming voice that matched the rest of her, big and imperious. "You all look on the verge of swooning like maiden aunts at a poetry recitation. Come, come!" She clapped her hands and everyone in the room winced. Matron's look of suspicion deepened. Charlie slid lower and lower into the bench until he was completely under the table.

"What is *wrong* with you milksops? Wilting like daisies, all of you! *Speak!*"

She swung around to glare at them all in equal ration, and Pudge spread his wings briefly to keep his balance. There was a collective intake of breath as he *almost* tipped over Matron's head and onto the floor, but he only ruffled up his feathers and settled back down again. Charlie began army-crawling on his belly down the length of the table, sneaking past legs and feet to where he could just make out Biscuits's tail, twitching, twitching, twitching.

"Matron!" Aggie's voice rang out, and Charlie glanced back down the length of the table to where her feet (surprisingly large and in un-sensible shoes with little straps across the ankles) had sprung upright as she stood. Behind Matron's back, another nurse was trying to work out how to grab Pudge without alerting Matron to his presence. So far, this seemed to involve a lot of being too scared to move aside from waving her hands around a bit in the air.

"Yes, Miss Carlisle? Do you have some insight into what has transformed you and your compatriots into a pack of fluttering moths?"

"Yes! I—that is to say—do you ever think about Antarctica, ma'am?"

"Do I ever think about Antarctica? Is that what you just asked me, Miss Carlisle?"

Charlie slunk out from underneath the table, his pajamas making barely a sound against the tile floor. He could see all of Biscuits now, her eyes huge as dinner plates, glued to Pudge.

"Yes, I just—I think sometimes we all just think about Antarctica and how very sad and lonely it must be there, what with all the snow, and we all, well, we all just feel a bit down. Don't we?" There was a hasty chorus of affirmative murmurings.

"So you mean to tell me that the *entirety* of my staff has been *overcome* by a sudden bout of *melancholia* about the lonely state of the Antarctic Circle? Miss Carlisle?"

Biscuits bunched her legs up underneath her. Charlie got up onto his hands and knees. There was a moment of total silence.

Pudge cooed. Biscuits leaped. So did Charlie. At which point the room promptly exploded. Charlie's fingers missed Biscuits by an inch, and she landed, claws outstretched, on Matron's head. Matron made a sound like a wounded bear, which startled Pudge into launching himself into the air, but because of his bad wing, all he really managed to do was fall with unprecedented flair while smacking Matron in the face repeatedly. Charlie managed to get hold of Biscuits's tail and yanked as hard as he could. But he underestimated his strength in his panic and sent Biscuits flying up into the air like a large, furry grenade.

Biscuits screamed. So did everyone else. The room was instantly divided into people trying to catch Biscuits before she could land on another victim and those who were trying to flee to safety, and all those people seemed to be running into each other. Someone's elbow knocked into Charlie and he careened into Matron, who promptly toppled over and—because of her considerable roundness—rolled under the dining table, where she became quite stuck, her thick legs kicking into space, sensible white underwear bared to God and everyone in the dining hall.

Charlie, dazed, saw Pudge toddling across the floor, oblivious to the chaos going on around him. Charlie scrabbled to his feet, trying to reach the pigeon before someone could crush him, but he was too far away to stop the foot that was blindly coming down to stomp Pudge flat.

The foot was intercepted in midair by a tiny, feathery missile. Bertie zoomed around Pudge at top speed, creating a tiny crater of still space amidst the screaming frenzy. Charlie ducked under a grabbing arm and scooped up Pudge, who chirped happily. He almost squashed Biscuits as she ran between his legs, but managed to keep his feet as he chased after her streaking form down the length of the dining hall and out into the hallway. There was a loud crash like several pounds of crockery being broken all at once, and a second blur swooped in front of Charlie as Bertie took the lead through the door, past the alley, and out into the snowy night.

18

THEY DIDN'T STOP RUNNING UNTIL CHARLIE'S lungs burned and wheezed with each gasping breath and even Biscuits's sides were heaving up and down with exertion. Bertie crash-landed into a snowbank, and Charlie flopped onto the ground next to him. Pudge hopped out of Charlie's hands and onto the sidewalk, where he began looking for crumbs. Even Bertie looked exasperated.

"This is," Charlie gasped out in between heaving breaths, "without question—the *stupidest*—thing I—have *ever* done."

Biscuits meowed.

"And you're not helping!"

She turned her back on him and began washing her face.

"Where are we, anyway?" Charlie squinted around in the darkness, looking for a street sign or a familiar building. But there were no familiar buildings, he realized as his eyes fully adjusted to the darkness, because there were hardly any buildings left on this street. Heaped on either side of the street were enormous mounds of rubble, broken concrete and stone with bits of metal and glass poking out at gruesome angles.

Charlie knew now why he was lost. He avoided coming to this part of London whenever he could. It was one of the neighborhoods hit heaviest by the Blitz, the months when all the German bombs had fallen on London, blowing apart buildings and whole streets. Some parts of the city had been cleared of debris, but not this one. Beams still stuck out of the surviving buildings like broken bones. It hurt just to look at them.

Charlie rubbed his hands together, trying to clap warmth into them. He wished he'd thought to bring mittens, or a hat. He wished he'd thought at all before he'd chased after a couple of pigeons in the middle of the night.

A soft, furry warmth ingratiated itself against his leg, and he looked down to see Biscuits staring back up at him, ears drooped in apology. He ignored her, his side still hitching from their sprint across town. "If you *really* want to say you're sorry, you could find a stupid *rat*, like Reggie said." Even as Charlie said it, he knew how silly it sounded. He had no idea how they were supposed to find a rat that would know where to find war wolves. But then, it wasn't as if he had any better ideas about how to continue their search. He kicked in frustration at a chunk of cement, succeeding only in stubbing his toe. If they couldn't find a rat, then there was no point being out here in the cold amongst all these ruins and cinders. They should just go home, maybe try again tomorrow. Charlie thought of his warm bed, which only made him feel colder.

"Bertie, do you know how to get back from here? Bertie?" Charlie turned in a slow circle, looking for the pigeons. "Bertie? Pudge? Where are you?"

An answering chirp echoed through the air, and Charlie carefully picked his way over the rubble, following the sound. Bertie was pecking at the ground, and a soft, tinny sound echoed back to Charlie.

"What're you doing over here? It's time to go. Do you know how to get us home?"

Bertie cooed and pecked at the ground again. The metallic ringing was louder this time, and Charlie approached, his breath hanging in front of him in wet ribbons. The pigeons were standing on a long metal beam, which gleamed dull silver in the moonlight. Charlie went closer to inspect it and tripped over an identical beam about a yard away.

"Trolley tracks." Brushing off the heavy coating of dust and ashes with his foot, Charlie followed the glint of the tracks as far down the unlit street as he could see before they disappeared into the quiet darkness. There was an odd, soft little clicking sound coming from somewhere just past where his eye could make out.

"No. Absolutely not," he said, scooping up Pudge and reaching for Biscuits one-handed. "We're going home. We can come back tomorrow." But the odd little noise came again, and this time Biscuits scrambled out of his grasp with a yelp and took off at a sprint towards the noise, racing farther away from him with every beat of his heart.

"Biscuits!" His throat went tight and sore. She couldn't leave him here, she *couldn't*. He was even colder and more exhausted than he'd been a moment ago, but some sense of urgency deep in the pit of his stomach drove him onwards, as fast as he could go, along the tracks. He ran too fast for the tears to dry on his face.

He couldn't hear the other pigeon following after him, but he was unsurprised when Bertie alighted on his shoulder a couple of minutes later when he finally stopped just outside the abandoned trolleybus. It was tipped at an angle off to the side of the road, lit by what moonlight penetrated the clouds and shadows. It had clearly taken some damage from a long-ago bomb, and nobody had had the time or energy to clear it away. Most of its windows were blown out, and mold and old plants seemed to be growing in the corners. *It looks dead*, he thought, and immediately regretted having done so.

There was a scraping sound from inside. *Biscuits*, Charlie thought, and he picked his way through the surrounding rubble and up to the door. It felt wrong, somehow, to climb in through the gaping ruin of the front door, a last insult to a bus that had served so long and so well. Charlie shuddered as he pulled himself inside—the shadows gathering in the corners and under the seats seemed to be moving.

No, they *were* moving.

One of the shadows detached itself from the others and ran, heading for the lopped-off end of the train, but another shadow

189

intercepted it halfway there. There was an earsplitting screech and the bigger shadow resolved itself into Biscuits, dragging something fat, heavy, and wriggling in her jaws.

A rat. It was the biggest rat Charlie had ever seen, nearly half the size of Biscuits herself and black as pitch.

Charlie got down on his hands and knees; there was no sense in mincing words, not at so late an hour and after everything he had seen in the last twenty-four hours. "Are you are a—a war rat?"

The rat continued to screech, but Charlie was too frantic to feel ridiculous interrogating a rodent. "Do you know the war wolves? Do you know where they go?"

"Wolfs," said the rat, and Charlie reeled back in surprise at its small, high-pitched voice. "Tongues and teeth, big claws, yes? Yes, yes. Wolf mouths. Bite and eat, eat and bite. Scraps sometimes. Morsels. Little sips, little gulps, yes, yes, yes."

Biscuits braced a paw on the rat's body, getting a better grip with her teeth. The rat squeaked, paddling his grimy feet in the air. "Cat teeth, no, no, no! Bad cat, stop!"

"Do you know where the war wolves are? Do you know where they meet? I need to talk to them."

"No talk, scurry, scuttle, run, run, run. Scraps sometimes. Eat and nibble. No talk."

"I *need* to talk to them. Do you know where they are?"

"Not know. Follow after, sniff out."

"You follow them? How? How do you know where they've been?"

"Bad smells, sad smells. Big puddles of it. Follow, chase."

"You can smell them? You can smell where they've been?"

"Yes, yes, yes, sniff them out. Follow. But guess sometimes, too. Get first and hide, wait. Scraps. Bite and eat, eat and bite."

"What do you mean, 'guess'? How do you guess where they'll be? What do they smell like? How do you *find* them?"

Charlie had gotten down on his hands and knees, inching closer and closer to the rat, trying to hear its chittering little voice. Its horrible naked tail lashed in that moment, sliding over Charlie's hand like a soft, furred worm. Charlie yelped, jumping back at the sensation, and Biscuits dropped the rat in surprise. Squealing with fear, the rat dashed for the door, but Charlie leaped on it, squashing it into the floor with both hands. The rat squeaked and cheeped piteously and Charlie loosened his grip, just a bit.

"How do you know where to look for them?"

"Bad, sad places," the rat wailed. "Dead places, death places, big gulps of fear. Wolfs go where the sadness goes, where the badness goes. Wolfs sniff it out and rats sniff out wolfs. Rubble, rubble, rubble. Rubble rumbles, yes, they can hear them. Big ground-shakes of sad. Deep earth-rumbles of bad. Bad hearts, sad hearts, eat, eat, eat."

"They go where . . ." Charlie gulped, his throat dry, his hands greasy with rat fur and sweat. "Where bad things have happened? Or where there's lot of people that bad things have . . . happened to?"

"Yes, yes, yes, that, that, that. Righto, righto!"

"Do you know where the War Room is?"

"Don't know! Don't know! Rats only follow. Rats don't know!"

"This place would be special, different to any other place you've followed them. The place where there've been the *most* wolves." Charlie did not completely know if this was true, but it seemed logical, if it was a meeting place.

The rat had begun to shriek, but then stopped mid-squeak. "The fear place. Yes, the *wolf* place. Yes. The biggest bites are there, the tenderest bits are there. Rats remember. But wolfs are there. Too many! Too many! Run, run, run!"

"You're going to take me there or, or . . . or I'll let my cat eat you." Charlie had absolutely no intention of letting Biscuits eat a war rat, or any kind of rat, ever, and Biscuits almost certainly knew this. But she let out a bloodthirsty little growl all the same.

"Noooo!" the rat squealed, squirming in his grip. "No eats, no eats! Bad cat!" Its little paws scrabbled in place at high speed.

"So you'll take us there? To the, the wolf place?"

"Rats take! No eats, no teeth." It nodded its snout up and down.

"I'm warning you, though, my cat is fast, and if you try to trick us and run away, she'll catch you."

Biscuits lashed her tail around for emphasis. The rat quaked and whimpered piteously.

Slowly, Charlie let go of the rat. It ran around in a tight circle on the broken floor of the trolley before skittering away. Biscuits gathered herself for a flying leap, but the rat turned to gesture at them with a paw.

"You come, yes? Onwards, yes? Wolf place."

Feeling equal parts hopeful and grim, Charlie hurried after it, Biscuits running ahead, her bright eyes trained on the war rat.

The creature took them down alley after alley, street after street, and Charlie was about to call the whole thing off, since the rat was clearly leading them a merry dance, when the rat took a sudden hard turn and scurried down a set of stairs.

"Oh no," Charlie whispered. "Oh no, no, no, no."

Anywhere but there.

The Goodge Street Station shelter had been built before Theo had left, before the war got really bad, before the German planes came to London, and the two of them had watched its progress with fascination, great piles of earth erupting like the spines of a sleeping dragon (or so Theo had insisted, back when Theo insisted on things like that). He'd only been little when the air raids began, and he remembered the earliest ones more like a sort of slumber party, with bunk beds and ladies singing, food in special tins. He didn't remember being afraid, not the first few times, but probably he'd been too small to know how scared he should have been.

He had learned to be scared, though, by the time he and Theo and Mum and Grandpa Fitz had had to evacuate down into the

Goodge Street shelter during the worst of the bombing, four years ago now. It had felt to him like they were walking into the mouth of an enormous monster. They were supposed to stay calm and orderly while waiting for it to swallow them.

He felt much the same now, walking down the shelter's maw again after so long, except this time he knew for a fact that monsters were waiting and that they were always hungry for more.

He was so afraid. His body didn't feel right, as if his bones had gone too hollow and loose to hold him upright anymore. He shook with it. And in that moment, he remembered something from the last time he'd been here, something that must have been pushed down to the very bottom corner of his mind, underneath all the piles of rubble:

The horrible silence, before the shells hit. The scream of a missile plummeting through space and then—nothing.

It swallowed him up now, rising over his head and blocking out all the light and air. It was as if the silence before the explosion had always been there, waiting. As if he'd never really left it. This was the place where his nightmares lived. The screams of the sirens, the screams of the bombs, the screams of people running from the bombs. Charlie remembered exactly where they had huddled, Grandpa Fitz holding him in an iron grip while Charlie cried, trying to get back outside. And he remembered when they had come home, their house was still there, and Biscuits on the front step, looking very put out. He had never cried so hard in his life. He remembered everything about that night.

But he did not remember the door he was staring at now.

It wasn't metal and stone and tile, like the rest of the walls in the station. It was wooden and almost black, with strange, patternless lines laid into its surface in something off-white and hard. Porcelain, maybe. Or bone.

On its right-hand side, standing out against the faint design, were three mismatched locks. A small silvery-looking one in the center; above it a fat, rusted one that looked like it hadn't been used in ages; and below, a lock with an impossibly narrow keyhole, the whole thing dented and covered with verdigris like lichen. There didn't seem to be any kind of handle or doorknob.

Charlie pushed at it, first with one hand, and then both, and then he shoved at it with his shoulder. It was only on this attempt that it occurred to Charlie that perhaps he did not want the door to open, that in fact he would prefer maybe anything but that door swinging open beneath his hands to reveal monsters that fed only on hearts.

When the door did not so much as shake, the relief of it took his knees out. He sat down gracelessly on the cold floor. Biscuits meowed and sat down as well, and the rat took that as its signal.

It tried to take off, but Charlie lunged at it blindly and found its tail and then its fat little body. Though he doubted the rat had any idea how to open to door, it was the only lead he had.

"Let go, run, run, run, go!" it squealed. The rat pushed its feet against Charlie's hand, squeezing his beady eyes shut, straining with effort. It was sad, really. The rat was sad. It was a miserable little parasite of a thing, and it would never know light or happiness or kindness. It would never know joy, whether it tasted better than misery.

Charlie let it go.

When Biscuits yowled and started to leap after it, Charlie scooped her up, reassuring his frightened hands with the downy softness of her fur, the warm-toast smell of her body, the worn-smooth gentleness of her little paws. "No, Biscuits," he said into her fur, and her dear little ears twitched and pricked at his voice. "Let it go. Just let it go. It's too sad. It's all just too sad."

Biscuits let him hold her, trembling and cold, for a long time.

19

A WAR WOLF WAS WAITING FOR HIM WHEN HE came outside.

The sight of it was like hitting an extra step on the stairs in the dark, the unquestioning expectation of open space and instead: something that should not be there. And, behind it, the sudden possibility of falling.

It was white, and perfectly clean. Dishonor had been dirty and matted and mangled. This one was pristine and pretty and immaculate as a dusting of snow over a bomb site. There it sat, perfect as a statue, so tall even on its back haunches that its head was even with Charlie's, maybe even a little taller.

Blood rushed in his ears. Well, he had wanted war wolves, hadn't he? This was why he had chased the rat, this was why he was out here in the darkness without anyone knowing where he was or how to find him should he not come home. This was what he had been chasing after. And now that he had found it, he wanted to run away.

"Hello, sweet boy," she said. He was quite sure it was a she.

"Hello." Charlie's voice was a hoarse whisper, squeezing past the chunk of ice that had formed in his throat. He couldn't breathe right. His face stung with cold.

"Aren't the stars lovely tonight?" she said, moving for the first time, her body seeming to ripple as she inclined her head towards the sky. "All that dead light falling down on us like ashes. Would that I could eat them whole."

Charlie opened his mouth but no sound came out.

The white wolf's paw flashed fast as lightning, coming down on something in the snow. "For me?" she said, looking down at the ground. "You shouldn't have."

Pudge. Charlie's breath came out in a soft wail.

The wolf held her great paw down delicately on the pigeon's tail. He was trying to waddle back to Charlie but couldn't get out of her grip. "Don't be unwise, little one." The white wolf looked up with a flash of her icy blue eyes and pointed her nose at Biscuits, who growled, low and hoarse, her tail thrashing against Charlie's ankles. Bertie was frantic, launching himself into the air and down again, over and over, until Charlie grabbed him for fear he would fly at the wolf.

"Please." Charlie's voice rattled in his throat. "Please let him go. He's just confused."

"You have been *noticed*, sweet one," said the wolf, looking up at Charlie even as she sniffed at Pudge, her breath leaving frost on the pigeon's lavender feathers. "An impressive feat in and of itself."

"I wanted—" Charlie had to clear his throat until his voice came out right. "I was hoping you could tell me how to get to the War Room. So I could talk with you—with the leaders."

"You were hoping? Darling boy, didn't anyone warn you about that? It makes the heart so much sweeter."

"Please," Charlie repeated. Pudge squeaked and flapped his bad wing. Bertie struggled harder in Charlie's grip, and he held on tighter, afraid to break those tiny hollow bones but even more afraid to let go.

"They called us both Remembrance once, my twin sister and I," the white wolf said. "But now my sweet sister goes by Regret, and I call myself Remorse." She cocked her head at a strange angle, as if listening to something only she could hear. "Or the other way around. I find I quite forget. Ironic, really." And she bared her teeth in a grin, the corners of which seemed to stretch back, back, back across her cheeks to meet somewhere behind her ears. Her teeth were like marble, and as sharp and spotless as scalpels.

"Can you—" He couldn't breathe right, the air wouldn't go back out of his lungs each time he breathed in. "Can you tell me how—" *Breathe out, breathe out, breathe out, just breathe out.* "How do I get through that door back down there? Please. Please, I'm begging you."

"Oh, sweet boy, that is not a place for you. Ask for something else."

"No, *please*. I'm begging you, I need to get inside, it's the only way."

"Who sent such a tender creature as you to look for it? Who would send you out into the dark?"

"Another war wolf, Dishonor, he—he said maybe the wolves in the War Room could give me my brother's heart back. If I could find them."

"*Ah.*" Remorse's razor-sharp smile spread, somehow, even wider. Charlie half imagined he could hear it creaking with the effort, a sound like cold metal gears turning, turning, turning. "Naturally. No doubt he was drunk on the flattery of being noticed. Of course, even if you do find a way inside, you'll still need to deal with the ones there. The ones who never leave, or never have to. But even so." She stretched back on her legs and her claws sank just a bit into Pudge's feathers. Biscuits wailed. After that, it was silent for a moment, their breath cloudy in the starlight, until Remorse spoke again.

"I can help you on your quest. For a price. Capitalism is the true marker of an advanced society, yes?"

"What do you want?" Charlie asked, but he already knew it didn't matter what she said. It wasn't as if he had any other options.

"A taste."

"A taste of what? Of my *heart*?" Charlie was already shaking his head, stepping back, and Bertie flapped his wings in panic. *Never.* He could *never* let a wolf get even a tooth into him, not willingly. His heart had scars already. If it was eaten, who would save Theo?

But Remorse just smiled, her tongue lolling slightly out of the side of her wide mouth. "Oh, no. Each of us deals in our own currency. You'll see. Do you accept?"

He could still say no. No one could blame him, surely, for not making a deal with a monster he met in the night, like some terrifying bedtime story. He could say he'd changed his mind, run away, forget about the wolves. And he would forget, he was almost sure of it. That the memory of them would begin to blur and melt until it slipped through the fingers of his mind entirely. And he would forget that there was anything he could have done to save Theo. And Theo would never get any better, not with a missing heart, and Charlie wouldn't remember *why*. He would just watching his brother slip through his fingers, too.

He drew in a shaky breath.

"I accept."

Remorse threw back her lovely, awful white head and howled so loud and so long that Charlie's vision blurred with it, his knees buckled and then gave way, his blood trying to crawl its way out of him and away from the sound.

It was like looking at the world through a sheet of warped glass, or a jarful of honey. Everything was blurred and tilted just a little. Everything was just a bit too bright or a bit too dark to see.

It was a year and a half ago. Charlie was sitting on Theo's bed. He looked up into Theo's face, but it wasn't Theo. Or at least, it wasn't the real Theo, not Theo way he was now.

His brother tied on his uniform boots, his enlistment papers burning bright holes in his back pocket. "You have to be the man of the house now, Charlie. You have to look after Mum and Grandpa Fitz. They'll think they're looking after you, but you and I know better, yeah? You have to be tough for them, okay? But it won't be forever. Just till I get back, and then I promise you won't have to worry about anything worse than which kind of candy to filch from the corner store, all right? I promise."

The light changed or the world slanted too far in one direction and toppled over. Now it was three years earlier. He was in the kitchen, at home. It was late afternoon or early evening, bright orange sunlight spilling in sideways through the windows.

"Don't worry, Charlie, I'm going to take care of us. All of us. Everything's going to be all right, you'll see."

Theo was in Dad's black suit because Dad was going to be buried in his blue one because it was the least nice. ("Never did believe in a waste, did Rob," Grandpa Fitz had said, sad but approving.) The cuffs hung down over Theo's wrists and shoes, but the shoulders mostly fit.

"Say it back to me, Charlie. Say, 'Everything's going to be all right,'

and it will. It's like a witch's spell, I promise. Okay? I promise."

"Everything's going to be all right," Charlie whispered. Charlie knew now what he hadn't known then, when he said the spell: it was a lie.

It was a week before that and Mum wouldn't get out of bed. She was holding Dad's sweater and sobbing into his pillow.

"Mum?" Charlie tried shaking her shoulder, but it was like she couldn't see him. "Mum, please!" She wouldn't get up, she wouldn't get up, she wouldn't get up.

The world shook itself like a snow globe. Charlie closed his eyes.

When he opened them again, he was kneeling in the rubble, his pajamas wet with snow and his cheeks wet with tears.

Charlie choked out a sob past the thick stone wedged in his throat, past the lumps of ice he must have swallowed whole, past every word he he'd had to eat down like a bruised, stale, rationed potato. Like ash.

"Please. Please don't take him away."

Remorse or Regret or Remembrance or whoever she was smiled her impossibly wide smile again and padded over to him on creamy paws, leaving Pudge to scurry free. She dropped her great, lovely head even with his—and lapped up every one of his tears, closing her eyes to savor each and every drop. Biscuits howled and spat and tried to leap at the wolf, and Charlie caught her more by instinct than intention, clutching her tight even as her claws scratched sharp lines of pain across his chest.

"Oh, you've been distilling that for a while, haven't you, my dear? I can taste it. Let my brothers and sister have their hearts and eat their fill—this is the only liqueur I need." Her soft tongue washed his eyelashes dry, thorough and greedy. "Oh, sweet boy, for that I'll give you all you need and more." And she winked an ice-blue eye at him. "I *promise*."

He didn't want to cry even one more tear for Remorse to swallow, but he couldn't stop them.

After what felt like hours, he managed to breathe past the choked-off feeling in his throat and he scrubbed hard at his face with a sleeve while glaring at the wolf, half daring her to stop him and half afraid she would. But Remorse just wagged her tail, once, before letting her tongue loll out of her mouth like dripping caramel before she gave three hacking, choked-off coughs and spat something out onto the ground, where it fell with a metallic *clink*.

A key.

"You'll need that before the end. And two more just like it. Or at least, of a kin to it. Siblings, if not exactly twins."

"Keys?" Charlie croaked. "One for each lock in that door down there, is that what you mean?"

"Quite so, my dear one. And next, I think, you should visit St. Paul's. So many hearts were broken into little bite-sized pieces there, it might as well be a confectionary. Trust your fear and your sweet heart to guide you. Be on time, but don't worry: you are *expected*, darling boy."

"By who?"

"Oh, I won't ruin the surprise." Remorse winked her other eye and gave each cheek one more lavish wash of silky tongue. Then she turned away and trotted into the darkness on nimble paws, where she seemed to blur into the snow or the snow blurred into her, and then he was alone.

It took much longer to get back home than it had to run away from it. Bertie led the way, sweeping around corners and chirping the all clear while Biscuits brought up the rear. Every time the little clicks of her claws against the cobblestones were muffled by snow or mud, Charlie spun around, Pudge tucked into his shirt, to make sure she was still there. He was so cold. He tucked the hand not supporting Pudge under his arm to thaw his fingers out a bit, switching hands every few streets. He could *just* feel his toes, and they hurt. Soon it was all he could do to force each foot to take one more step, one more step, one more step. Little pinpricks of pain sparkled in his vision with each footfall.

He was quite unprepared when Pudge struggled out of his grasp and flopped with great inelegance down to the street and waddled at high speed away from Charlie. Bertie rocketed past Charlie's head and after the other pigeon.

Were they giving up? Abandoning him to find his own way or freeze trying? A sob was halfway out of Charlie's mouth when he saw the birds alight on a familiar bench, with a familiar lump of blankets and newspaper in the center of it. Charlie waded into the sea of sleeping pigeons and reached out to shake Mellie awake. She gave a little shiver in her sleep and his fingers stilled just shy of her bony shoulder.

Charlie drew back and shrugged off his Sunday jacket. It was far too small for him now—he seemed to have grown quite a bit recently—but it was just the right size for Mellie's thin shoulders and bony arms. He tucked it around her while she slept. Her pigeons cooed sleepily around her, and Mellie sighed in her sleep. Charlie picked Biscuits up (she had politely ignored the pigeons) and continued walking.

The cold sliced through his pajamas and it drove him the last few steps down the street to his front door. The house seemed to be in conspiracy with him—the front door opened without so much as a squeak, and not even the tricky floorboards by Mum's door gave their usual groan of complaint at being trod upon.

Safe in his room, Charlie stripped off his damp socks, put on his thickest, scratchiest wool ones, and pulled on two jumpers over his pajamas. Then he pulled the key Remorse had given him out of his pocket, his fingers trembling, from chill or fear or both.

The key was a bright nickel color and icy cold to the touch. Frost rimmed around Charlie's fingers where the skin touched the metal. He dropped it on the bedside table and he stopped shivering quite so badly.

Biscuits was already burrowed under the covers when he crawled into bed, not bothering even to change out of his wet pajamas, and he curled himself around her.

He found he still had a few tears left for Remorse after all.

20

HE DID NOT SLEEP, NOT EXACTLY. SOMETIMES HIS thoughts would drift, go a bit fuzzy, and he would think that maybe some time had passed. But mostly he stayed shivering in the darkness of his room, familiar and unfamiliar all at once, until the sky turned blue enough that he could pretend that it was morning. His pajamas, when he swung his legs out of bed, had dried mud caked to their cuffs and were still a little damp at the knees. And sitting on his nightstand, its shine dulled by the morning haze outside, was the key.

It was smaller than he remembered, just barely as long as his little finger and quite a bit thinner. It looked like one of those little keys to open music and jewelry boxes. There was a lacy pattern of frost on the wood of the nightstand around the key. Charlie didn't want to touch it, but neither did he want to leave it there.

A bit of twine he dug out of the nightstand drawer sufficed as a makeshift necklace. He held the key with the edge of his pajama shirt to keep it from touching his skin as he threaded the twine through the top of it. Only when he was fully dressed in fresh, dry clothes did he pull the twine necklace over his head, careful to always keep at least one layer between the cold, bright metal and his skin.

He only noticed Biscuits was gone when he went to pick her up to carry her downstairs. It was silly, probably, to feel a stab of panic at her absence. And it was probably even sillier to want his cat like little kids wanted their blankets or stuffed toys. But he didn't care. He was scared and sore and his heart hurt. That wasn't silly.

Bone-tired, Grandpa Fitz liked to say, and Charlie had always thought he'd known what he meant, but he hadn't. He was bone-tired now.

He went downstairs and into the kitchen and told himself quite sternly that he wasn't embarrassed by the way he could breathe again at the sight of a familiar white-and-marmalade shape standing guard in front of the door. Biscuits chirped to let him know she'd heard his approach but didn't move her clear green-gold eyes from the door.

Charlie glanced out the window into the street, still shadowy in the earliest light of morning. A pair of lights, just about the same height as a pair of wolf eyes, blinked. But instead of being scared, Charlie just felt tired.

"Dishonor?" he said, his voice hoarse and scratched raw in the empty kitchen, the sound bouncing off the walls in too-loud echoes that hurt his head. "Please just leave. Just go away and leave us alone."

The lights, whatever they were, vanished. Biscuits, declaring the danger past, sat up and stretched with elaborate slowness, first her front end and then her back, culminating in a silent yawn. She rubbed her whole furry length up against his shin to say good morning, then searched around for a warm spot of rug to nap upon. She'd had a long night, too, after all. Charlie left her to her beauty sleep while he mixed hot water and just a tiny bit of milk in a deep pan for porridge. He stirred and the warm steam woke him up a bit with each rotation of the spoon round the pan. And the more he woke up, the more the fear and the pain seemed to wake up, too.

He spooned his share of the porridge (he didn't like porridge anyway) into a coffee mug, taking the rest of it off the burner and putting a plate on top of the pan to keep the warm in. He tugged on his boots, still damp from last night. Had it really only been last night? It seemed very far away now, like it had happened to someone else, someone much smaller than he. He went for his Sunday jacket, and then remembered it was gone. His fingers hesitated at the large coat hung up at the very end of the line of coat hooks.

Dad's coat was heavy navy wool and the sleeves hung down past Charlie's hands when he pulled it on. He turned his nose to the collar and the faint smell of pipe tobacco punched Charlie's still-sore heart, hard enough to sting his eyes a bit. He rubbed at his face with the sleeves and then rolled up the cuffs so his hands were free.

Biscuits followed him out the door into the chill morning. The city was just starting to wake up, lights slowly turning on in houses and apartments, and smoke beginning to curl up from chimneys. A paperboy on a fast, thin bike nearly collided with Biscuits as they turned the corner towards Mellie's favorite bench, and the boy tipped his cap to her in apology.

Charlie, who had forgotten his scarf, turned up the collar of Dad's coat against the cold and another pang of earthy tobacco smell wrapped around him. He shoved the hand not clutching the mug of porridge deep into a pocket (he had forgotten mittens as well), and worried a hole in the lining with a fingernail. He was thinking that he should mend it so he wouldn't make the hole any worse when Biscuits gave a very *particular* yowl and streaked off down an alley across the street, narrowly avoiding a truck filled with construction debris. The truck honked first at Biscuits, then at Charlie as he chased after her past a ruined building that looked like a carcass being slowly picked clean. Men in hard hats were crawling all over the soot-black ribs of an old restaurant and pulling out buckets of debris like scorched bits of fat. Everything on the street looked dead this morning. Everything looked lost and done-for.

He could feel the ache and scratch of the tooth marks on his heart. His chest and throat felt too tight and seemed to burn, almost. His hand went to rub at his neck, but instead his fingers closed on the key around his throat. The icy metal burned his fingertips numb and he saw the red flash of rats' eyes in the deepest shadows of the building's corpse.

"Go *away!*" he screamed, his voice brittle and cracking as his numb fingertips sought and found a hunk of brick to fling at the little dark shapes. They scattered and re-formed like a school of fish.

One of the men in the hard hats shouted something back at Charlie, but he couldn't make it out over his own gasping breath. There was a loud chirp and flutter of wings right next to his face, and then a bundle of feathers and bright black eyes was settled on his shoulder.

Bertie. Charlie could have cried.

"What on earth have you gotten my birds into, Charlie?"

"Mellie!" Charlie yelped in relief. Pudge was cradled in one of Mellie's gnarled hands, fluffed up and content. "Pudge and Bertie found me last night and we went to the hospital, and a trolley car, and an air raid shelter, and we found a war wolf and she *licked* me—"

"Slow down, boy." Mellie stomped her way over to her bench and sat down with a grunt, gesturing at the empty space next to her. Charlie's Sunday jacket looked quite sharp on her, the tiny part of his brain not swirling about in a mad panic observed. He handed the mug of porridge to her and she pulled a dirty-looking spoon from somewhere in the depths of her many jumpers. She placed Pudge into Charlie's arms and he began to stroke his silky head without thinking.

"Now," she said around a mouthful of porridge. "From the beginning."

The sun was fully up by the time Charlie was done talking. Mellie had long since finished her porridge and begun serving the pigeons their breakfast of stale crusts. Pudge had gone to sleep on Charlie's lap and Bertie had huddled up next to him to keep warm. The street was milling with people, who now and then tossed Mellie and Charlie curious glances. Charlie was too distracted to care.

"Now, *that*," Mellie said finally, "is a right predicament."

"What should I do?"

"Never mind 'should,' should is philosophy and poppycock. Stuff and nonsense. What *can* you do? Lay out your options, Merriweather. Assess the weapons available to you. Warcraft 101."

"I don't have any weapons. I have Biscuits and this coat—that's it." Biscuits swatted at his ankle to remind him that that was certainly not *nothing*. He scratched at her ears.

"Well, a good coat is a good start," Mellie said, running her thick-knuckled hands along her sleeves. She looked immensely proud of it. Charlie's shoulders felt, for a moment, just a tiny bit lighter. "But that's a shield more than a weapon. Defensive, not offensive. We need to think carefully. We need more intelligence."

"I'll say," Charlie said, rubbing at his head.

"I mean *facts*, not brains, boy. Although, seeing as you chased after a pack of war wolves in the middle of the night without a plan of attack, a few more brains might not hurt you."

Charlie nodded, heavy with misery.

"You can't open the door without the keys, yes?"

"Right."

"And you can't get the keys without the wolves."

"Right. I mean, I think that's right. I can't imagine anyone but a war wolf would have the keys to the War Room. And I don't know any locksmiths. And even if I did, those locks didn't look . . . standard-issue."

"No, I'd imagine not. So," Mellie said, resettling herself. "You'll probably have to deal with more wolves, if you need more keys. How will you get them? What do they want? Your heart?"

"I . . . I don't think so. The war wolf last night said that they each have their own . . . *currency*, she called it."

"Hmm" was all she said, glaring thoughtfully out into space. After a long minute, she finally said, "How's your heart?"

"It hurts."

"Hearts do that. It's mostly what they're for: breaking and hurting. The hurt's how you know it's still there. Come back tomorrow," she said, standing up, pigeons flurrying around her. "I'll give it a think and we'll make a plan."

Charlie, knowing when he'd been dismissed, got up to his feet. His knees crackled a bit from sitting for so long, and he wished that he'd thought to bring his bicycle. He didn't feel much like going home, but it was too cold to go anywhere else without a scarf and mittens.

Bertie swooped overhead to make sure Charlie made it down the street safely, although, here in the daylight, it felt like Bertie's droppings were the main danger. And as Charlie finally arrived back at home, at little lighter, perhaps, than he'd been when he left, the bird did a little loop in the air that Charlie reckoned was a pigeon salute.

21

CHARLIE STOOD IN THE KITCHEN LATE THAT
night, or perhaps very early the next morning, and truly looked
at his brother for the first time since he had first spoken to the
war wolves.

He had woken up that night from a fitful sleep, wolves and
pigeons and cats chasing each other in endless loops all through
his dreams. Theo was up, walking around the kitchen downstairs.
Charlie recognized the *THUMP-drag, THUMP-drag* of Theo's
walk, moving in an endless loop. *Checking the perimeter*, that's
what Grandpa Fitz called it.

Charlie had punched his pillow a few times, trying to get
comfortable. Biscuits had made a grumpy noise from somewhere
under the blankets, and teeth nipped at his ankle, as if to suggest
that he settle down or leave certain other parties to get their
well-deserved beauty sleep. With a sigh, Charlie had gotten out
of his warm bed and padded in stocking feet downstairs.

Now, Theo was standing by the kitchen table, his eyes flickering
from the door to each of the windows in turn. He was pale. He

looked so very, very tired.

"Couldn't sleep?" Theo asked without turning around.

"No," Charlie said, sitting down in the chair to Theo's left. "I keep thinking about all the things I have to do tomorrow."

Theo gave a dry huff of a laugh. "That I understand."

"How *is* the new job?" Charlie winced, wishing he could snatch the words back. The job Charlie had made Theo miss because he had thrown a snowball at him because he was a thoughtless idiot? The job they needed the money from so Mum could unclench her shoulders just a little bit? That job?

"It's fine," Theo said, his voice indifferent.

"It's not . . . too early? For you to go back? After . . . ?"

Theo just shrugged. "There's nothing for it."

"But do you . . . like it? The job, I mean? Do you like the factory?"

"Not really." He shrugged. "But I don't really think there's a job anywhere in London I would enjoy, anyway."

In the dark, Theo didn't look so tired, so angry, like he always did now. In the moonlight it could almost be like before—before the war, before the wolves, before the whole world had gone wrong.

THUMP-drag, Theo marched. *THUMP-drag.*

Charlie could only blame the fact that he was exhausted from hunting monsters who ate hearts when he said, without thinking, "You always did say I'd make you go all lopsided."

Theo's face went strange, blank and then red, and then his shoulders began to shake.

Oh no, Charlie was so stupid, he should've known it wasn't funny, he should've *known*—

Theo was laughing.

The laughter didn't stop. Theo was barely making any noise, just sucking air and shaking, his mouth wide open, tears leaking out of the corners of his eyes.

"Theo?" Charlie finally said, rising, crossing to his brother and tapping his shoulder. "Are you all right, Theo?"

Theo just waved a hand dismissively at him and wiped the tears from his eyes.

Some mad impulse took over Charlie's mouth. He wanted it so *badly* all of a sudden—the life, the world, the Theo he'd had before. "Will you tell me a story?"

Theo looked over at him in surprise, his breath still coming in fits and starts.

"Just a short one," Charlie added quickly. "Just so I can sleep."

His brother was silent for a long minute, and Charlie had almost decided to go back to bed, but then Theo began speaking, his voice a little hoarse.

"Once upon a time, there was a baker," Theo said, carefully sitting down at the kitchen table, his bad leg stretched out in front of him. Charlie sat down beside him, trying to be soundless so as not to break the temporary spell. "He was the best baker in his whole village, some people even said in the whole world. He loved to make cakes and pies and iced buns and soft, flaky pastries for all the villagers. He thought he could give them sweetness, to lessen the bitterness of their lives. The town had been stricken with a plague of sadness by a wicked sorcerer. Not the crying kind of sadness, but just a wet blanket of unhappiness that clung to everyone like mildew. Joy couldn't push its way through to any of them.

"The baker loved his village; he wanted to see the people smile again. But no matter how much sweetness he put into their bellies, he could never seem to put any into their hearts. With each passing day the sorcerer's curse weighed heavier on the village, until the villagers were so sad they could barely get out of bed to milk the cows or tend their fields.

"Finally, the day came when no one came to the baker's shop for sticky buns or bread studded with berries and nuts. They were all too overcome by a grief they didn't understand. All day the baker waited and waited, but no one ever came. So that night, he began laying out the dough for something new. The last bit of sweetness could he offer up to the village he so cared for. He took all of the love out of his chest and baked it into a pie. He made the crust a latticework of all the hopes and dreams he had for his friends in the village. He dusted it with sugar like an early snowfall, and then he set out into the dying light."

The blue light of the dark room only illuminated the highest planes of Theo's face, so Charlie saw him only as a flash of cheekbone, the bridge of a nose, the occasional flash of teeth.

"He gave a slice of the pie to each of the villagers in turn. With each bite he saw the joy come back into their eyes. But with each slice there was less and less of him left, too. Finally, he'd given a piece of the pie that was his love to everyone in the village. There was just one sliver left. Just enough for one more person—the piece he'd saved for himself. But as he lifted the pie to his lips, he saw a long, dark figure walking down the road towards the village square. It was the wicked sorcerer who had cursed the land with sadness. He had felt the curse lifted with each villager that tasted the baker's heart.

"'How did you fix them?' the sorcerer asked the baker. 'How did you get rid of the sadness? How did you make it go away?' The sorcerer was crying. And the baker realized that the sorcerer had cursed the land because he, too, was cursed to never feel joy. He had wanted someone else to feel what he felt, and now that the village was saved, he was alone in his unhappiness again.

"So the baker took the sorcerer's hand, and placed the last slice of pie in it, and lifted it to the sorcerer's lips. And with that last bite, the sorcerer's own curse was lifted, and the sadness fell away from the land, not just the village. The sun shone brighter than anyone could remember.

"But the baker's love was gone, every crumb of it given away.

The village prospered and the sorcerer went through the land undoing all the wickedness he had wrought. But the baker never smiled again. The end."

His story finished, Theo got back up and began walking the perimeter of the room again. *THUMP-drag, THUMP-drag.*

There was something Charlie should be saying, he knew. Exactly the right thing to make Theo understand that Charlie was helping the best way he knew how; a magic word to break the curse, a pie with all his love in it.

Was that what it would take, in the end, to fix Theo? All of Charlie's love, his whole heart on a plate? But how could Charlie possibly make himself love Mum less, or Grandpa Fitz, or Biscuits, or even Mellie? He couldn't. And what was more, deep in the pit of his stomach he knew he *wouldn't*, either. Just like he would never give a wolf his heart to eat, and that Theo wouldn't, either. He couldn't have.

"You're home now, Theo." Charlie's voice came out in a hoarse squeak. "I missed you for so long, did you know that? But you're home now, you really are."

"I don't think I am, Charlie." Theo's eyes caught the firelight, two small torches against so much darkness.

"Theo . . ."

"I think, maybe, I'm still there."

"No, you're right here," Charlie insisted, grabbing Theo's hand. But Theo eased himself out of Charlie's grip, and stood so the moonlight slipped off him like a closing curtain.

"Good night, Charlie," Theo said as he made his way to the stairs.

"Good night, Theo," Charlie said, and found himself alone in the dark.

Charlie knew who it was before he opened his eyes. The briny, fishy smell of the docks spiced with the metallic tang of the metalworks factory that was next to the harbor: Dad.

"Charlie, wake up." Dad's voice was a whisper, but still deep and thick with smoke from the docks and the burr in his vowels from where he'd grown up, somewhere far to the north, Charlie couldn't remember where.

Charlie blinked, eyes blurry with sleep, Dad just a big, soft shape interrupting the dark of Charlie's bedroom. "Dad? Did you work a double shift again?"

"Yes, and a good thing, too. Otherwise I might never have found this little one as needed looking after."

Charlie sat up as Dad pulled something out from deep inside his coat. At first he thought it was a balled-up fur cap like he'd seen posh ladies wearing downtown. Then Dad put the fur cap into Charlie's sleep-clumsy hands, and Charlie almost dropped it in surprise. It was warm and vibrating. A tiny mouth with nubs where the teeth should have been latched onto Charlie's finger. It didn't hurt—if anything, it tickled a bit. The fur hat's vibrating got louder.

"I found her hidden under some netting, all alone. I think her mum lost track of her when she was moving her other babies. Such lungs she had, wailing away so loud I could hear her over the foghorns. So I dug around until I found her and you know what she said?"

"What?"

"She said she needed someone to take care of, once she got big enough. She said she just needed a little help getting to the big enough part. Do you think she could look after you, Charlie? Would you mind? Since I'll have to work a few more doubles before winter sets in and Theo's got his paper route?"

"I don't mind," Charlie whispered in the dark. The kitten had crawled up his pajamas with tiny, sharp claws and tucked itself into a tight ball between his shoulder and chin. "We can look after each other."

"I think that's a wonderful idea, Charlie. What'll we call this little one?"

"I don't know," Charlie said. "She's my favorite thing. She's my favorite thing I've ever seen."

Charlie didn't see so much as hear Dad smile. "What's your second favorite thing, then? We should mark her place of honor."

"Um . . ." Charlie had to think, but only for a moment. "Biscuits."

Dad laughed and flicked a biscuit crumb at Charlie from where they were clustered by the candle on his nightstand. "That sounds about right. Biscuits she shall be, then."

Biscuits made a little brrrrpt noise against Charlie's neck. Charlie felt the sound bouncing around inside him like a moth tapping against *the windows of his rib cage.*

"I love her, Dad."

"And I love you, my Charlie boy. Sleep tight, my little ones."

Charlie's cheeks were wet with tears when he woke up. Biscuits licked them away.

22

CHARLIE WENT TO GET BREAD FOR TOAST AND
hit empty cupboard wall instead.

"Grandpa Fitz, we're out of bread again," Charlie said over
his shoulder.

Out of the corner of his eye, he saw Grandpa Fitz's shoulders
slump as he tucked some mail into a drawer. "Thank you, Charles,
I'll take care of it."

Charlie felt something like delayed panic. He hadn't meant
to upset anyone, he didn't *need* toast, no one *needed* toast. "I'm
going out for a bit," he said, hoping to distract him. "Have you
seen Biscuits?"

"She saw a mouse on the windowsill outside and screamed
until I let her out to give chase. I'm sure she'll be back soon, with
all sorts of grisly little presents."

Charlie felt sweat bloom on the back of his neck. "Are you
sure it was a mouse and not a rat?"

"Hmm? I didn't actually get a very good look at it; I suppose it could have been a rat. Biscuits *has* always been ambitious in her attempts at slaughter. Why?"

"No reason." He kissed him on a whiskery cheek and went to pull on his coat. "I'm going out for a bit, see you later."

As he stepped outside, he called for Biscuits, but she was nowhere to be seen. "Be careful," he whispered, and walked into the street.

There were so many people out, he still wasn't used to it. All the young men, milling loose, and women, too, a lot of them probably like Rosie Linton's sister and suddenly without a job to be at during the day, now that those men had come home. It made him feel crowded. Everything seemed to be pressing in on him lately.

St. Paul's wasn't a short walk, and his cheeks were burning with cold by the time he arrived at the right street. This one, like so many others, was mostly abandoned buildings and, every few houses, one that had been blown apart, like a missing tooth in a rotten smile. Charlie could sort of go numb to it in the other streets, the odd sort of evenness. He could almost trick himself into thinking it looked normal. But entire streets around St. Paul's were simply *gone.* Looking up in London, he was still used to buildings around him, stretching up on all sides; here, there was nothing but piles and piles of red brick and gray cement in the blasted craters where whole lives used to be.

You could see so much of the sky from here, but in a backwards, mirrored sort of way. It felt wrong to look at, like being able to see the space behind Grandpa Fitz's missing arm.

For the middle of a weekday, there were a surprising number of people milling about, some of them sitting on the church steps talking or eating their lunches. None of them, of course, could see the wolf waiting for him, sitting quite matter-of-factly on the walk by the steps to the front of the huge domed cathedral. People coming up and down the stairs gave him a wide berth without seeming to realize what they were doing, or why.

This one looked old, but not the way Dishonor looked old. His face was masked in white and gray, but his eyes were a clear sharp yellow and the muscles underneath his coal-dark fur were strong, and waiting. It followed his approach but made no move to stand up or come any closer.

Charlie forced each foot forward until he was an arm's length away.

"Good afternoon," said the war wolf, his voice neither quiet nor loud.

". . . Hello." It was a bit mad that Charlie felt almost more worried about people looking at him speaking to no one than he was about the fact that he was, in point of fact, speaking to a monster with very large teeth. Grandpa Fitz would have said there was a lesson in there somewhere, but Charlie was not in a fit state to go searching for it.

"My sister told me to expect you," said the wolf. "One never can tell with her, though. Half the things she remembers the most clearly never happened at all. The mind is a strange country."

"Does that mean you're . . . Regret?" Charlie asked.

"Oh, no. Hunger's children, we are all of us brothers and sisters. Perhaps you'll get to meet us all, eventually."

Charlie wasn't sure if he was supposed to say something in reply to this, so he just tried to make himself as small and unappetizing as possible. Someone behind him laughed at something, and the sound made him jolt with alarm.

"Come. Walk with me. Let us take the air."

Charlie absolutely did not want to take the air with this latest monster, who had waited for him by appointment, but neither did he see an alternative. He trailed along behind the wolf, careful to keep enough distance that there was no chance of that great, shaggy tail brushing him by accident.

"Do you think it beautiful?"

"What?" Charlie did not think he had heard the war wolf correctly.

"The church. Is it beautiful to your eyes?"

"I guess." Churches were churches.

"I came here because I heard there was stained glass." The war wolf looked up at the cathedral, then sighed. "But none of the stains are interesting. Not enough reds." The wolf pawed a bit at his face, as if wiping his eyes would reveal something different. "There was a church in France that I saw, as the bombs fell all

around. Blue, like sorrow, were its windows. I liked those. They were honest. All this golden hope feels disingenuous."

"It's church," Charlie said, a bit offended for some reason. "You're supposed to be hopeful in church."

"Why?" The wolf sounded only curious.

"Because church is about how things get better eventually."

The war wolf cocked his head at Charlie. "I don't understand this God and his hope. The only god I know is Hunger. Before there was anything, there was Hunger. Every war wolf knows that."

Charlie thought about what Father MacIntosh said on Sundays, about the Before There Was Anything time in the Bible. *In the beginning God created the heavens and the earth. And the earth was without form; and void.* "Void" meant "empty," he knew. And empty things usually wanted filling—stomachs, shoes, teacups, arms for hugging.

"I guess that makes sense," Charlie said, slow and cautious. He didn't like agreeing with a war wolf. It seemed a very bad habit to get into.

"'Hunger: to desire with longing, a need,'" sighed the wolf. "Do you know the roots of the word 'need' in your human English? It comes from an older word, in an older tongue. 'Danger,' that's what 'need' was first."

"How do you know that?" This wasn't the question Charlie had intended to ask, but it was the only one his voice could shape around all the ice that had found its way into his throat again.

"As long as there has been war there have been war wolves.

231

And there has always been war."

"No, there hasn't." The words, once more, were out of Charlie's mouth before he could think better of them.

"No? There have never been two humans in the world who never wanted to fight each other. Not ever. Where human hearts go, wolves cannot help but follow." The war wolf sat down on his haunches and sighed, squinting his yellow eyes at the leering gargoyles on the roof of the church. "The work is never done."

"No rest for the wicked," Charlie said under his breath.

"Do you think me wicked, little human boy? Do you think me evil and cruel? Think of all the pain felt, and caused, by those hearts you cling to so greedily. Heartache, isn't that what you call it? Wouldn't it be better, kinder, just to do without? It is a mercy, what we do. One day, when your heart is eaten, or hardened beyond pain, you will realize this, and you will thank us."

Charlie took a thick, shaky breath, licking lips that had gone dry and cold. He tasted salt. He didn't remember when he had started crying.

The war wolf was agitated now, restless and fidgeting, lashing his thick tail back and forth as he paced. "Do you think that you alone have a monopoly on suffering? I have always been hungry," the wolf moaned, pawing at his eyes again. "I cannot remember anything else. Hunger is never satisfied, the work is never done. So we can never stop hunting." He let his great paw fall to the ground and fixed his bright yellow eyes on Charlie's. "Insatiability is a kind of holiness."

As quick as the strange fit of emotion had come upon the wolf, it passed, and he shook himself and started walking without looking back. "Come. Walk with me a little longer. I will show you how I worship."

They were now on one of the streets that had been completely destroyed by the Blitz. Flattened, turned inside out like tilling soil in a garden. Charlie was startled to realize that he couldn't quite remember what it had looked like before.

"This is my church," the war wolf said, looking out at the ruinous crater where street and buildings and whole lives had been. "Carnage and Shrapnel and Blunt Force; these are my saints. I return to Hunger each day with new devotion, for it will never forsake me. Can these people say the same?"

"No one knows anything about God for sure," Charlie repeated in his best Father Mac impression. "That's why they call it faith."

"I have no need for faith, boy. I have knowledge. My god is straightforward, and as plain as night." The wolf's yellow eyes were wide and saliva dripped from each great fang. "What would you give for such certainty, boy? I fancy a good deal more than you think."

"What do you *want*?" When Charlie got scared, he usually froze up, like a rabbit in front of a truck's headlights. But now he wanted to run, far and fast. He legs burned with unspent miles, and his breath was coming in fast, shallow laps.

"What was there before there was anything, boy?"

"Hunger," Charlie whispered. *Run, run, run, run,* sang his blood.

"What do you think I want?"

"To eat." His fingers clenched into fists and then stretched back out, over and over. Charlie had to concentrate to make them stop.

The mad look had returned to the war wolf's eyes and his long red tongue lolled out of his mouth, dripping hot saliva onto the stones beneath them. The snow hissed and steamed where they fell.

"Then feed me."

"I can't give you my heart," Charlie said, unable to look away from the gleam of those teeth catching the light. "I won't. I need it." *Need,* Charlie thought madly. *Danger.*

"A heart is a main course, little morsel. I'm only asking for you to present me with an appetizer. Something *precious,* if you want my help." The wolf made a strange yawning gesture with his wide mouth, and snapped his jaws shut with a whine. Then he shook his head violently and pawed at his white mask again. "You have until tonight."

"Tonight?"

"Midnight, to be precise. Now run along, little morsel. You've work to attend to."

Charlie's legs propelled themselves into action and he was down the steps and heading for the street before he realized he was moving. But something bone deep made him pause and turn to look the wolf in his yellow eyes. "What's your name?"

"Wrath."

Charlie didn't stop running for a very long time.

23

WHEN HE FINALLY GOT BACK TO HIS NEIGHBOR-
hood, Charlie saw Mellie feeding her birds beside her usual bench.
She waved at him, but he pretended he couldn't see. He felt like
he had grease or coal dust all over him, like he was contaminated.
He needed to be quarantined until he was safe for other people
to be around. He tried not to think about the way her face fell
when he ignored her, or how small and frail she seemed in the
empty, icy street.

If he could just get inside, lock himself in his room, and take
a hot bath until he scrubbed away all the traces of Wrath on his
skin . . . but there was something going on inside the house.

Grandpa Fitz was running around the kitchen holding a towel
in his hand and shouting. "I'd never begrudge anyone their war
spoils, but that has to be for your outdoor horde, tiny hellion,"
he boomed.

Biscuits zoomed between his legs as he made a grab for her,
and leaped up onto the table to give a proud, muffled welcome
to Charlie. "Oh, Charlie, excellent, she listens to you. Please tell

your general to spit out her prize."

"What—oh, Biscuits, that's disgusting." Biscuits had a long, snaky rat tail between her jaws like a gory earthworm. "Spit it out," he said sternly, picking her up by her scruff.

Disgusted by his lack of gratitude, Biscuits dropped the tail to the ground with a soft plop. Grandpa Fitz snatched it up in the towel before she could change her mind and tossed it outside.

"Don't know what's got into her today, she's not normally quite so bloodthirsty," Grandpa Fitz said, running his hand under the tap. "Or at least she's less obvious about it." Biscuits routinely presented Mum with mice on the front mat, but all she really wanted was to be sufficiently praised and assured that she was an unparalleled huntress. This tail business was just ghoulish.

Charlie carried her up to his room to sequester her, shutting the door behind them after he set her down. "Biscuits . . . tell me you didn't."

Biscuits looked insufferably smug.

"You cannot be hunting war rats," he ordered. "It's not safe and it's . . . sad. And disgusting," he added, pointing at her. She ignored him and craned her neck to look very purposefully at the wall. She held this pose as if it was perfectly comfortable.

"I have a problem, anyway, and I need your help."

Biscuits made a low, annoyed chirp.

"A war wolf needs me to find something 'precious,'" Charlie continued, "and *no*, he did not mean a rat's tail, I don't want to hear it."

With a great show of dignity, Biscuits swung her head back around to squint up at him.

"Come here, help me think." He flopped onto his bed and Biscuits leaped up beside him obligingly. "Something precious. Something precious to Wrath . . ." he murmured.

He did not mean to fall asleep, but the next thing he knew, he was jerking awake. Biscuits was snoring, but had thankfully found no new, horrible gifts to leave around. Bleary and headachy with sleep, he lurched upright, and looked at his clock in a panic. Seven o'clock. Half the day was gone and he had nothing to show for it, no ideas, no help. Panic was wrapping itself around a spot right in the center of his chest. He wasn't breathing exactly right; it was like he was trying to hold his breath without meaning to, taking big gulps of air and just holding them as pressure mounted inside him.

There was still time. He made himself let out a breath, slowly, and then another. And another. There was still time. Five hours. He would go out; maybe he could find Mellie. If Bertie and Pudge could help him find Remorse, surely they could help him find something precious to Wrath. Yes. Yes, he could find Mellie and the pigeons and they would suss out what to do.

He was almost at the bottom of the stairs when he heard Mum and Grandpa Fitz talking in hushed voices.

"I'm not discussing this with you."

"Well, you need to discuss it with *someone*."

"Dad, I have to be realistic. If they keep letting girls go from the phone company—"

When he walked in, the voices abruptly cut off.

"Charles, there you are," Mum said. "Set two extra plates for dinner, please, our guests will be here any minute." She glanced at the clock and fussed with a pin in her hair, looking fretful.

"Who's coming?" he asked, trying to look as unsuspicious as possible.

"Mr. Cleaver's son just returned to London, and I thought it would be nice to give them both a proper meal."

"Was his son in France, too?"

"Oh, no, he was evacuated to the country. He's your age."

Some—most, probably—of the children in London had been sent out of the city when the bombing started, either to stay with family or with strangers who offered to take them in. They had been trickling back home in fits and starts. Eustace from church had stayed on his grandparents' farm in a village so small Charlie couldn't even find it on a map. He had said only that cows were scarier than they had any right to be and should be treated as hostile, should Charlie ever meet one, and had refused to speak further.

"Well, that doesn't sound too bad."

"Imagine how you'd feel, Charles, being away from home for so long, in a strange place where you don't know anyone."

"Yes, that must be simply *awful*," Theo drawled. Charlie wasn't sure whether he was meant to laugh to or not.

"Now I expect you all to be on your best behavior for our

guests," Mum went on as if Theo hadn't spoken. Theo rolled his eyes at Charlie over her shoulder, and Charlie grinned in surprise.

But when a jaunty series of knocks came from the front door, the grin slid off Charlie's face onto the floor like a wet snowball.

"Hullo, hullo!" Mr. Cleaver said in his stupid voice that was somehow nasally while also being far too loud for the space. "So lovely of you to have us over, Beth. Theodore, Charlie boy, how are you? Fitz! There's a good man!" Mr. Cleaver went about in a whirling dervish of handshakes and shoulder slaps and "Call me Stuart"s through his rather thin mustache. The three of them muttered an unenthused chorus of "how do you do"s in response, as Mr. Cleaver shoved his son at them like some sort of prize ham.

"This is my boy Tommy; say hello to the Merriweathers, Tommy."

"Hullo!" Tommy's cap of blond hair gleamed in the light, like someone had taken a very well-polished bowl and stuck it on his head. His cheeks were a ruddy pink and his jumper didn't have a single darning scar on it. Charlie disliked him immediately.

"Nice to meet you," Charlie lied.

"Is that your cat? Here, kitty, kitty!" Tommy made a swipe for Biscuits as she wound round Charlie's ankles to assess the newcomers. She hissed as Tommy's grabby fingers reached for her, and then streaked up the stairs to safety.

"Let's everyone sit down, before the food gets cold," Mum said with an aggressive sort of cheerfulness.

The Cleavers kept up a bubbling stream of conversation, mostly about themselves, for the better part of an hour. Every time they slowed down a bit, Charlie was careful to shove a large portion of food into his mouth so as to discourage them from asking him to speak. It only worked sometimes.

"They sent us back for winter hols, but now that the war's over with, we all went home," Tommy barreled on, taking second helpings of everything. "Are you still on winter hols, Charlie? From school?"

Charlie blinked. He couldn't tell if Tommy was trying to make fun of him, or if he was just stupid. He glanced nervously around the table. Both Grandpa Fitz and Theo looked as if they were imagining socially acceptable ways to throttle Tommy. Mr. Cleaver—Stuart—just looked politely curious, a bit like how Charlie imagined a cow would look if presented with a maths equation.

"I left school. To help with . . ." He glanced at Grandpa Fitz and decided that was none of the Cleavers' business. "To help around the house while Mum works."

"Oh, well you must be having loads of fun, then, running around with no schoolwork."

Ah, so he was just dense, then. "Not particularly," Charlie said, slicing up a piece of cabbage with medical precision.

"We're hoping to send Charlie back to school in the spring," Mum piped in with a bit too much forceful cheeriness.

"Well, that'll be a real corker, won't it, Charlie? Exciting to get back to normal, eh?" Tommy's teeth gleamed white in the dim light. Charlie felt a sudden and intense urge to throw something at him. A plate, maybe, or Biscuits.

"Yes," said Charlie, dead-eyed. "A real corker." Theo made an odd choking sound. Grandpa Fitz rubbed at his temple.

Tommy didn't even seem like a real person. He was like one of those war posters of a boy, red-cheeked and smooth-haired and with stupid, perfect shiny teeth, telling everyone that Britain would prevail over the German Reich. Charlie half expected a Union Jack to unfurl behind him and Tommy to suggest he start a victory garden. He probably never jumped when he heard a car backfire, didn't still keep his drapes drawn shut at night because it made him feel safe to know that no planes could see the light from his window as they flew overhead. Instead he just kept droning on about how nice the country was, how clean the air smelled, how delicious fresh food straight from the earth tasted. Meanwhile, Charlie ate his rations, which tasted like the memory of the food they were supposed to be, rather than the real thing. Something was coalescing inside Charlie, a hard little stone like a coal that was burning.

"Oh! Do you want to see something brilliant?" Tommy asked, bright eyes beaming.

"Sure," said Charlie, who absolutely did not.

Tommy reached into his pocket and pulled out a wood-handled pocketknife. He snapped it open carefully, so it gleamed bright in the dim light. Charlie, who did not care for knives, especially near him, gripped the burning coal inside himself hard enough to almost hurt.

"I got it from my cousin in Surrey, who I was staying with. He says every young man ought to have a knife, at least in the country. And it's ever so useful."

"For what?"

"Oh, cutting things up and the like."

Charlie watched the light play off the sharp edge of the knife, and thought of fangs, of things that sliced and tore. "You don't say."

"Yes! My cousin says it's a family heirloom. He said people don't make things like they used to anymore, and I should clean it with a special cloth and not get it in water, in case it rusts."

Charlie wanted to dunk Tommy and his stupid knife in a mop bucket. "Amazing" was what he said, though, just as Theo said the same in perfect unison, their voices both dry as match paper. They stared at each other in startled silence for a moment before bursting out laughing. And it felt for just a moment like it had before—before the war, before they made each other angry all the time, before everything. When all they had to do was look at each other and *know*. Theo looked up at Mum with a lopsided grin, but there was something brittle and nasty in his voice when he said, "Mum, didn't Dad grow up on a farm?"

Mum's face didn't change, but something about her seemed to sink in on itself, her shoulders drooping. And Charlie, to his great surprise, felt . . . almost triumphant at that, the piece of coal compressing tighter and tighter, being forced into a new shape, something jagged and angry and sharp as any knife.

"Careful now," said Grandpa Fitz, his voice very low and calm.

"Beth, I think perhaps young Thomas and I ought to go," Mr. Cleaver said, his words coming out in a weirdly cheerful rush that seemed to get caught up in his mustache before freeing themselves.

"Yes, I think that's for the best, Stuart."

"D'you fancy a spot of cricket next week, Charlie?" Tommy asked as he pulled on his scarf and mittens. Grandpa Fitz's hand closed over Charlie mouth before he could reply, but Theo's voice carried past them.

"I'm sure Charlie would love nothing more," Theo drawled.

"*Theodore*," Mum hissed, but the Cleavers were already pulling on their coats, oblivious.

Charlie forced himself to hold still and endure a hug from Tommy, who did a great deal of hearty slapping at Charlie's shoulders. Charlie, whose arms were pinned, could only pat his fingers weakly in the general vicinity of Tommy's pockets.

Then Mr. Cleaver ruffled Charlie's hair, which gave Charlie fresh insight into what Biscuits felt like when her fur was rubbed the wrong direction. When he kissed Mum on the cheek, Charlie understood Biscuits's general willingness to bite people.

In a quiet voice, he excused himself to his room, and waited.

Once he was sure everyone had gone to their rooms for the night, he sneaked back outside—*easy, it was so easy now*—and into the alleyway behind the houses. He shivered, despite the heft of his dad's coat, scanning the shadows for what he knew would be there, somewhere.

Even knowing he was looking for it, he still went rigid when he saw a pale shape that might almost have been a skull hovering in the darkness. The vague skull coalesced into Wrath's gray-sprinkled face, his eyes brighter, somehow, than they had been in the sunlight, the yellow deep and opaque. He said nothing, looking as patient as stone. Gingerly, Charlie reached into his pocket and pulled out what was hidden inside.

Tommy's knife gleamed bright in the dim light.

"Is this . . . is this what you meant? Is this what you wanted?"

"Open it," Wrath suggested, his voice silky, gentle almost.

The gleam of the light off the knife was somehow entrancing, and Charlie flicked it open. There was nothing special about it, really, except that it was Tommy's, and Charlie had taken it from him, right out from under his ridiculous, oblivious nose. Maybe he would realize as soon as he got home that it was gone, or maybe he was too clueless to even notice for days or weeks. *A family heirloom.* Ridiculous. If it was so important, he should have looked after it better, he should have just kept his obnoxious mouth shut about what a pleasant, relaxing war he'd had—

Shame flooded Charlie in a wave.

"There it is," Wrath whispered.

Charlie's mouth felt cottony and sour. Tommy was annoying, infuriating even, but he wasn't *bad*, he wasn't *cruel*. He had tried to be friendly in his blundering way. Charlie was the one who was bad. Charlie was the only one who had done something just for the sake of meanness, because he'd been angry, *so* angry, because he had wanted Tommy to feel it, a little jagged piece of the loss that was always following him around.

He snapped the knife closed, and pain flashed bright across his palm. He dropped the pocketknife with a yelp, clutching his hand. He'd cut himself on the stupid, *stupid* stolen pocketknife. He hissed as blood seeped sluggishly in between his fingers.

Without a sound, Wrath padded forward, his head snapping out like a snake, making Charlie yell in surprise. But he didn't bite. There was only a soft splash of tongue as Wrath licked the trickle of blood off Charlie's smarting palm, which went numb at the touch, then started to burn worse than before.

Charlie snatched his hand away, Wrath's eyes following its every move.

The gray-masked war wolf drew back and pawed at his face, so hard Charlie almost told him to stop before he scratched his eye and hurt himself. But then he remembered that he didn't care if Wrath hurt himself, and clenched his hands into tight fists until the pawing stopped. Wrath shook himself violently, and something fell to the ground with a heavy metallic chime.

Charlie was too horrified—with Wrath, with himself—to say anything.

"Thank you," said Wrath, inclining his head towards the house. "And you're welcome."

***

Charlie didn't touch the key for a long time. Wrath had long since disappeared, but Charlie couldn't make himself reach down and pick it up. It was bigger than the key Remorse had given him—thicker than his thumb and longer, too. It was iron, maybe, dark and a little rusted at the edges.

Only when it started snowing did he slip his twine necklace over his head and untie it, threading the large key onto the cord next to its smaller cousin. He made to slip the loop of twine over his head, but found he couldn't bear the thought of the keys so close to his heartbeat.

He shoved both keys into one pocket and Tommy's pocket-knife into the other and walked inside without looking back. He didn't want to know who or what might still be watching, but deep inside him, a wild anticipation was unfurling.

There had been three locks on the door. Three locks, then, would need three keys. And now he had two. *Just one more to go.* One more war wolf, one more key, and then it would be over. One more key and he could open the door. One more key, and he could enter the War Room and get his brother's heart back. Somehow. It wouldn't be easy, he knew that. The wolves would try to trick him, almost certainly. They wouldn't give up the heart without a fight.

But neither would Charlie. He was ready.

Mum opened her bedroom door on the second soft knock.

"Charles? Oh, darling, are you all right?"

The thrill he had felt at the second key popped like a soap bubble.

"I'm so sorry, Mum." His voice was a whisper. It was the only sound that he found he could make. "I'm sorry I was horrible at dinner. And I'm sorry I—Tommy left his knife here, and I should have told him, I should have given it back, but I didn't, because I was angry with Tommy and I didn't want to do something nice for him. I'm sorry."

"Oh, Charlie." And Mum swept him into her arms and wrapped her housecoat around him like a blanket, and she smelled like clean laundry and lavender soap and, underneath that, just a bit like shoe polish. She smelled exactly the way a mother ought to smell, but her arms felt just a little less substantial than they should have around Charlie's shoulders. His face pressed into her ribs instead of her hip. He didn't fit into her arms quite right anymore.

Charlie was ashamed when he started to cry.

"My sweet boy," Mum said into Charlie's hair, rubbing one hand up and down his back and making little crooning humming sounds. "My poor, sweet boy. My littlest one, it's all right. Hush. It's all right."

Mum pulled him under the covers with her and hugged him close so his snuffling was somewhat muffled by her shoulder.

"I'm sorry I was so awful to everyone. I just—nothing's the way it's supposed to be."

"I know, darling. I know it hasn't been for a long time."

"I know I could fix things if, if they would just hold still long enough."

Mum sighed into his hair. "Nothing ever holds still, I'm afraid. I would hold it still for you if I could."

Mum's heart beat a strong, steady rhythm in Charlie's ear where it was pressed against Mum's side. For the first time he could hear the scars on her heart scraping and rasping against the bony cage of her ribs.

"Tommy didn't leave his knife," he said into her shirt. "I took it."

"I know," Mum said, and stroked his hair. "But I also know that you're sorry, and that you'll make it right." Charlie gave a snuffly nod.

"I could learn to like Mr. Cleaver. If you really like him, I mean. I could find a way."

"Good Lord, Charles. That's not something you need to worry about, nor is it something I feel inclined to discuss with you. All right?"

"All right." After a moment, he added, "You're always careful at your job, aren't you, Mum?"

"Whatever do you mean, sweetheart? It's a switchboard center, there's really not much uncareful to get into."

"But, I mean, walking there? You're always careful? And you never—never take bad roads or anything?"

"Bad roads? The bus stops at that same corner every day and it takes me the same twenty steps to get from that corner to this door. The walk's a bit slick in winter, but it's hardly dangerous, Charles."

"I *know*, but—" Charlie was horrified to realize he was about to cry again.

"Oh, *Charlie*." Mum brushed his hair back away from his eyes and cupped his wet, snotty face in her warm hands. "What can I do, my love?"

"Is Grandpa Fitz going to die?"

"We're all going to die someday, darling. But not today. Not for a good long while. Your granddad will outlast all of us, you wait."

"But not you?"

"Not me what?"

"He's not going to outlast you, is he?" Charlie's breath came in a shaky rattle. If he couldn't do it, if he couldn't fix Theo, if Grandpa Fitz got bad and didn't get better, if Mum—he'd be alone. He'd be all alone. "You're never going to die, are you? Promise me you'll never die."

Mum crushed him tight into her arms and hummed quiet nonsense songs to him until they both fell asleep.

But she never promised.

24

A DAY WENT BY AND CHARLIE WAITED, BUT A wolf did not appear. The wolves up until now had made themselves known. Dishonor had materialized when summoned. Remorse had simply been there, waiting and prepared, and with instructions about how to find Wrath. And Wrath had been waiting, just where she had said. But Wrath hadn't said where to find the next wolf—the last wolf, with the last key.

So Charlie waited more. The day went by with exaggerated slowness, honey dripping off a spoon, each minute dragging out into hours. No wolf outside. No eyes flashing in the darkness. No paw prints pressed into the snow. The minutes dripped off the hands off the clock. Nothing.

One day became two days. Three. On the third day, Charlie started walking and did not stop. He left right after Mum and Theo went to work in the morning, the sharp chill of the morning giving way to the blunted cool of the afternoon as he walked down street after street, looking down each alley as he passed, under each bench, behind each tree. Five times he stopped and pressed a pin into a tender fingertip, and called for the war wolves. At the end of the day, each finger on his left hand stung and his voice was hoarse.

Nothing.

On the fourth day, he started walking in the opposite direction. He came home with the fingers of his right hand scabbed over.

Nothing.

By the fifth day he was not sleeping, couldn't make himself eat, and the confusion at the wolves' absence and the anxiety at his inability to find them had coalesced into a panic from which Charlie could not extricate himself, not even for a moment. He ate breakfast and his heart pounded. He helped Grandpa Fitz get dressed and his hands shook. He buttoned his coat and his breath came in a gasp. He saw himself do it again—take a breath and hold it as if he were underwater, until his lungs burned—and was unable to stop it.

Just breathe normally, it's not that hard, you do it every day, he ordered himself, and it would work for a few minutes, a few streets, until he tried to call for the war wolves again and he had no breath with which to speak.

And still, nothing.

On the sixth day he had a plan.

Charlie set out after breakfast, an extra piece of toast for Mellie clutched in one lobster-claw mitten—it was not *really* an extra piece of toast, it was Charlie's breakfast, but if Mellie asked, that's what he would say. Charlie was wearing Dad's coat again; Mum had given him a long look when he'd pulled it on, but hadn't said anything. He hoped that meant she didn't mind. It really was the warmest thing he'd ever worn. Not even the sharp north-blowing wind could get through the thick navy wool.

Mellie grinned when she caught sight of him, and Charlie could see pink gums where some of her teeth were missing. She was wearing his Sunday jacket—although it was *her* Sunday jacket now, he supposed—and had a lumpy knitted thing that could maybe be a hat, if you screwed up your eyes, tugged down over her ears.

Charlie gave Mellie her toast. She carefully tore off the crusts, which she tossed to her pigeons, and ate the rest in small, efficient bites in a few seconds. As she did, Charlie sat on his hands to keep himself still and silent. He was about to upset her, he was pretty sure, and he didn't have to be impatient in addition to being rude.

When she was finished, he made himself look at her. "Mellie, I need to ask you something, and you're not going to like it, and I'm sorry, but I need to know."

Mellie looked at her pigeons for a long minute, and the space between her and Charlie stretched and filled with the quiet sounds of contented pigeons. It was peaceful. Charlie was sorry to ruin it.

Finally, Mellie looked at him.

"You've seen the wolves before," he said, his voice going thin and reedy. It came out like a question, but it wasn't one. Mellie

didn't answer; she just stared at him with her dark blue eyes and waited him out. "I need to know where you saw them."

She didn't say anything at first. She didn't sigh or grumble, but something in her face closed itself off from him. It felt like walking down a street in the night and being able to see inside an illuminated window, to see a flash of the hidden life inside, and then the light being turned off.

"I saw them everywhere, at first," she said, looking at the ground. "After . . . I lost my boy. David. I saw them outside, I saw them inside buildings, peeking out of windows like house cats. I saw them at the cemetery. Everywhere. People didn't like that, of course, a woman saying she saw wolves behind every corner. No one wanted me around for too long. But then I started feeding the pigeons and . . . and I saw them less, after that. By the time I could tell the pigeons apart, by the time they each had names, I only saw the wolves now and again, and I had learned to pretend, by then. That I couldn't see them. I learned how not to react. It's a rule, I think. Once you can see them, then you're in danger, because they can convince you to give them your heart. But if you can't see them, then you can't bargain. I think I tricked them, eventually. Or they got bored. Or my heart's just not good eating anymore."

She reached down and scooped up a pigeon Charlie didn't recognize, and stroked its soft wings with a fingertip.

When he realized she was done talking, Charlie spoke.

"So there was . . . nowhere in particular they went? Nowhere you saw them more often?"

"No."

Charlie sagged on the bench. He'd upset Mellie for nothing, then. "I guess I'll have to try talking to Reggie, then." Another person he didn't want to upset, but was going to anyway. He kept causing all this *damage*, and hoping it would be worth it in the end.

"Who?" Mellie was distracted, agitated, and the pigeons were picking up on it. Around her the pigeons cooed and flapped their wings, fretful.

"Reggie. He's a soldier I met at the hospital. He told me about the war rats, that's how we—the pigeons were with me, you remember—that's how we found the War Room. And Remorse."

"*Don't* say their names," Mellie hissed.

"Sorry," Charlie said in a whisper, wincing.

"Right," Mellie said, seeming to gather herself. "Hold this." She pushed the pigeon into Charlie's hands and began to gather up her things and stuff them into her pram with great purpose.

Charlie and the unknown pigeon blinked at each other. "Er, Mellie. Where are you going?" The pigeon trilled, too, its tone demanding answers.

"To the hospital, of course. I've had enough watching you scour this wretched neighborhood for—*creatures*. It's exhausting to watch you. You're going to make yourself sick if you don't stop, and you're not going to stop until you've found the things, so. The hospital."

"You want to come with me?" Charlie asked, dumbfounded. The pigeon cooed and he petted it, distracted.

"Right you are," she said, checking around the bench for any misplaced essentials. "We've got a fox in our henhouse."

"It's a wolf," said Charlie.

"It's a figure of speech and don't interrupt your elders. Hmm." Mellie sucked on a piece of her gray hair thoughtfully. "You need allies. That's how we won the war, isn't it? Allied forces? So we'll go to the hospital and talk to your soldier and then—then—"

Here she broke off, and she snatched the pigeon out of Charlie's hands and placed it with infinite gentleness on the ground with its family. "I need to leave my things somewhere. They won't let me bring them inside. I know they won't." It was the first time Charlie had ever seen Mellie timid. Her eyes kept skipping back and forth between the pigeons and the pram.

Charlie reach out and took hold of her gnarled hand in his mittened one. "We can leave your pram at my house, don't worry." He paused, worrying a scab on his lip between his teeth. "You know . . . you don't have to come, Mellie. I wouldn't think any less of you." He squeezed her hand. She squeezed it back, hard.

"I know you wouldn't," she replied, and pushed the pram down the street in the direction of Charlie's house, her jaw set at a stubborn angle. "But I would."

✳ ✳ ✳

"This is my friend's! I'll be back for it in a little while," Charlie shouted up the stairs at Grandpa Fitz as he parked the pram just inside the door.

"What the blazes—" Grandpa Fitz began, but Charlie shut the door as fast as he dared. Biscuits *just* missed getting her tail smashed as she materialized between his feet.

"No. Not a good idea. Not after last time."

Biscuits chirped and wrapped her tail around her paws, angelic and innocent of all crime.

"*No.* They'll recognize you in a *second* and they'll run us off the property or—or have us *arrested* or something. You can't come, do you hear me? You are going to stay *right here*."

"You're bringing that cat with you?" Mellie asked from where she was waiting on the sidewalk.

Charlie sniffed and didn't answer. Biscuits rubbed herself against Mellie's legs, purring so loud Charlie knew she was just being petty.

"Don't even think about it, beast," Mellie said to Biscuits. They glared at each other for a long minute before Biscuits turned on her heel and started off down the sidewalk, her tail held high as a flag. Pudge cooed a greeting to Biscuits as they marched past. Biscuits was careful to ignore him.

258

25

CHARLIE WAS OF THE OPINION THAT THE WHOLE business of walking up the steps and shouldering open the brass-handled doors of Mary, Queen of Peace Convalescent Hospital was quite a bit more dramatic than was necessary. That it took multiple attempts and some considerable coordination between his scrawny arms and Mellie's even scrawnier ones to drag the door open did nothing to set him at ease. It made all intents of secrecy a bit of a nonstarter, which was a rather dispiriting note to begin on.

He escorted Mellie with as much dignity as he could muster up to the high counter of the front desk, where a woman with round spectacles was watching their progress with raised eyebrows.

"Do you need medical attention, sir?" The woman behind the desk looked from Mellie's gnarled hands to her unwashed hair and finally down to Charlie, whose coat suddenly felt far too big.

"Er, no," Charlie started, his voice cracking. "I'm actually here to visit Mr. Pemberton-Ashby? Lieutenant Pemberton Ashby,

I mean? Reginald Pemberton-Ashby?" Charlie said. Saying Reggie's fancy surnames so many times in a row made it sound like gibberish.

"The dashing lieutenant himself! But I'm afraid he's not accepting visitors right now."

The woman had to crane her neck to see him. He stood up on his tiptoes to peer over the desk at her. "Aggie let me visit him before. Aggie Carlisle—that is, Agatha. Ma'am. Miss. Um."

"Oh, Aggie! You should've said. *Everyone* knows Aggie." The nurse threw her head back and laughed. "Well, that makes sense. You just follow me, love."

Charlie looked over at Mellie and, after a moment's hesitation, offered her his own arm. She flashed her gummy smile at him and grabbed his elbow in a vise grip. He looked at her out of the corner of his eye—her deep blue eyes were darting all over the place, and she was very pale under her surface layer of grime and wrinkles. Her hand on his arm was shaking. Charlie put his free hand over Mellie's and squeezed it, very gently. She slowly let out a breath and they followed after Ward Sister Radcliffe.

The echoes of their footsteps seemed much louder in the empty hall than they should have been, and Mellie jumped a bit every time a door slammed shut somewhere else in the hospital.

After what seemed like a mile of clean, waxed tile, they were back at the door he remembered from his night in the snow. And there, in the same bed, was Reggie, reading in a wedge of lamplight and frowning in concentration.

"Lieutenant, we have some guests for you!"

Reggie looked up and saw him, something almost like relief in his expression. "Quite lovely, Nurse Radcliffe. I'm so very popular lately, you mustn't let it go to my head."

Nurse Radcliffe gave a tittering laugh and blushed pink. "I'll leave you lot to it, then."

"It's wonderful to see you, Charlie. Reggie Pemberton-Ashby, madame," he said to Mellie, offering his hand. She presented her own with great dignity, and Reggie gave her knuckles a polite brush of his lips. Mellie did not blush, but she seemed *pleased* in a way that caused her to glow slightly.

"Melinda Jenkins," she said primly, and Charlie gaped. It had somehow never occurred to him that Mellie was short for anything. Or that she had a last name. These were shocking revelations.

"What can I do for you today, Charlie—"

"You have got *some cheek* showing up here again, my friend," said a voice from behind them all.

A bucket of ice water dumped itself down Charlie's back. Aggie was framed by the curtain circled all round Reggie's bed, hands on her hips and her red-lipstick mouth pursed underneath furrowed eyebrows.

"I—"

"You are quite lucky you've got the face of an angel or we would be having *words*, my friend." Aggie strode forward and bent down close enough that Charlie could smell her perfume— and then she was holding something small and furry and white-and-marmalade-y, which she was frowning at with great authority.

"I will have none of that tomfoolery this time, young lady. Do we understand each other? Yes? Good. Introduce me to your friend."

Biscuits leaped down to the floor and butted her head against Charlie's knee, purring about as loud as a Spitfire plane.

"Yes, I know sweet Charlie. I meant the rest."

"*Brrrrrpt!*" said Biscuits.

"Well, that's hardly declarative. Charlie, would you take over for your miscreant friend . . . ?"

"Biscuits," Charlie finished, mortified.

"Would you take over for Biscuits and kindly introduce me to your friend?"

"Oh, this is Mellie," Charlie said.

"Pleasure," said Aggie. Mellie ignored her, her set shoulders and serene expression giving her a very Biscuits-ish air.

"Same to you, love," said Aggie, smiling. "Now, Charlie, what on earth can I do for you and your varied and sundry compatriots?"

"I—you—that is—"

"Charlie here was hoping to have a word with me about his brother, Ward Sister Carlisle," said Reggie, smooth as butter.

"Mmm, his *other* brother, I suppose? Does he bear more of a family resemblance?"

Reggie smiled, wide and charming, and for just a second Charlie could see who he must have been before the war. He had the sort of smile you could only get with a lot of practice, deep lines crinkling up his eyes.

"There may have been a slight communication error on that front, for which I, in my fragile state, take full responsibility."

Aggie rolled her eyes heavenwards. "*Fine*, don't tell me, then."

Now Charlie wanted to crawl under the bed. He wiped sweaty palms against his knees. Even rolled, the sleeves of Dad's coat came down almost to his knuckles. He focused on the scratchy itch of wool against chapped skin.

"My brother—my *real* brother, Theo, the one who I was actually telling you about last week—he . . ." He swallowed hard, twice, his whole face feeling very hot, then the wooly itch against his hand was replaced by a warm, downy silkiness.

Biscuits crawled into his lap, tucking her feet underneath her, quite dainty. *She said she needed someone to take care of, once she got big enough. She said she just needed a little help getting to the big enough part. Do you think she could look after you, Charlie? Would you mind?* Dad's northern burr echoed in Charlie's mind, steadying his hands.

"I'm going to help him," Charlie finally said. He looked up to meet her eyes, stubborn and determined.

Aggie stared at him for a long moment before plopping down on the foot of Reggie's bed with a loud sigh. "God help the poor girls when you grow a few feet, Charlie. How on earth does your mum ever say no to that sweet face?"

Charlie was torn between explaining that Mum was *excellent* at saying no to him, or throwing up from embarrassment all over the glossy hospital floor; he wasn't quite sure which. He opted to never speak again, instead.

"All right," Aggie went on, squinting with deep suspicion at each of them in succession. "Walk with me, Charlie." Charlie looked back at Reggie, anxious to speak with him about the war wolves.

"Actually, I was going to speak with Reggie about—" Aggie pointed at him with one eyebrow raised to menacing heights.

"I am the nurse in charge of this ward and everyone in it, which currently includes both of you. And how I manage the welfare of every in my charge is up to *me*."

Aggie's tone brooked no argument. Charlie had to scramble to catch up with her rapidly retreating footsteps. Biscuits made to follow him, but he made a frantic shooing gesture and she planted herself on Reggie's lap, as though that had been her plan all along.

When he caught up to Aggie in the corridor, she had her hands on her hips and was looking at him with an expression somewhere between fond and exasperated. Charlie was quite familiar with this look. Mum wore it often.

"C'mon, love, let's get some medicine into you and we'll have a chat about it."

Aggie stashed him in a small room with a sign that read "Lesser Lounge," which he suspected might actually be a broom cupboard that had gotten notions. Against one wall sat a squashy-looking sofa where there was a lump of blankets that might have begun the day as a nurse.

"Don't worry about waking her, she'll be out like a light till swing shift starts," said Aggie, and she gestured towards a smaller sofa that had a few obvious holes but otherwise looked very comfortable. "You have a seat and don't go off on any adventures till I'm back."

She ducked out the door and returned a minute later ladened with two enormous white mugs of tea. Then she settled herself down next to Charlie.

"Drink your tea and then tell Aggie what's weighing on you." Aggie kicked off her pointy shoes and tucked her feet up underneath her in a very Biscuits-ish way, then took a sip of tea that left a cherry-red kiss-print behind. After a moment, she nudged him with an elbow. "Go on. Unburden yourself."

Charlie twisted the mug around in his hands.

"What happens if your heart gets too hard, Aggie? Can you . . . does it hurt?"

"D'you mean like hypertrophic cardiomyopathy?"

Charlie blinked several times.

"No, I thought not." Aggie paused to gulp down half her mug of tea in one go. "Hearts are beastly complicated things, Charlie. There are so very many things that can go wrong with them and they're the very devil to fix."

"I know," Charlie said into his tea.

"I know that's what a lot of people—nurses and doctors, you know, the people I worked with—took away from the war. How very fragile the human body is, all the different ways there are for it to get hurt. But you know what always struck me from day one over there?"

Charlie shook his head.

"How bloody *resilient* the human body is. It is absolutely astonishing what you can live through. The most incredible things can go wrong and the body finds a way to fix itself enough to keep going."

"Hearts, too?"

"Hearts *especially*, darling. The heart's the strongest muscle in the human body, did you know that? Think about all the different muscles you use every day, how much work you do with them. But the heart doesn't ever get to *stop*, does it? Just about every other muscle in your body gets to take a breather occasionally, but the heart? Always awake, always working like anything to keep you going. So hearts *have* to be strong; they're made that way, made to never stop."

"That sounds exhausting." Charlie now considered himself something of an expert on exhaustion.

Aggie made a clucking sound, very much like one of Mellie's pigeons, and touched her thumb to his cheek, quick as a kiss. "And that's why you've got to be as kind to your heart as you can, whenever you can, Charlie. Our hearts work so very hard for us."

"But what if you haven't been kind to it? Or you just can't? What

266

if it's already . . ." Charlie searched for the right word. "Wrong?"

"You can live for a long time with a broken heart if you learn to take care of it right. Did you know that sometimes broken bones heal stronger than they were in the first place? Not always, I mean. Sometimes they just break in the same place over and over again. But that's usually because they weren't set quite right the first time."

"But what can you do if it wasn't set right? A long time ago, I mean. Is it too late? To make it like it was?"

"Well, did you know there's talk about actually transplanting a heart from one patient into another someday soon?"

"What, when you're still alive?"

"Like, if someone died in an accident, you could take out that person's heart and swap it in for someone with a damaged or unhealthy heart. Isn't that absolutely and beautifully mad?"

"I wouldn't want someone to have to die so I could have a new heart."

Aggie smiled at him and pulled the blanket back over the sleeping nurse, who had wriggled out of it a bit in her sleep. "I know. That's how I know your heart isn't hard at all. Listen, sometimes having a hard heart is worse than having no heart. Don't let the world make your heart hard. Keep it soft, and wide open, as long as you can, as much as you can bear. And even when you can't bear it. It's all right that your heart hurts—that's how you know it's still there."

"Why are you always so nice to me?"

"Why on earth wouldn't I be? What did being horrible ever get anyone?"

"Lots of things, I'm pretty sure."

"Nothing worth having has to be taken from someone else. You can quote me on that. Ask your mum to cross-stitch it on a pillow for you." Aggie stretched out her legs in front of her and her arms towards the ceiling and rolled her head around several times, knees popping and neck cracking like machine-gun fire. "Come on now, your granddad will be waiting for you, and I've got a round of bed checks calling my name."

Charlie got up and set his cup down on a little table by the blanket-nurse, who gave a contented snore. One had to admire the absolute dedication to her nap.

Down the hall and back to Reggie's room they went, where they found everyone asleep, except for Reggie himself, who was doing his best to read his book around the lump of sleeping cat that had grown on top of his chest.

Reggie met their eyes over the top of his book and held a finger to his lips, which were curved into a smile.

"I'll leave you here for now, love," Aggie whispered into Charlie's ear. "Leave whenever you're ready. But don't forget, Charlie: your heart can take just about anything the world can throw at it. It's the very strongest part of you."

Then she leaned down and kissed his cheek. Charlie felt himself go very red, but he it made him feel warm and safe right down to his toes. He kept his head ducked down until he heard the tap of her shoes fade away. When he had managed to compose himself a bit, he looked up to find Reggie and Biscuits smirking at him.

"*What?*" said Charlie.

"Nothing," said Reggie.

"*Brrrpt,*" said Biscuits.

Mellie startled awake and glared up at him out of sleep-squinted eyes. "Well, now that you've concluded your pressing business," she said testily.

"Yes, what brings you to visit, Charlie?" Reggie's smile was warm, but there was a tired sort of resignation there, too. He already knew what Charlie was going to ask, but was hoping he was wrong.

"You said you saw the wolves here in the hospital, when you were first admitted?"

Reggie's shoulders fell, just a little. "Yes." It was as if the word hurt coming out of his mouth. "I saw one, here in the hospital, when they first brought me." His dark eyes were huge in his pale face. "It was night. I heard it walking down the corridor, its *nails* . . ." He closed his eyes and took three long, deep breaths before continuing. "I didn't bother pretending to be asleep. It's so horrible, you know, to feel dread but not fear. To know that it was just . . . waiting. Looking for its next meal. You can't warn people; I'm sure you've tried, too. How could you? If you can't see them, you don't know to be afraid of them until it's too late. And once you can see them . . . it's too late anyway." He seemed to realize what he'd said, wincing. "I didn't mean

269

that. It's not too late for *you*, Charlie."

But Charlie waved him off, wild excitement buzzing inside him. "No, I'm *close*, Reggie, I'm so close. I only need one more key, and then I can find them, I can get into the War Room, and I can make them give me Theo's heart back. Don't you see? I can really do it, Reggie." And saying the words, just then, he believed it, that he could make everything okay again. He almost grinned in frantic excitement. "I just need your help to find the last wolf."

But Reggie was shaking his head no, rubbing his forehead hard with his knuckles, like he was trying to keep the thoughts inside. "The wolves found me, they find you, they always find you. If they've left you alone, Charlie, that's a *good* thing. Don't you see? It's an absolute blessing that you can't find them, that you can let this go."

"No, you're not listening—"

Reggie was shaking his head again. "I've had a lot of time to think since the last time you were here, asking about the wolves. I shouldn't have told you all that, I should never have encouraged this. If I really were your brother, I would tell you that you've done enough, Charlie. How much has it cost you already? How much have they taken from you?"

Charlie thought of Remorse and Wrath, licking their lips. *Blood and tears, that's all. I've got plenty of both. More than enough.*

"I didn't know how to say this before, but I'm saying it now to you: you can't get his heart back, Charlie. It's eaten, it's gone. You need to accept that this is who you brother is. It's not fixable. There's no cure."

"You're just saying that because you've given up," Charlie snapped. That coal from the disastrous dinner with the Cleavers flared to life again in his chest. "You don't want to be with your family, so you don't think Theo should be with his. But he's different, he's going get better, because I'm going to *make* him like he was before, you'll see."

"You don't understand what happened to him over there—"

"He was in a war, *I know*. I *know* bad things happened to him—"

"Stop, Charlie. You *can't* know, you *can't* understand because you *weren't there*." Reggie squeezed his eyes shut and took a deep breath before opening them again to look straight at him. "He gave his heart up, Charlie. He let them eat it. That's how it happens. You can't get it back."

"You're wrong!" Charlie's own voice startled him, how loud it was, how sharp, how angry. And he *was* angry, he was furious with Reggie, with Aggie, with everyone, saying such things when he was so close.

Reggie flinched away from him at that, his body shrinking in on itself. And in it, Charlie saw Theo fall to his knees in the snow, felt the cold of the snowball in his hand. Shame burst inside him. He kept doing this, he kept hurting people without meaning to, without thinking. He kept making everything worse.

Reggie pinched at the skin on his arm, so hard it hurt to look at, over and over, shaking his head like he was trying to clear it. Without touching him, Mellie sat down on the edge of his bed.

"It's all right to be scared, Reggie," she said. "My son, David,

271

he used to get scared of things. I told Charlie here that he was even afraid of birds when he little. And he was little. So much smaller than the other boys. Afraid of birds, can you imagine that? But he was clever, David was, so much cleverer than me. I don't know where he got it from, but he always was. Anyways, he was so afraid of birds that he decided he would learn everything there was to know about them, because if you understood how a thing worked, you didn't have to be afraid of it. So many books he read. Textbooks, too, like veterinarians use, I've no idea where he even found them." She laughed, a dry little huff of a sound.

"But that's how he got the pigeons. He read about homing pigeons and how easy they are to keep, so he built a coop on the roof of the flat where we lived, and he left out food until the pigeons started sleeping there, and laying their eggs. The ones that hatched there would eat out of his hand. They were so small, I was afraid to touch them, afraid I would crush their little bones. But David was so gentle, and so sure. He took such good care of them.

"And I used to make fun of them a bit, I asked why he liked such ridiculous little birds. They're not very clever, not much to look at, common as rain. He told me that the one thing—the *one thing*—pigeons are brilliant at is coming home. That no matter how far away they were, they always knew the way.

"He even let the army use some of his birds during the war. They would drop the birds where they thought there might be resistance groups with no way to communicate, so people could send intelligence back. A lot of birds died that way. Guns and hawks and weather. David even sent his favorite bird, because he knew Pudge was the brightest, that if anyone could get a message home, it would be Pudge. But weeks and weeks went by and Pudge didn't come. Months, even." Reggie's breath was still shaky, but it was slowing down, his chest casting a shadow every time it rose and then fell.

"And then, one day, there he was again. He had a mangled wing and he couldn't really see straight, but he was the same bird. 'You see?' David said. 'They'll always find their way home, if you give them enough time.'

"He said . . . he said, 'That's you and me, Mum. You're my home, and I'm yours. If we get separated, we'll always find each other, even if it takes a while.' And then David died, a few weeks later. Everything he was, everything he'd learned, all the love inside of him—just gone. And I thought, David was wrong, you can't find your way home if there is no home. So I threw open all the doors to the coop. And I left. And I never went back. But one day, I woke up outside, and there were pigeons all around me. At first I thought they were just pigeons, but then I saw one with one bright white wing that I recognized, and there was another with a soft green head, and there was the pigeon with the bad wing. David's pigeons.

"The pigeons didn't think the coop was their home, they thought *I* was their home. Because David was right, because he was right about everything, because he was the cleverest person

273

I've ever known. He was my home, and I'll find my way back to him. It will just take longer than I'd prefer. You'll find your way eventually."

She patted his hand, once, with her thick, veiny hand with its papery skin. Reggie, his eyes still closed, gripped her hand tight.

Charlie felt sick. He had to make this worth it. If he could find the last wolf, the last key, if he could get Theo's heart, this would all be undone. Because it would have *been* for something, for the most important thing in the world. They would see. He would show them. Soon.

26

CHARLIE WAS WALKING TOO FAST FOR MELLIE to keep up. He had never realized how much Mellie leaned on her pram when she walked, how slowly she moved now without it, but she wouldn't ask him to wait and he couldn't make himself slow down. By the time they got back to his house, it was starting to snow, just a light dusting of confectioner's sugar over everything. London, spread out in every direction, glowed new and promising, but Charlie just felt wound-up and sick.

A burst of warm air enveloped them as he pushed the door open, like one of Mum's very best hugs. Wanting the real thing now, Charlie started towards Mum where she was washing dishes in the sink.

He stopped short halfway there. Mum's face was red and puffy from crying.

"What's going on?" Charlie spun around. Theo was sitting at the kitchen table, his shoulders hunched up by his ears; Grandpa Fitz was standing by the door, but there was something in the drooping set of his shoulders that spoke to an absence. Just out-side the doorway, Mellie fretted in place, as if she were afraid to let the light from inside touch her. Charlie was torn between the warring urges to go to everyone at once. Everyone needed his help right now.

Mum wouldn't want Mellie here for this, whatever this was. He grabbed her pram from where he had stashed it earlier and pushed it out to her. She grabbed its handle like he would try to snatch it away, and pushed it away from him and down the street, wilting against the handle as she slipped away into the dark.

Charlie shut the door and turned back to the horrible little tableau in the kitchen. There was a letter open on the table, which looked as though it had been crushed and then smoothed out again. Mum and Theo were both angled towards it, as if it were a bomb that had gone off and all they could do was look at the empty space left behind.

No one tried to stop him as he picked it up.

Mr. Theodore Merriweather,
We are pleased to inform you that a space has become available at the Rosehill Home for Returning Soldiers starting May 5. Please reply to confirm your acceptance with the enclosed form by the above date. Space is limited and in high demand.
Best regards,
The Rosehill Group

"You're leaving," Charlie said from somewhere underwater. "You want to leave. After everything, after *everything* I did to fix it—" Charlie had found war wolves. He let them lap up his tears, his blood, his pain. He cried and he stole and he lied over and over and Theo was just going to give up. "What is *wrong* with you?"

"Everything," Theo said with a bitter laugh. "And even if there weren't—there's no place for me here, you don't even need me anymore, you can take care of everything yourselves. Everything except me. I'm just making things worse."

"I'm taking care of everything *because you told me to!*" Charlie's voice in his own ears sounded like he was shouting from a very distant room. "You *told* me, you said I needed to be the man of the house, you told me I had to take care of things, even though I didn't know how and I had to work it out all on my own because *you weren't here.*"

"I didn't want to leave, Charlie—"

"But you're leaving *now.*" His voice was coming out in a high, babyish whine, but he couldn't stop it. "No one's making you, you're just giving up."

"Charlie, I'm—" Theo put his face in his hands and gave a ragged sigh before looking up again. "Charlie, I'm trying to get *better.* I can't do that here."

"Yes, you can. You *will*, you'll seen, soon." Charlie's voice was all mangled, his throat was swollen and itching.

"He can't," Grandpa Fitz interjected. He sounded so tired.

"But he has a chance to, Charlie, somewhere else. They've got special doctors at this place, new ideas for treatment, just for people like your brother. It's not like it was when I was young. He could have a real chance with their help, Charlie."

Mum started to cry again, very softly, and something strange and fragile inside Charlie wrenched and tore.

"You said you'd take care of me, but you didn't," Charlie said to Theo, ignoring his grandfather. "You won't even take care of yourself. You left and I had to do everything. Grandpa Fitz is old and he's going to die, and someday Mum will be dead, too, just like Dad—or she'll be old and confused and she won't even know me and that'll be worse. Someday I'm going to be all alone because you won't even be there because you're already gone."

"Charlie, listen—"

But Charlie wasn't finished. "If you were just going to leave again, you shouldn't have come back."

As soon as the words were out of his mouth, he couldn't believe that he'd said them. But he could see from Theo's face that he had.

You shouldn't have come back.

He didn't mean it, he wanted to scream.

But part of him did. Just a tiny, angry, hurt little part of him, but that little sliver of him meant it. And Theo had seen. And Theo had known.

And now, in the After of the bomb he had just dropped on them all, Charlie found he couldn't face the full, crushing shame of what he had said, what he had done. He wasn't a good brother, or a good son, or a good person. He wasn't generous or openhearted or selfless or kind. He was a monster, as sure as a war wolf was. Different, but no less vicious or any less bloody.

Mum choked a sob into her hands. And Charlie ran out the door and away, like the coward that he was.

Grandpa Fitz must have followed him out, because he caught him in the street, snagging him gently by the shoulder and spinning him around. But there was still something *not there* in his expression that Charlie couldn't understand, like he still hadn't fully woken up from his haze.

"Stop this, Charlie. Theo leaving for this Rosehill place, it's not what you think."

"But he doesn't have to." Charlie's voice came out in a broken sort of sob. He squeezed his eyes shut and shook his head back and forth, trying to clear the shrapnel from his mind. "I can fix it. I'm almost done, I just have to get one more key, Remorse told me—" Charlie bit his cheek to stop the stuttering flow of words.

Grandpa Fitz grabbed him with his one hand, his long fingers wrapping easily around Charlie's skinny arm. "What did you say, Charlie?"

With a savage push against his grandfather's chest, he broke free, and the force of it sent them both stumbling. Grandpa Fitz kept his balance, but Charlie landed hard on the slippery ground. Charlie scrabbled to his feet, his shoes slipping and stumbling beneath him. He heard Grandpa Fitz calling Charlie's name as he started running. Charlie didn't dare look back. If he did, he might lose his nerve, and he couldn't, not now, not when he was *so close*—

"Charlie, come back!" Grandpa Fitz shouted into the cold empty street, the echoes biting at Charlie's heels like teeth.

27

CHARLIE RAN UNTIL HE HAD TO WALK BECAUSE his side with seizing bright with pain. It had felt like an incantation, almost, the horrible power of those words. *You shouldn't have come back.* So Charlie ran to the spot where Theo had returned, as if he could go back to before all this, to before he knew about war wolves or Hollow Chest, as if he could yank the words out of the air before he ever had a chance to say them, to *think* them.

The train station was so much farther away than he remembered. But he didn't dare stop.

It was waiting in plain sight under the sickly orange wash of light coming from a soot-coated lamp. Huge it was, almost twice as big again as Wrath, its bones jutting out under its skin, its fur a muddy brown color, like rust. Or old blood.

"What do you want?" Charlie gasped. He was still out of breath from running. Or maybe he was just scared.

"Lots." The wolf grinned, wide and yellow. Saliva dripped down each great fang to land, hissing, in the frost.

"What do you want from *me*?"

"Everything."

"What's your name?"

"Poor, stupid boy," the wolf said, his voice so low that it thrummed through Charlie's bones and made his teeth grind. "Alone in the cold with Agony and Anguish."

A laugh rumbled up from behind Charlie. He spun around and a second, nearly identical war wolf winked a yellow eye at him as it stepped out of the shadows and into the dim light. One of its ears was half-missing and a scar stretched the left side of its face into a mad rictus grin.

"Heh heh, heh heh." Drool pooled in the ruined corner of its mouth and dribbled down its chin.

"Too right, brother," said the first wolf. "Manners. That one is Agony," he said, jerking his head back to face Charlie. "This one is Anguish."

"I'm Charlie." His voice came out in a whisper.

"We know you, little Merriweather. We know bigger Merriweathers, too." Anguish licked his chops and Charlie smelled something coppery. "Sweet, sweet hearts." Anguish padded closer to Charlie, sniffing the air, his nose pointed at Charlie's chest. "And legs. And hands."

"Heh heh, heh heh."

Charlie couldn't breathe. Grandpa Fitz, with his neatly pinned sleeve. Grandpa Fitz, trying to pet Biscuits with his missing arm. Theo, his leg sticking out at the wrong angle, the fat snake of

282

scar tissue twisting up around his knee that would never bend right again. And Agony just kept laughing.

"You need a key, yeah?" Anguish asked. "You need a way *in*. To the War Room. Maybe Agony and Anguish can help. Something for something, yeah? A key for a just a little something?"

"Did you eat my brother's heart?"

"Heh heh, heh heh."

The wolves began to circle him, their claws making soft clicks on the ground as they moved. There was a dull chattering sound coming from somewhere. Charlie clenched his jaw shut and the noise stopped.

"Did you eat my brother's heart?" he repeated.

"Yeah," said Anguish. "And it was sweet. Love and tenderness, and all hope lost. The finest flavors. Succulent, it was."

"Something for something," Charlie whispered. "I can't . . . I *won't* give you my heart. You must know that by now. So what do you want that I can actually give you?" He thought of wolf tongues—licking his cheeks and knuckles. The intimate horror of it. If Remorse had craved tears and Wrath blood, what would Agony and Anguish ask for?

"Just a little thing. Just what the middle Merriweather keeps hidden." Anguish's wide, wet smile oozed wider still, like a wound tearing. "Hidden where his heart should be."

A splash of dread washed over Charlie, straight through to his guts. What did that mean, hidden where Theo's heart should be? He had a horrible vision of sticking his clammy hand into the

283

wet inside Theo's chest and rifling around like Mum searching for lipstick at the bottom of her handbag.

He swallowed down the wave of nausea that brought on, keeping his gaze firmly on the ground in front of his feet. He did not see the wolves leave, only heard the click of their nails fade away as they retreated to wherever it was monsters went to wait.

Knowing he had a mission was the only way he could make himself walk through the door. He wanted to die rather than face the shame of what he had said, he wanted to curl up in the snow and suffocate under it, but he couldn't. Getting into the War Room was the only chance now, the only way to keep Theo from leaving, to have the chance to make right what he'd said. If he could get Theo's heart back, it wouldn't matter, it would all be undone, atoned for, back to the way things had been before any of this had happened. He could still fix it.

Theo's coat and boots were gone from the front room, as were Grandpa Fitz's. Charlie's knees buckled with relief. He didn't know where they'd gone, but he knew he couldn't face Theo, not yet, not empty-handed, not after what he'd said. Mum was asleep in the chair by the fire, her face still red from crying. Charlie did not dare wake her as he crept upstairs.

Theo's room both was and wasn't exactly how Charlie had left it before his homecoming. Theo's things he'd brought back were spread across it, but they felt somehow apart from the room, like a fungus spreading somewhere it didn't belong. The picture of Charlie and Theo on the dresser was turned facedown.

Charlie started badly when he saw the shape of a coat in the mirror, hanging off the back of the closet door like a flat, bulky ghost. It was the drab, thick military coat Theo had worn as he had come off the train that day a hundred years ago. The coat seemed misshapen somehow, bits of it stuck out strangely, as if parts of someone were still inside it. It didn't seem scary, just . . . sad, the way things that had lost their purpose sometimes did. It was a coat for a soldier, but the war was over.

Charlie went over to it and investigated the lumpy bits, finding one pocket filled with wrappers and strings and a small, smooth rock. The other had three thin gloves stuffed inside, all of them with the fingertips worn through. The breast pocket of the coat was bulging from the inside—

The breast pocket of the coat.

Hidden where his heart should be.

Charlie's fingers felt numb and shaky as he pulled open the coat and felt around the smooth lining. His finger hit a lump of what felt like paper, and he pulled it out with some difficulty. A crumpled pack of cigarettes fell out.

And then a thick brick of letters.

Charlie's letters? Mum's? What else would he keep so close to him, what else would he never give up? Warmth flared bright as a match tip in his chest as he grabbed the letters, and died just as quickly as he looked at the address in confusion.

To: Charlie Merriweather

He flipped through the envelopes; all of them were addressed to Charlie. But Charlie *had* all the letters Theo had sent him; he would have noticed if Theo had taken them back. Confused, he opened the first one—it wasn't sealed; Theo would never know.

Dear Charlie,
A comprehensive but incomplete list of things I miss:
- *You*
- *Mum*
- *Grandpa Fitz*
- *your cat Biscuits*
- *actual biscuits*
- *my bed*
- *any bed*
- *normal tea*
- *normal anything*
- *eggs*
- *knowing what day it is*
- *dry socks*
- *Dad*
Theo

Dear Charlie,
I tried to imagine what it will be like when this is over, and

I couldn't. I couldn't picture it. All I could think of was you turning eighteen and being called up into service, like me. But I couldn't picture you at eighteen, so I just imagined you with a coat with sleeves that came down past your hands onto the floor, and the gun was so much bigger than you and the helmet kept falling down over your eyes.
Theo

Dear Charlie,
I had a dream last night that I came home, but I was sick, I was covered in black mold, and when Mum went to hug me the mold spread all over her and she dissolved. In the dream you swept up the mold with a broom and put it in the wastebasket. In the dream I was still reaching for you, even though I knew it would make you dissolve, too. In the dream I told you to run away from me, but you wouldn't.
    You wouldn't, would you?
Theo

Dear Theo, Love Charlie.
Wait, that's not right.
Dear Theo loves Charlie.
Theo loves Charlie, who is dear.
Who is Theo, dear?
Charlie.
That's not right.

Dear Charlie,

I'm so lonely I could scream. I'm so lonely I do scream. You can scream sometimes and people don't even look at you, they just keep going as if screaming is a normal thing to do. How can they not look? Do they not see me? Do they not hear me?

Sometimes I think that I'm a ghost, that I died and just didn't notice, that I died with everyone else last month. I think I died with Johnny and Philip and Stephen and Pip. I keep having dreams where I'm a ghost and no one can see me but I can't leave and I wake up and I don't know if I actually did wake up.

I think that I'm a ghost.

Theo

Dear Charlie,

Disregard last letter. Ghosts can't hurt this much.

Theo

Dear Charlie,

Did Grandpa Fitz ever tell you how he lost his arm? He told me, when I was your age. He said that he was crawling on his belly towards someone, another soldier, his friend, and he was trying to pull his friend out from under something when a shell landed and that he didn't even notice his arm was gone at first because his friend was gone, too. Both of them, the friend and arm, just gone, as if they never were.

I made friends here, does that surprise you? In a place like this? It probably doesn't seem strange to you, you make friends so easily, you're so good at that, you see someone and you see everything in them worth liking. I made friends, Johnny and Stephen, Philip and Pip (not to be confused), and because I was their friend, they trusted me. They trusted me to get them across the field and if we could get across the field, then maybe we could go home, one day even if it wasn't that day. I made friends, and I made them trust me, and I made a mistake and now they're dead. Gone, like they were never there.

Grandpa Fitz told me he didn't regret losing the arm, because it meant that he was reaching for someone. He told me that reaching out is always worth it.

But Charlie. I think he lied to me.

My leg hurts. All of it hurts.

I don't know if it was worth it.

Theo

Dear Charlie,

I want you to understand why I did it, but I hope you never do.

Theo

Charlie couldn't breathe right. His pulse was hammering in his chest like he was underwater and needed to come up for air.

I want you to understand why I did it.

Dishonor was right. He'd been right the whole time. Theo had let the wolves eat his heart and then he had forgotten, in that slippery, magic way of theirs. Something had happened to him, had changed something inside him in a way Charlie simply could not know. And it was so bad he had been willing to let war wolves eat his heart out of his chest rather than feel it anymore.

Charlie couldn't stand it, the thought of it, the idea, the knowledge, it was intolerable, unbearable. Anger tried to bloom inside him, a knife-edged flower—*after everything I've done for you, for our family, you just gave up, you gave up before you even got here, you said you'd always find me, you promised me you'd always find me, but you left, you left me, you let them take you away*—but it struggled and shuddered and died. He just felt numb.

With clumsy fingers, Charlie began stuffing letters into his pocket.

"Mmmm, that's it," Anguish said, licking his chops. "You brought the good stuff."

Drool pooled under his tongue and spilled out on the ground in spatters. He let his mouth fall open wide, and then his jaw seemed almost to *unhinge*, like a snake's mouth, his dark red tongue lolling loosely in invitation.

The space between Charlie's fingers and that mouth seemed so far as he stretched out his hand, the letter crumpling with the force of keeping himself from shaking. Each fang lining Anguish's jaws seemed to lengthen as Charlie laid the last letter on the wet ribbon of tongue.

The paper began to dissolve like sugar, even before Anguish's jaws closed with luxuriating slowness.

"The good stuff," Anguish said with a wet grin. "But not enough."

"Heh heh, heh heh." Agony's voice seemed to drip down Charlie's neck like a smear of oil.

"I gave you what you asked for," Charlie said, his voice croaking in the quiet street.

"But not enough. Never enough."

Charlie reached into his pocket for those other letters that Theo had kept where his heart should be, the ones Anguish would eat like crisps or candy floss. Like they were nothing.

In the dream I told you to run away from me, but you wouldn't.

Charlie closed his searching fingers into a fist. No.

You wouldn't, would you?

No. They didn't get to have those. They didn't get to have more of Theo, they didn't get one more morsel of the memory of his brave, battered heart.

I want you to understand why I did it.

"Something for something," Charlie said. Agony and Anguish, who let pain melt like candy in their mouths. "Show me," he breathed. Then, louder, "Show me what he felt. Show me what he felt, and give me what I need."

This time it was Anguish who laughed, as Agony bit into Charlie's leg.

It hurt so much that the pain turned into a separate thing from

Charlie, like it was an enormous rock or a wave of water or a bomb was going off very slowly inside his body. He had to become a sort of Far Away Charlie just to look at it. It was extraordinary, that anything inside a person could feel like this, that when God was thinking up human beings, he thought he should make them so that they could ever feel this way. Far Away Charlie would ask Father Mac about that later, someday, if he lived through this, if you *could* live through fire and ash and broken things all crawling through your veins and skin and ripping you apart.

Theo lived through this, Far Away Charlie thought. *Theo felt this. Theo's still here.*

And just like that the pain was gone. Charlie opened eyes he didn't remember squeezing shut.

Agony was licking his chops. Anguish was drooling, his breath steaming out around him in a fog.

Charlie made himself look down, knowing the ruin he would see where his leg used to be. But when he rolled up his trouser leg, the skin underneath was smooth and unbroken, nary a scar to be seen, except the little one from when he'd crashed his bicycle into a tree when he was seven and hadn't quite gotten the hang of corners yet.

And he was surprised to find that he wasn't afraid of Agony and Anguish anymore. It was the same as when one had been waiting for something really terrible one knew was going to happen—when it finally did, afterwards there was really only room for relief.

I want you to understand why I did it.

But I hope you never do.

The numbness that had settled over him turned to stinging pins and needles, like the very guts of him had fallen asleep and were waking up. *Oh, Theo.* He had just wanted it to stop. He had just wanted it all to stop. The sweet, blessed relief of that, the stopping. It felt like a mercy.

"You have something for me," Charlie said, his voice breathless with pain, but steady. Certain. "Something for something, that's what you said."

Anguish sneered at him, but jerked his head towards his brother. With one last mad chuckle, Agony threw his head back as a convulsion rippled through his meaty body, starting at his tail and spreading all the way up to his mouth, where he made a hacking sound like something detonating underwater, and in a spray of bloody spittle, spat out a key that looked too tiny and delicate for the violence of its expulsion.

Charlie knelt to pick it up, then immediately dropped it, sticking his fingers in his mouth. Its edges were sharp as a razor. A thin line of blood bloomed across his fingertips.

He heard Agony's laugh once more, but when he looked up, the war wolves were both gone. Agony's laugh seemed to echo much longer than it should have.

Mum was still asleep by the fire when he came home. Charlie wanted to tuck her blanket around her shoulders. But he couldn't risk waking her just yet. He walked past and back upstairs to Theo's room.

The envelopes were still there on the floor in a pile. He wanted to shove all their letters back in, as quick as he dared, but he couldn't. He just couldn't. He folded each one up along its seams and placed it into its envelope as carefully as tucking in a baby, as carefully as if it was a small and precious thing as breakable as it was dear.

Back into the breast pocket of the coat they went. It would be a tight fit to get the cigarette pack in, too, and he considered throwing it out, empty and crumpled as it was. There was a picture of a horse on the front, and someone had drawn spectacles on it in smudgy ink. Charlie thought of Mellie's pram, full of chipped vases and teacups and tattered ribbons. Charlie didn't get to decide what was rubbish and what was precious. He shoved the pack in the pocket with the letters, crumping it a bit further in the process.

"Sorry," he whispered, and patted it, smoothing down the coat's lapels.

Three keys clinked quietly against his heart.

28

"CHARLES?"

Charlie froze.

"Charles?" Mum repeated, her voice coming from the wingback chair, still slurred with sleep.

"Yes, Mum?" He stepped closer and the weak light caught the slick tear tracks on each cheek.

"He's so scared, Charles. I'm scared, too. I never thought I could be this scared, not of anything, not after your father. But I think about losing him all over again—I think about losing one of my boys—"

"Hush, Mum, it's okay," Charlie said, kneeling down beside her and smoothing down her sleep-mussed hair. "It's okay. I'll take of it. I'll take care of everything, you'll see."

Mum shook her head and tried to push herself out of the chair, but her strength seemed to fail her halfway, and she collapsed back into it with sigh.

"Listen," Charlie said, touching her shoulder to keep her in place. "Listen. Once, there was a king and queen who had no children."

Mum ground the heels of her hands against her eyes and made a noise like she was about to say something, but Charlie put a finger against her lips. His hand looked much larger next to Mum's face than he remembered it being.

"The king and queen wanted a baby to love more than anything. And they wished and wished and wished for one, but no baby came."

Charlie picked up the blanket that had fallen from Mum's lap and wrapped it snug around her shoulders, the red-and-green tartan wool scratchy and safe against his skin. Still talking, he stood up and walked over to the sink. The kettle was waiting, patient and big-bellied, by the draining board.

"So one day, the king and queen went out riding and they met an old lady by the side of the road. Now, most people thought the old lady was quite mad, because she talked to herself a bit and didn't care much for other people and she fed a lot of the animals that the other people thought were pests."

Water went into the kettle. The kettle went onto the stove. The flame on the burner jumped to life with a soft *whoomp*, like getting the air knocked out of you by a flying cat that had missed you very much. Or a little brother who rugby-tackled you as you came off a train. Like someone loving you with all they had.

"'I know how to help you get a child,' said the old lady. The queen was suspicious, but the king was so excited that he insisted they listen to what the old lady had to say. 'I will give you a task to complete, and you must agree without knowing what the task is. But if you can complete it by the end of one year, you will have a child of your very own. It will be hard, and scary at times, but—'" Charlie smiled a little into the cups he was carefully spooning loose tea into. "'There's no cure for scary like a job that needs doing. And I'll tell you that for free,'" he added, just for authenticity.

"The king and the queen discussed it over lunch and tea, and finally they both agreed that it would be worth whatever the maybe-mad old woman wanted them to do if they could have a child to love more than anything. So they went back to where the old lady was waiting and agreed to her terms. She smiled a great big smile, even though she didn't have all that many teeth left. And she had the king and queen follow her to the local orphanage, where she yelled and yelled until a wild little girl with absolutely filthy hair and no manners to speak of coming hurling out to meet them in a big cloud of dust."

Hot water went into each cup and along with a splash of milk for Mum, because that was how she liked it and milk rations could just jog on. Mum was watching him with big, liquid eyes and he wrapped her fingers around the teacup carefully. He sat down in the other chair and blew on his tea to cool it off before he went on.

"'Your task,' said the old lady, 'is to civilize this wild creature. Her parents died a long time ago and the kind people of the village brought her here to be taken care of until someone came to claim her. But no one ever did, and she's so wild that she won't let anyone get close enough to care for her. If you can teach her to comb her hair and wash her hands and mind her manners enough that someone can manage raising her on their own, in one year's time, I will give you the child you so desire.'

"The task didn't seem so bad, honestly, so the king and queen took the wild little girl back to their castle with them. Except they realized very quickly that the wild little girl didn't want to be civilized. She kicked and screamed whenever anyone tried to brush her hair. She bit anyone who tried to come near her with soap. She cried all night so that everyone in the castle was half-mad with being so tired.

"Finally, the queen and king—their crowns at funny angles and big dark circles under their eyes—went into the wild girl's room and said something to the effect of, 'What on earth do you *want*, you strange, unwashed little thing?' And the little girl started to cry again, the big ugly kind of crying that's kind of embarrassing to look at. She cried so long and so hard that eventually she tired herself out and fell asleep on the floor, right between the king and queen. The king and queen were afraid they'd wake her up by leaving or moving or breathing too loud, and so instead they just fell asleep right there on the floor next to the little girl. None of them had ever slept better."

Mum had finished her tea at some point after the king and queen had taken in the little girl and had closed her eyes to listen.

"Now it went on like this, back and forth, for a year. The queen and king were soon so caught up in wrestling the little girl's hair into braids and insisting she use spoons and forks instead of her hands to eat dinner that they quite lost track of time. So they were surprised when the old lady came back, and asked if they'd finished their task.

"'Oh!' said the queen. 'Could we maybe have just a little longer?' The king agreed that the little girl was not quite civilized yet, but that with just a little more time could definitely pass for human rather than beast.

"'Very well,' said the old lady. 'You may have one more year. After that I will return and see if you have completed your task and are ready to receive your child.' Now things went on like this and the next year, when the old lady came back, the queen and king felt it would be an awful waste to interrupt the wild little girl's schooling just when she was starting to figure out her times tables and hadn't bitten her dancing master in several weeks. So they asked for another year to complete their task, and the old lady gave it to them. And so on, and so forth, until the little girl was almost grown and considered by just about everyone in the castle to be delightful, even if she did seem to have a moral opposition to wearing shoes.

"When the old woman came back the final time, the queen and king began to cry when they greeted her, because they knew the wild little girl was thoroughly civilized now, and would be a welcome addition to any home. They didn't want to see her go, as they had grown quite fond of her. Sometimes they still let her sleep in between them when she had nightmares. They loved her more than anything, you might say.

"'Please,' said the queen, 'we don't need a child of our own. Just let us keep her, please.'

"The old lady looked quite shocked at this. 'Don't you know you already have a child of your own? Look, here comes the princess now!' And the formerly wild little girl came down to see what all the fuss was about, and the king and queen scooped her up into their arms and kissed her all over her face until she was quite embarrassed and threatened to bite them all. By the time the queen and king had wiped away their tears and scolded their daughter that she really ought to be wearing shoes in the courtyard, the old lady was gone. And they all lived happily ever after."

Mum was asleep, and Charlie didn't wake her. He just tucked the blanket up under her chin and kissed the very top of her head.

"Only dream of lovely things," he whispered.

Theo and Grandpa Fitz came back very late. Charlie heard them downstairs. No voices, only the sound of the door and the dry rustling of coats and then footsteps, the *THUMP-drag* of Theo's walk distinct from Grandpa Fitz's. The sound of it, the thought of his bad leg dragging, the tight scar tissue keeping it locked in place, brought with it a rush of some emotion Charlie couldn't identify.

Charlie made sure he made a bit of noise as he walked, stepping on all the creakiest floorboards down the hall until he was outside Theo's room. He heard Theo pacing back and forth inside.

I'm going to find a way to get your heart back, he wanted to say. *The war wolves have taken so much, but I won't let them keep it. Not if I can help it. You're brave if you do brave things, and I want to do a brave thing for you.*

He knocked at the door, just once, soft. He heard Theo pause, then keep pacing.

"Theo, it's me," Charlie said, still soft. "I just—I wanted to tell you that I understand, if you really do want to go to that Rosehill place. But whatever you decide to do, I didn't mean what I said before. And I want you to know that I'm going to prove it to you. I'm going to do whatever it takes to help you. I promise."

He heard Theo pause, and take several steps towards the door. But the door between them stayed shut.

29

"I THOUGHT I'D BE SEEING YOU AGAIN."

Remorse tilted her head towards him, her coat silky and silver in the moonlight. Charlie was holding Biscuits in his arms, and turned his face into her fur. When he didn't say anything, the wolf continued.

"My brothers and sisters, with their vast, aching hunger for hearts, they eat their fill and they are done. But I? I love you, all of you, all of your lovely, rich tears. I can follow my flock their whole lives long. Hearts can be eaten, or harden until there is no sweetness left to be sucked out of them. But tears? Tears are a wellspring which never runs dry. Regret alone may last forever. Have you done something you regret, lovely boy? Have you brought me something sweet?"

Charlie turned his face away from Biscuits's coat.

"I was cruel to my brother."

Remorse's tail wagged a snow angel into the soft fallen powder. "And?" she panted.

"And I won't ever be able to make it okay. I told Theo that he should never have come back." He thought the tears would be slow to come, knowing their fate. But it was as if they had been waiting for this, for release. He put Biscuits down on the ground, and she hissed at Remorse, squaring her body to the wolf.

"And?" Remorse slunk towards him, slow and languorous, her tongue rolling red and steaming from her mouth.

"I can never make it right, because it was true. Even if it was only true for a minute, I can't take it back. And now every time Theo sees me for the rest of his life he'll know I wished that. He's going to leave because of me."

"Sweet boy," Remorse whispered, her breath hot against his cheek.

"This is all my fault."

Charlie crumpled to his knees. Remorse sat down on her haunches next to him, and without quite knowing why or how, he wrapped his arms around her chest and buried his face in her thick, silky fur. Her coat muffled the sounds of his wet sobs and soaked up his tears even as they fell.

Charlie was little. Maybe four, or maybe younger. He had been playing hide-and-seek with his big brother for hours, all day practically, but Theo always found him easily. This time he'd been sure he'd found the perfect spot. He'd smothered his giggles when he heard Theo walk past the front stairs he was hiding under, calling for Charlie to come out, come out, whenever he was. But Theo kept looking. And looking. And looking, and not finding him. And it was cold under the stairs, and there were maybe spiders, and the shadows were wrapping thicker and thicker around him with every minute.

It was dark by the time Theo crawled under the porch, a smear of dirt across his nose and a worried expression in his bright blue eyes. Charlie had immediately burst into tears and been too upset to move, so Theo had scuttled on his hands and knees under the stairs until he could reach Charlie and grab him up in a hug.

"I didn't think you would ever find me," Charlie had snuffled into Theo's neck. "I thought I hid too good."

"Oh, Charlie, I'll always find you, don't you know that? No matter how long it takes, I'll always find you."

"I regret it, the things I said, the things I thought about Theo. But . . ."

Remorse looked at him, and there was something in her expression he didn't have a name for.

"But that's not your name. Regret, I mean. Remorse . . . it's not always bad. It's not always bad to remember things that hurt. Because it means you know what you've done wrong. And if you know that, then you know how you can be better." He hesitated, then stroked the silky fur of Remorse's head, just once. It felt like touching silk that was also somehow snow. "Will you walk with me? Just to the entrance?"

"My boy," Remorse murmured. She sounded . . . sad. "I will go with you wherever you would take me. For I fear you and I may never be done with each other. I get so lonely. My poor boy."

Biscuits walked between them the whole way, her ears flat to her skull and her claws ready for anything. But they walked together all the same.

He left Remorse outside the shelter entrance. He did not turn back to see if she would watch him go down into the old subway station. Instead he picked up Biscuits—the way he hadn't been able to the last time he was here, when he'd had to rush to the shelter, the time he thought that she was gone forever—and carried her down into the tunnel. She was trying to growl and purr at the same time, and was succeeding at neither, instead just making an odd snuffling sound against his neck.

The first thing to remember was that monsters always wanted something. Well, he knew what these monsters wanted, had always wanted: his scarred, scared, still-beating heart. To make a meal of it.

But the second thing to remember was that there was always a way, somehow, to win against them.

He had to set down Biscuits to pull the heavy twine necklace of keys over his head. They clinked against each other and Biscuits mewed in answer.

"I have to," he said to her without looking down. If he even glanced at her lovely yellow-green eyes now, or stroked her soft fur, or felt the thick rumble of a purr from her warm cat body, he might change his mind. If he remembered that there were soft, good things in the world, and that he wanted to be one of those soft, good things, too, then he might lose his fragile nerve and run away. And then Theo would never get any better and Charlie would always know that he had had a chance to make it right, and he had run away.

Theo couldn't run away from what had happened in France. Charlie wouldn't run away from what had happened to Theo.

Wrath's lock first, at the topmost edge of the door.

"I understand," he said as he slid the heavy key into place and turned it with a heavy *clank*.

Next came Remorse's lock, right at hand height, the tiny silver key tinkling against the bright metal of the lock.

"I'm sorry," he said as he turned the key with barely a sound except a soft, musical *clink*.

Agony and Anguish's lock was last, and he had to stoop down to reach it.

"I won't forget," he said, and shoved the key into the hole. The lock fought him the whole way, turning only with a whining metal groan.

Finally, there was a deep *thunk* and the door creaked open, just a bit.

"This is it," he said, looking down at Biscuits. His cat lashed her tail—once, twice—then puffed out her fur to its battle proportions and hissed a silent warning to anyone who might be listening who thought she would back off without a fight. She was brave. Charlie could be brave, too.

"No," he said.

Biscuits turned to look at him, distracted, her ears pinned and ready for war.

"No, Biscuits. You can't come with."

Biscuits ignored this and began marching towards the door, but Charlie grabbed her around the middle. She squirmed and yowled and clawed and he almost dropped her twice. "I love you so much," he whispered into her fur. Then he tossed her as gently as he dared and ran through the door, slamming it shut behind him. A second later a cat-sized something smacked into the door over and over again. He could hear her wails. She sounded so far away.

"There's no cure for scary like having a job," Charlie whispered to himself.

"Oh, I don't know about that, Charlie Merriweather."

He opened his eyes to find himself in a large room, although how large, he couldn't tell, darkness swallowing up the corners. It was dimly lit by a lone, bare bulb overhead, swinging just a little in a breeze he couldn't feel. And underneath the bald glare was set after set of eyes, like gas lamps, gleaming in the shadows beyond the bulb's light. The eyes—there were so many—didn't seem to be reflecting the light from overhead, but instead seemed to wink back at him with a glow that was entirely their own.

"Manners," one of the war wolves growled, and Charlie recognized Anguish, hulking and grinning next to his brother. Charlie

squeezed his eyes shut and gulped down, hard, swallowing every memory of light and hope and love like a spoonful of medicine or a warm cup of tea or a magic potion. *Please help me. Please keep me safe. Please don't let them win.*

"He-hello," he said, opening his eyes again. "I'm Charlie. Charlie Merriweather. I came here for my brother, Theo. You ate his heart. I—I want it back. Please. Please, give his heart back to me. He needs it."

One by one the wolves began to grin, red wolves and black wolves and wolves the color of gunpowder and grease and old ash. Their teeth gleamed brighter than their eyes in the dim light. Then, one by one, they began to fall back, to edge away, their claws scraping against the grimy tile floor. And as Charlie stepped farther into the room, they formed a great circle around him, and only one war wolf remained in the center beneath the bulb.

The last wolf was smaller than the rest, but being smaller made her scarier. She was bony, her fur matted and dull, but her teeth were a perfect, well-tended white.

"I do believe it's time for us to meet, dear Charlie. I apologize it's taken so long, my fault entirely. I've just been so very busy these last few years. Agony and Anguish have feasted during this war, of course," said the small wolf, and Agony and Anguish licked their chops. Very briefly, Charlie smelled old meat. "But I always get my share. I pick off every straggler, I follow them home and then I eat their flocks' hearts, too, sometimes."

"Who are you?" whispered Charlie.

"My name is Acceptance. How very nice to meet you, Charlie Merriweather." And the small, wicked wolf smiled at him with her horrible teeth, gleaming beautiful and pristine in the ruin of her mouth. "A brave heart, now that's good eating if you can get it. Tough meat to soften up, but any heart can be eaten if you're willing to work at it. Why, my sister Melancholy's been worrying your Mr. Churchill's heart for years now, long before this war business ever got started. She's his oldest friend. She greets him every morning and curls up right on the center of his chest each night. She hasn't been this devoted to a man in a suit for decades," Acceptance mused, almost cheerfully, stretching out her rangy legs and crooked tail.

The wolf padded closer to him, until Charlie felt his bones turn to tuning forks, humming with terror under his skin with a sound he was certain she could hear.

"But enough with this small talk. Tell us again, dear Charlie, what it is you want."

"I want my brother's heart." His voice was so small and squeaky he sounded like Biscuits. Or worse, like one of the mice she liked to catch.

"No. You don't."

Agony and Anguish snickered, a strange snorting sound that pushed itself out wetly from their cruel, pointed noses. Anguish bumped his furry shoulder into Agony, who grinned yellow and huge.

"I do," Charlie persisted, swallowing again and again until his voice came out almost like his own. This was when the hero was supposed to spring the trap to trick the enemy. This was when he was supposed to realize how to win. But he had nothing. "I want my brother's heart back."

"Well, I'm afraid that's long since eaten, dear Charlie," Acceptance said, very polite, inclining her head towards Agony, who winked one enormous yellow eye at Charlie.

"You're war wolves," Charlie forced past his thick, dry mouth. Something was building up in Charlie's chest, gaining momentum every second like the train that had brought Theo home and started Charlie down the path that had led him to this room. "You can do anything."

Acceptance tilted her ears, pleased. Agony and Anguish woofed with agreement.

"That may be," Acceptance allowed, wagging her many-times-broken tail just a bit so a light cloud of dust billowed up around her. "But it remains: the heart is just the means, Charlie. It is not what you want."

"It is, too!" Charlie was surprised that his voice came out like that, strong and true and quite angry. "*You* don't know what I want."

"Oh, but I do, sweet Charlie. Longing is the sharpest smell there is. It's how I find all my very best meals. Nothing tastes sweeter than longing stamped out into nothing. It distills in the heart and gives the richest flavor. I love to suck the memory of wanting out of the softest parts of a heart."

311

"I want his heart." He was whispering again, mouse-quiet and papery. The thing in his chest was pushing at the edges of him, searching for a way out. He could feel it, shoving itself against his mouth for release.

"No, you don't."

"I do!"

"What you do long for, my own dear Charlie Merriweather?"

The thing in Charlie's chest burst forth, shoved itself past his tongue, his teeth, his trembling lip, barreling out into the open, unable ever to turn around. *"For things to be like they were!* For Theo to be *nice* again, and happy, and funny. For Mum to smile again and have a pink dress for church. For there to be butter and jam for toast and eggs on Sundays. For a Sunday jacket that fits and shoes that don't pinch. For Grandpa Fitz not to forget things. I just want things to go back to the way they were. I just want to go back."

The only sound in the room was Charlie's breathing. One by one, the war wolves' mouths split into red grins, their teeth catching the light.

"Not even war wolves, Charlie, can go back. There is only forward; all other directions are a myth, made up by scared men to comfort themselves around fires. Myths keep no one warm, Charlie. There is no back."

"You can't give me his heart, can you?" Charlie felt like *he* had Hollow Chest, empty and wrung out.

"Eaten is eaten, Charlie Merriweather. You can't un-eat a heart any more than you can un-fire a bullet or un-birth a pup. We are war wolves: we are made for one thing. We do it very well."

The truth of it landed heavily inside him like a stone. Theo's heart was gone. It had all been for nothing. All of it. Nothing.

Acceptance cocked her head at him and sniffed the air deeply. "Your heart is broken. A deep crack runs through the center of it." She padded over to him, her nails clicking on the tile of the floor. She pressed her nose to his chest just as Dishonor had done, but instead of freezing him, her touch burned.

Charlie gasped and tried to shrink away from her.

"I know you think us cruel, Charlie Merriweather. I know you think us beasts and monsters that only maim."

Charlie thought of Remorse. Of her mad, sad eyes, the feel of his face against her fur.

"But we can be kind to you, truly. Let us be kind."

Charlie closed his eyes. He didn't want to hear what she would say, because he knew now, knew how it would sound to him here, alone in the dark and surrounded by monsters and all the hope draining out of him like lifeblood.

"Let me ease your burden, young one. Too young to carry something so heavy."

Here, in the dark and cold and more alone than he had ever been in his life, it sounded . . . nice, almost. *This is how it happens*, Charlie realized. They wear you down to nothing, they heap the weight on top of you and then say they can remove it. The relief of the pain stopping seems like a kindness. How could he have ever blamed Theo for accepting? Monsters had herded him into a trap and sprung it. They had made his heart intolerable to bear.

Charlie shook his head, so hard a tear went flying from where it was clinging to his chin. His voice only came out as a paper-thin croak.

"No."

"We need good, strong hearts to sustain us, sweet Charlie, and we have perhaps overindulged ourselves these last few decades. Eat too much of a flock and eventually there will be no more sheep, correct?"

"Y-yes?" *Thump-THUD. Thump-THUD.*

"I cannot give you back your brother's heart, Charlie Merriweather, any more than I can give you back your father's life. Therefore, I could not accept your heart for tender, with nothing to exchange. But perhaps . . ." And Acceptance licked her chops, and he smelled smoke and singed hair.

"Perhaps what?"

"Perhaps another bargain could be struck. A partial exchange for a partial return."

A partial exchange for a partial return. In return for what? What was there left to want, when the thing he wanted was impossible? An idea flickered to life in his mind. In front of him, Acceptance's tail began to wag again.

Things could never be as they were again. He knew that now. A part of him, perhaps, had always known. But neither could Theo. Or Mum. Or Grandpa Fitz, or Mellie or Aggie or Reggie. All they could do was keep pushing forward. Together, if they could.

"A heart is a stubborn thing," said Acceptance. "A weed, really. Give it an inch and it will grow, even just a seed of one."

Theo would never again be who he had been before the war. Charlie understood that. But maybe, *maybe* Charlie could still help him become someone new.

"My heart," Charlie whispered. "I could give you *part* of my heart."

They would get what they wanted anyway, the war wolves. There had never been a way to win, he realized, not against this. There were just different kinds of pain, different kinds of damage his heart could take. If Theo left again, if anyone left Charlie alone again, he didn't think his heart could take it. It would break, or it would harden into stone, and not a war wolf alive would want it. His heart would be safe.

But that wasn't what Charlie wanted. Not anymore.

"A piece for a piece," agreed Acceptance. "I shall take . . . half, shall we say? A decent mouthful. But of that mouthful, I will leave you just a bite. Just enough to plant. I cannot promise that the earth of your brother's chest will accept the seed of your heart, but neither can I promise it will not. If you give Theodore Merriweather a piece of your heart, he may yet accept it. A new one may grow in its place. Perhaps, anyway."

Charlie thought of what Acceptance had said. That there was only one direction, and that direction was forward. He thought of all the things he would never get back again, no matter what he did, no matter if Theo grew a new heart or not. And he thought of tall, strong Theo crying himself to sleep when he believed no one could hear.

I'll always find you, don't you know that? No matter how long it takes.

"I accept your bargain."

It hurt.

It hurt so much more than he had thought it would.

It hurt like every bruise and broken bone Charlie had ever had squeezed into one. It hurt the way Theo's hands around Mum's arm had hurt, the way Mum's tears had hurt, the way Dad never coming home had hurt. It was all those hurts at once, encompassing and overwhelming them.

It was every kind of hurt a body and a heart could endure, every pain he had felt and all those pains yet to come. All at once. Her teeth sinking into his heart. His heart leaping and wriggling in her jaws, the slick, velvety caress of her long pink tongue. He felt it when her teeth found the fault line in his heart, the place not stitched up quite right, where the scarring of a small lifetime's worth of hurt hadn't healed cleanly. Acceptance bit down harder, harder, harder, and Charlie Merriweather's broken heart cracked clean in two.

Charlie crumpled to his knees. There was no blood, which was strange, and he couldn't feel the wet oil slick of an open wound on his chest where he knew it should be. But the pain was bright as a beacon, the half of his heart still in his chest thrumming with pain and loss, almost hiccuping with the shock of it.

Acceptance pulled away from Charlie and held something wet in her awful jaws—it was wriggling weakly and glowing, very faintly.

"Better do it quick, sister," said Agony, eyeing the hunk of something in Acceptance's jaws with eyes yellow as lanterns. "You know how they fast they harden in the open air."

Acceptance made a noise that sounded like agreement, then tossed the lump of glowing flesh in the air and snapped her jaws down on it. It fell on the ground in two pieces, one much larger than the other.

"A bargain is a bargain, Charlie Merriweather," said Acceptance, nudging the smaller piece towards him with her pointed nose. "You take this piece and we shall take ours."

Agony picked up the piece of Charlie's heart delicately in his fangs and carried it off. Aguish followed after, heading towards the end of the room. Acceptance went after them, looking small and no less terrifying in comparison to their looming bulk.

But before she disappeared, Acceptance paused and turned

317

around to face him, Agony and Anguish flanking her on either side. "Very seldom have we had the pleasure of a heart such as yours, sweet Charlie. Take care of what is left of it. It would be such a shame to waste it."

Charlie didn't know what to say to this, so he fainted instead.

30

WHEN HE WOKE UP, BISCUITS WAS LICKING HIS face with her rough little tongue. It hurt, actually, but it felt good, too, because it meant that he was alive and Biscuits loved him. Sitting up, Biscuits twining anxious figures of eight around his feet and mewling in concern, he pulled up his sweater to look at his chest where Acceptance had chewed out half of his heart, but there was no blood, no gaping wound. Just the pale, smooth expanse of his skin and a hollow ache in his chest. Looking up, he was surprised to find that the War Room was just a supply closet, not big at all. It was odd, really, that he hadn't recognized that before.

Then he looked down. Clutched in his hand was his half of the bargain.

It didn't look very much like a piece of heart. It was spongy, a bit like modeling clay. He ran his fingertips along it and felt the tiny ridges of old, healed scars. Tooth marks, just like Acceptance had said.

This is a piece of my heart, thought Charlie, feeling very strange and a little sad but also a little hopeful. *I grew this myself. This was inside me.*

And now I will give it to Theo.

He tucked the piece of his heart safe in his pocket, then scooped up Biscuits. Out they walked into the cold, snowy night. Pudge and Bertie were waiting for them outside the door. Charlie followed them out into the street and around a few corners to where Mellie was sleeping in a little nest she had made of blankets and newspapers. Charlie set Bertie down at her feet and kissed the top of her grizzled head. She mumbled in her sleep.

"I love you, too," Charlie whispered.

When he softly opened his front door, it was to Grandpa Fitz, asleep in his chair by the embers of the fire in the main room. His hand was resting on his chest, keeping Grandma Lily safe against his whole, unbroken heart. Charlie kissed the top of Grandpa Fitz's head as he walked past. Grandpa Fitz let out a loud, content snore.

Up the stairs and down the hall, Charlie peeked into Mum's room. She was sleeping soundly on the left side of the large bed. The other side was waiting for Dad, who would never lie there again. But Mum was smiling in her sleep.

Charlie closed the door as quietly as he could and then crept into Theo's room, avoiding the squeaky floorboard and sitting down on the foot of Theo's bed.

Theo was muttering in his sleep. A bad dream, maybe, but not a nightmare.

Charlie fished the bit of heart out of his pocket and held it up to the moonlight creeping through the curtains. It was awfully small. Underneath the dirt it had picked up on the floor, and the lint it had picked up in Charlie's pocket, it was gold.

Charlie pressed it against Theo's chest and thought, as loudly and strongly as he could, *This is for you, Theo. I grew it for me, but I'm giving it to you. Please take it. Please let it grow. I love you.*

When he pulled his hand away, the piece of heart was gone, as if it had never been.

When Theo woke up, a moment later, Charlie held out his hand. Theo took it.

"Charlie . . . ?"

"You can go back to sleep now," said Charlie. "Don't worry—I'll keep you safe."

Theo looked at Charlie with sleepy eyes and smiled, just a little. It didn't fit quite right, but it was stretching.

"I believe you," he said. "Will you—will you tell me a story?"

"Yes," Charlie said. "Once there were two brothers, and one got lost. But the other brother found him. Because they loved each other. The end."

"That's it?"

"That's the only story that matters."

Biscuits curled on top of Theo's chest, keeping Charlie's heart safe and warm and ready to grow, if only Theo would let it. Underneath her purring, Charlie fancied he could hear it beating.

31

"DON'T READ IT UNTIL I'M GONE," THEO TOLD HIM as he pressed the letter into Charlie's clammy hands.

Charlie stood on the platform between Mum and Grandpa Fitz and watched the train carrying Theo away to the Rosehill Home for Returning Soldiers until it disappeared from sight, and for a while after that, too. Mum kept the knuckles of one hand pressed against her lips, and kept Charlie's hand clasped tight in the other. Grandpa Fitz let his hand rest heavy on Charlie's shoulder. But even with the two of them anchoring him in place, there was a strange sensation. That he was almost weightless, that if they let go of him he would blow apart like a dandelion.

But they did let go, eventually.

And he didn't blow away.

They could have taken a cab or a bus back home, but they agreed without seeming to discuss it that they would all prefer to walk. Charlie went slowly, a bit behind Mum and Grandpa Fitz, watching the slow drip of water melting off gutters and tree branches. Ragged bits of green were dragging themselves into daylight everywhere he looked. He hadn't even really needed his coat.

A street from home, Biscuits catapulted up into the air over a rubbish bin she'd been hiding behind, startling a laugh out of Charlie as he caught her in his arms. Mum and Grandpa Fitz turned back to see them, and Mum smiled. It was only a little watery around the edges.

The letter in Charlie's pocket rustled a bit as Biscuits climbed up to his shoulder with the focus of a mountaineer. He should read it. He wanted to read it. But then he thought about the echoing spaces inside the house, and he found he could not go inside to a place where Theo didn't live. Not yet.

"Mum, I'm going to visit Aggie and Reggie," he said, pushing Biscuits's back feet the last bit up onto his shoulder.

"One day, you're going to have to introduce us to these new mysterious friends of yours," Mum threatened, but her smile was easy.

"One day," Charlie promised.

"Biscuits, keep him out of trouble!" Grandpa Fitz said with a big, booming laugh. The locket with Grandma Lily's portrait gleamed through a gap between the buttons of his shirt. Charlie waved to them as he turned around towards the hospital and started walking.

He missed Theo. It was a physical sensation as plain as being hungry. Sharp but bearable. His brother hadn't seemed that different when he left. "You know I'm no good with goodbyes, and Mum'll be a mess, so—here," he had said, shoving the letter at Charlie before going back to double-checking all his bags. Charlie focused on the memory of that piece of his heart sinking into Theo's chest.

It felt different. His heart. He could feel the edge where it had been torn, could feel the empty space around it that made it every heartbeat feel as if it had an echo, an afterimage like the kind you got from looking at the sun. There was the feeling, and just behind it, the memory of how it felt before, before Acceptance's jaw hinged shut around his beating heart. A ribbon of sadness ran through him now, wrapped around his heart, such as it was, and through everything around him.

But ribbons, after all, could hold things together.

"Oh, hello, love. Are you here to see the lieutenant again?"

The lady with spectacles—Nurse Radcliffe, he remembered now—was minding the front desk. She had a very large nose, but the nose matched her rather large spectacles, which in turn made her eyes look as large as an insect's. The spectacles evened out her features. She really had a very pleasant face.

Charlie realized he'd been staring at her for what was fast approaching a strange amount of time. "Er. Yes. Please. Thank you."

She smiled, wide and bright. "You're such a dear. You go right on in. And I'll make sure Aggie knows you're here," she added with a wink.

"Thank you, Miss Radcliffe," Charlie said, feeling rather red and sweaty.

"Oh, look at you, with your sweet little face," Nurse Radcliffe said, waving her hand at him. "Get out of here."

"Um. Okay." Charlie scuttled into the hall, thoroughly unsure as to whether he should be pleased or mortified. There was a long wooden bench running along one wall, and he took a seat the very end of it, his feet just barely touching the ground. Had they touched the last time he was here?

"Charlie!" Aggie appeared after a few minutes in a swish of gray-and-white uniform. "What brings you here today, my fine young friend? You know what? Don't answer quite yet. I've got loads to do and I'm avoiding Matron because she'll make me do it, so come hide with me and once we're in the clear we can have a nice sit-down."

Charlie opened his mouth to respond, but Aggie was already off and running, striding down the busy hall with a clarity of purpose that dared anyone to question it. He jumped to his feet and scrambled after her, dodging around doctors and nurses and patients in their drab white hospital clothes.

She stopped by a door and waved her hand about frantically behind her. Charlie scooted inside and she yanked the door closed. There were more empty beds than Charlie remembered seeing before.

"Oh, hullo, Charlie!" Reggie was sitting up in bed, reading a newspaper and looking rather . . . whatever the opposite of worse for wear was. Better for wear? Repaired, maybe. "What are you doing here on such a fine and lovely day?"

"I just . . . wanted to see you, I guess. To see how you were doing."

"Well, I'm very glad to hear it. Let me know if you need me to shove off so you can chat with Aggie. I haven't wandered the halls half-dressed in several months now. I rather miss the thrill of it." Aggie grabbed a page of unattended newspaper and swatted at him with it.

"Do you need me to get rid of him, Charlie?" Aggie said, pretending to be annoyed. "Because I'd be happy to. Possibly permanently."

"No, it's fine." He pressed his hand to his coat's breast pocket and felt the crackle of the letter again. "I just wanted to talk to someone for a bit. I'm building up to doing something, but I don't know if I'm brave enough yet."

"You're one of the bravest people I know, Charlie," Reggie said without hesitation.

"Why don't you think you're brave enough?" Aggie asked, seating herself at the foot of Reggie's bed.

Charlie just shrugged. How could anyone ever explain the state of their own heart?

"Well, it seems to me that the sort of person one is, is quite dependent on the sort of things one does," said Aggie, her voice firm and thoughtful. "So if you do something that's brave and good, even if you don't think you're a brave and good person, doesn't that *make* you brave and good?"

"Maybe." Charlie remained unconvinced. Before he knew it, he'd blurted out, "Will you tell me a story, Aggie?"

"What, like a bedtime story?"

"Any kind you like." Charlie's cheeks burned, but he didn't regret asking.

"Oh Lord, this is like when someone asks you what your favorite food is and you can't think of anything you've eaten even once," Aggie said, brushing her hair back with a laugh.

"Well, how about this," said Reggie. "Once there was a handsome prince with an even handsomer mustache."

Aggie rolled her eyes. "Typical."

"There's always a handsome prince!" Reggie protested.

"Tradition is just a long line of dead people looking down their noses at you," Aggie said in a tone that brooked no arguments.

"Er . . . Once there was an average-looking man of no particular social standing, who still possessed a very handsome mustache nonetheless. Is that better?"

"Well, it's not worse, at any rate."

"And he was cursed to . . . hmm, what's a good curse?"

"Not in front of the children, please," Aggie said crossly.

"That's not what I meant!" Reggie spluttered, but Aggie

winked at Charlie over her shoulder.

"What about muteness?" she suggested.

"There was an average-looking man of no particular social standing who was cursed to never be able to say what he really meant. So if he was ill, he would say he was well, and if he was sad, he would say he was cheerful or hungry or sleepy or something."

"How is that any different from lying?" Aggie crossed her arms, and something about the angle of her eyebrow implied she was deeply unimpressed.

"Because he wasn't doing it on purpose!"

"Hmm."

"And one day the cursed average-looking man of no particular social standing met a princess."

"A *princess*, naturally. There are no poor girls in this entire country." Aggie's eyebrow was pure disdain.

"All girls are secretly princesses, that is the *rule*, there is a *precedent*," Reggie said, making a sweeping gesture with both hands.

"Tosh."

"There is!"

Charlie had the strange sensation that he was only hearing half of their conversation. Their faces never seemed to quite match the words they were saying. He kept almost-remembering what it reminded him of, and then it would slip through his grasp again. He realized with a start the conversation had quite gotten away from him.

"Well, obviously they rule the kingdom together in harmony."

"Oh, 'obviously,' is it?" said Aggie tartly.

"Happily ever after! It's the *rule*." Reggie raked a hand through his dark hair in apparent frustration, not seeming to realize he was making it stand up on end like a cockatoo. Aggie looked at him with a face that was clearly supposed to be despairing, but wasn't. It reminded him of Mum, actually, that look, but he couldn't place who she would be looking at. Grandpa Fitz? Mr. Cleaver?

"Thank you, both of you." Charlie rose to his feet. "Hopefully I'll see you soon," he said, feeling now like he was intruding on something private and a bit fragile. He got up and gave Reggie a quick, impulsive hug. With his ear pressed against Reggie's chest, he thought for just a moment he heard a sort of . . . noise. He drew back in surprise.

"What?" Reggie asked, furrowing his black-dash eyebrows.

"Nothing," Charlie said with a hasty smile. "I'm just distracted, sorry."

"Oh, Charlie?" Reggie said. "Do you think you might go see Mellie soon?"

"Sure, why?"

"Do you think you can give her this? It's my card. I asked her to come see me the last time you were here, but I haven't heard from her. If she's nervous about being in the hospital, I can meet her in the front lobby, or anywhere. The thing is, I've been talking with my family, just a few phone calls, and . . . oh, bother." Reggie raked a hand through his hair again. "Listen, Charlie, metaphorically speaking, one can't hide under one's bed for one's whole life. They're making noise about discharging me from this place, lovely though the stay has been, and we all know I'm going to need a bit of help. Even if my head was in perfect working order, I never really learned any practical skills regarding being a person in the world. I don't know how to cook, and I can't fold a shirt to save my immortal soul. I'm hoping Miss Mellie will be willing to lend her services. Of course, she'd need to come live with me, and we'd have to get her kitted out in some new jumpers, and I've no idea how to build a pigeon coop."

"You want to build a pigeon house?"

"Well, they certainly can't stay inside. Mother would have a fit."

"You're going to stay with your family again?" Charlie asked, surprised. Reggie waved his hand back and forth indecisively.

"Maybe. Eventually. Only if there's a pigeon coop."

"Mellie would never leave the pigeons behind."

"And rightly so; they're war heroes."

Could I come visit you when Mellie moves in? Charlie wanted to ask the question, wanted to toss out a rope and tie it to the idea of Mellie and Reggie in a big house, having tea in a sunny garden, pigeons picking at the crumbs of fancy cakes made just for them. He could sit under the table like when he was little, and break the iced cakes into little pieces for the birds. Occasionally Mellie would pass down another cake for the pigeons, and Aggie would pass down a biscuit for Charlie with a tiny nibble taken out of it, her red lipstick smudged into the icing. Because of course Aggie would be there, too. How could she not be?

But Mum would never let him sit under the table, even if Reggie said it was all right. And it wasn't much of a perfect day to imagine if Mum wasn't there. Or Grandpa Fitz, who would probably start bickering with Mellie or maybe just napping in the sunshine with his bristly chin on his chest.

Or Theo. Maybe Theo was asleep in the sunshine, too, dreaming of only lovely things.

Maybe that was what being a grown-up really was. Not sitting in a chair and making conversation, but doing something you didn't really want to do because it made someone else happy; because it was *important*, even if it wasn't important to *you*. One couldn't sit under the table for one's whole life, either.

He tucked Reggie's card safely into his pocket.

"I'll make sure she gets it."

"Good man," Reggie said with a smile.

"I'm not actually a man," Charlie said, shrugging one shoulder and busying himself with his coat. "I'm just a boy, really." Just a boy with half a heart and a coat that was too big for him.

"*That*," Aggie said, appearing in front of him to straighten his collar and press a red-lipstick kiss into his hair, "is a matter of opinion."

Charlie was so distracted by this that the thought sneaked up on him as the door closed: *Dad*. That's what he had somehow remembered from so very far away while Aggie and Reggie were bickering.

It was how Mum had looked at Dad.

Biscuits leaped back into his arms from where she had been waiting, impatiently but politely, outside the hospital doors. He caught her more out of reflex than actual preparedness. He stroked her soft fur absently as he walked, her tail lashing in contained thrill at the promising trills of birdsong overhead. He slowed down as he drew close to home again.

He picked his way across the street, over potholes and wide puddles of greasy water, to Mellie's bench. She was hunched over her pram of trinkets. She looked very small in the bright light.

"How are you, Mellie?"

"Living and breathing, aren't I?" A dark gray pigeon with lovely green flecks on her wings alighted on Mellie's shoulder and began preening a bit of wild hair.

"Their bones are hollow, you know," she said, stroking the pigeon's soft head with a dirty fingertip. "That's how they make themselves light enough to fly. They can't carry even an ounce of unnecessary weight."

Charlie reached into his breast pocket to pull out the card, but his fingertips stilled against Theo's letter, still unread, and somewhere underneath it Charlie's heart still beat. It felt so much heavier, even though there was less of it. He would never make it off the ground.

"David told me that. He was a good boy." Mellie rubbed her cheek against the downy wing of the dark gray pigeon. Charlie pretended not to see her cry.

"I know how awful it is," he said after several silent minutes. "When someone you love very much dies." He got up and tucked Reggie's card into her chapped red hand. "Reggie wanted me to give you this. He knows he needs help sometimes, and that he probably will for a long time. You should let someone help you, Mellie. You should let people love you back." And without thinking about it too much, he hugged her and squeezed her as tight as he dared. She held herself stiff and unmoving, but Charlie felt wetness where his cheek touched hers. "Thank you for being my friend," he whispered.

He pulled away, scratched Pudge under the chin, and turned towards home.

They hadn't been walking long when Biscuits growled, puffing herself up double her size against his shin.

"Yes, I see it, too," he murmured to her. Something was keeping pace with them, just out of sight. But he wasn't afraid. He recognized those steps.

He sat down on a bench underneath a tree that was stubbornly pushing out a few shriveled green buds. A drop of water dripped down onto his neck, and he hunched over a bit to shield the letter as he opened it.

Dear Charlie,

I'm writing this the night before I leave. I know I won't be able to say everything I want to when I go. I used to be better at this, but for now this will have to do:

I know you worried when I stopped writing before. I don't know if I'll be able to write this time. It's hard, sometimes, to try to explain what I feel.

But I hope you know that even if I don't write, I'm always trying to. That's why I'm leaving. So I can come back.

I promise I'll keep trying.

Love,

Theo

"All that, and he still left you," came a voice off to his left.

Charlie didn't look up straight away. Her voice sounded just like he remembered. Remorse settled on her haunches next to the bench. Their eyes were almost even.

With a low growl, Biscuits slunk over his knees to place herself between them.

"He didn't leave me," Charlie said, smoothing the letter flat against his knee. "I let him go."

No one walking past paid them any mind. And anyway, what

other people thought didn't bother him so much these days.

Theo had told him that he had to leave if he wanted to get better. That if he wanted to try to get better, he needed to get help from people who knew how to help him. And he did want to try. Theo didn't know he was carrying around a chunk of Charlie's heart, and Charlie didn't even know if the heart could grow, or if Theo would ever bring it back to him.

But he thought of that soft, dark ribbon that ran through him and wrapped around the things he loved.

He thought of that invisible thread that guided carrier pigeons home, no matter how far away they flew.

I'll always find you.

"I don't have any tears for you today."

Remorse gave a little sigh, but didn't protest. Charlie folded up the letter along its seams, put it back into its envelope, and tucked it safe inside his coat before pushing himself to his feet.

"I'll see you around, though."

"You will," Remorse agreed.

She wasn't something to be afraid of—the feeling, at least. It was only when it curdled into shame that it could hurt you, poison you from the inside. It was okay to mourn mistakes. And Charlie had made so many mistakes, would probably make many, many more. But he'd had victories, too. Big ones—his heart, such as it was, throbbed faintly with remembering—and countless small ones, like cups of tea made just right, clean linens in the cupboard when someone reached for them, Biscuits eating from

a bowl that Theo had filled. No. No tears today.

He nodded to the wolf as he walked away, Biscuits at his heels. He turned back, just once, to look, and she was gone. Half his heart beat in his chest, and somewhere across the city the other half was gaining momentum, every second taking it farther and farther away.

Charlie lifted his face to the watery sunshine and started walking down a different street.

Acknowledgments

Writing is usually depicted as a lonely experience, something that by nature can only be done in isolation. I have never found this to be true. That we need to be lonely to be productive or creative or good is a lie I think we should stop telling ourselves or anyone else. I wrote, edited, and finished this book because of other people, because of the warmth, community, patience, expertise, advice, and shelter they shared with me. When I stumbled was when I tried or was forced by circumstance to do it on my own. I am saying this as a gentle reminder to whomever might be reading this, and a not so gentle reminder to the future version of myself who will look back on this time and wonder how on earth I did it. This is how:

My agent, Tina Dubois, and the intrepid team at ICM, a lighthouse of support, patience, and confidence, who guided me through rough waters with gentleness and grace.

The team at Walden Pond Press who designed, edited, and cared for this book from the very, very beginning. In particular, Debbie Kovacs, for her steadfastness, inspiration, and endless warmth—there is a fireside glow about you. And most especially, my editor, Jordan Brown, for his endless patience, precision, and vision. You could always see the shape of the thing while I was still mapping out the edges. You are a mentor and a friend. There is no getting rid of me now.

Dadu Shin for the incredible cover and illustrations. Seeing them for the first time was like a match being struck in my heart.

Mary Rockcastle, Kelly Krebs, and the sprawling family of teachers, students, and staff at the Hamline MFAC program. In particular, I would like to thank Swati Avasthi, who was the first person to make me take myself seriously as a writer, and Claire Rudolf Murphy, who never once gave up on me.

And most especially Anne Ursu, for being my teacher, my friend, my biggest advocate, and a lamplighter to my spirit. Now you are stuck with me, sorry.

My front row: Jennifer Coats, Jessica Mattson, Zachary Wilson, Josh Hammond, Sarah Ahiers, and Anna Palmquist, as well as Gary Mansergh, Kate St. Vincent-Vogel, Steph Wilson, and Ronny Khuri. For countless hours sitting across from each other at Jen's kitchen table or sprawled across the couches at Sarah's cabin or around the fire at Palmquist Farm. For being such a part of my daily life and thought process and heart that it is impossible to extricate who I am as a writer from the tangle of your friendship. For pulling me out of every dark hole I dug myself into like cheerful, relentless miners with pickaxes you weren't afraid to use. There's a sincerity for ya.

My friends and family. Jim, Sunilla and Jessica Eklund, and my favorite Australians, Andrea, Brad, Ollie, and Obi Philips. You are the net always ready to catch me. Sarah Dunworth, for living in my brain. Kristi Kontras Rudie, for being a sister to my spirit.

My grandfather, Perry Eklund.

And my mom, Joan Eklund Sandstrom, who keeps my heart safe.